HAVE YOU EVER GOTTEN away with something really, really bad? Like when you hooked up with that cute guy you work with at the bagel shop . . . and never told your boyfriend. Or when you created an anonymous Twitter profile and posted a vicious rumor about your BFF . . . and said nothing when she blamed it on the bitchy girl who sat in front of her in Algebra III.

At first, not getting caught might have felt amazing. But as time went by, maybe you felt a slow, sick roll in the pit of your stomach. Had you really done *that*? What if anyone ever found out?

You've probably heard the phrase *She got away with murder* a thousand times and thought nothing of it, but four pretty girls in Rosewood actually did get away with murder. And that's not even all they've done. Their dangerous secrets are slowly eating them from the inside out. And now, someone knows everything.

Karma's a bitch. Especially in Rosewood, where secrets never stay buried for long.

BOOKS BY SARA SHEPARD

Ruthless

A PRETTY LITTLE LIARS NOVEL

SARA SHEPARD

HARPER TEEN

An Imprint of HarperCollinsPublishers

HarperTeen is an imprint of HarperCollins Publishers.

alloy**entertainment**

Produced by Alloy Entertainment
151 West 26th Street, New York, NY 10001

Library of Congress card catalog number: 2011945748

ISBN 978-0-06-208187-2 (pbk.)

Design by Liz Dresner

14 15 16 CG/RRDC 10 9 8 7 6 5 4 3 2
❖
First paperback edition, 2012

To Farrin, Kari, Christina, Marisa, and
the rest of the fabulous Harper crew

Suspicion always haunts the guilty mind.

—WILLIAM SHAKESPEARE

YOU GET WHAT YOU DESERVE

Have you ever gotten away with something really, really bad? Like when you hooked up with that cute guy you work with at the bagel shop . . . and never told your boyfriend. Or when you stole that patterned scarf from your favorite boutique . . . and the security alarms didn't go off. Or when you created an anonymous Twitter profile and posted a vicious rumor about your BFF . . . and said nothing when she blamed it on the bitchy girl who sat in front of her in Algebra III.

At first, not getting caught might have felt amazing. But as time went by, maybe you felt a slow, sick roll in the pit of your stomach. Had you really done *that*? What if anyone ever found out? Sometimes the anticipation is worse than the punishment itself, and the guilt can eat you alive.

You've probably heard the phrase *She got away with murder* a thousand times and thought nothing of it, but four pretty girls in Rosewood actually did get away with murder. And that's not even all they've done. Their dangerous secrets are slowly eating them from the inside out. And now, someone knows everything.

Karma's a bitch. Especially in Rosewood, where secrets never stay buried for long.

Even though it was almost 10:30 P.M. on July 31 in Rosewood, Pennsylvania, a wealthy, bucolic suburb twenty miles outside Philadelphia, the air was still muggy, oppressively hot, and full of mosquitoes. The flawlessly manicured lawns had turned a dry, dull brown, the flowers in the beds had withered, and many of the leaves on the trees had shriveled up and fallen to the ground. Residents swam languidly in their lime-rocked pools, gobbled up homemade peach ice cream from the open-till-midnight local organic farmstand, or retreated indoors to lie in front of their air conditioners and pretend it was February. It was one of the few times all year the town didn't look like a picture-perfect postcard.

Aria Montgomery sat on her back porch, slowly dragging an ice cube across the back of her neck and contemplating going to bed. Her mother, Ella, was next to her, balancing a glass of white wine between her knees. "Aren't you thrilled about going back to Iceland in a few days?" Ella asked.

Aria tried to muster up enthusiasm, but deep down, she felt a niggling sense of unrest. She adored Iceland—

she'd lived there from eighth to eleventh grade—but she was returning with her boyfriend, Noel Kahn, her brother, Mike, and her old friend Hanna Marin. The last time Aria had traveled with all of them—and her two close friends Spencer Hastings and Emily Fields—was when they'd gone to Jamaica on spring break. Something awful had happened there. Something Aria would never be able to forget.

At the very same time, Hanna Marin was in her bedroom packing for the trip to Iceland. Was a country full of weird, pale Vikings who were all related to one another worthy of her Elizabeth and James high-heeled booties? She threw in a pair of Toms slip-ons instead; as they landed in the bottom of the suitcase, a sharp scent of coconut sunscreen wafted out from the lining, conjuring up images of a sun-drenched beach, rocky cliffs, and a cerulean Jamaican sea. Just like Aria, Hanna was also transported back to the fateful spring break trip she'd taken with her old best friends. *Don't think about it*, a voice inside her urged. *Don't* ever *think about it again.*

The heat in Center City Philadelphia was no less punishing. The dormitories on the Temple University campus were shoddily air-conditioned, and summer students propped up box fans in their dorm windows and submerged themselves in the fountain in the middle of the quad, even though there was a rumor that drunken junior and senior boys peed in it regularly.

Emily Fields unlocked her sister's dorm room, where

she was hiding out for the summer. She dropped her keys in the STANFORD SWIMMING mug on the counter and stripped off a sweaty, fried-food-smelling T-shirt, rumpled black pants, and a pirate's hat she'd worn to her waitress job at Poseidon's, a gimmicky seafood restaurant on Penn's Landing. All Emily wanted to do was to lie on her sister's bed and take a few long, deep breaths, but the lock turned in the door almost as soon as she'd shut it. Carolyn swept into the room, her arms full of textbooks. Even though there was no hiding her pregnancy anymore, Emily covered her bare stomach with her T-shirt. Carolyn's gaze automatically went to it anyway. A disgusted look settled over her features, and Emily turned away in shame.

A half mile away, near the University of Pennsylvania campus, Spencer Hastings staggered into a small room in the local police precinct. A thin trickle of sweat dripped down her spine. When she ran her hand through her dirty-blond hair, she felt greasy, snarled strands. She caught a glimpse of her reflection in the window in the door, and a gaunt girl with hollowed-out, lusterless eyes and a turned-down mouth stared back. She looked like a dirty corpse. When had she last showered?

A tall, sandy-haired cop entered the room behind Spencer, pulled the door closed, and glared at her menacingly. "You're in Penn's summer program, aren't you?"

Spencer nodded. She was afraid if she spoke, she'd burst into tears.

The cop pulled an unmarked bottle of pills from his

pocket and shook it in Spencer's face. "I'm going to ask you one more time. Is this yours?"

The bottle blurred before Spencer's eyes. As the cop leaned close, she caught a whiff of Polo cologne. It made her think, suddenly, about how her old best friend Alison DiLaurentis's brother, Jason, went through a Polo phase when he was in high school, drenching himself in the stuff before he went to parties. "Ugh, I've been *Polo'd*," Ali would always groan when Jason passed by, and Spencer and her old best friends Aria, Hanna, and Emily would burst into giggles.

"You think this is funny?" the cop growled now. "Because I assure you, you are *not* going to be laughing when we're done with you."

Spencer pressed her lips together, realizing she'd been smirking. "I'm sorry," she whispered. How could she think about her dead friend Ali—aka Courtney, Ali's secret twin—at a time like this? Next she'd be thinking about the *real* Alison DiLaurentis, a girl Spencer had never been friends with, a girl who'd returned to Rosewood from a mental hospital and murdered her own twin sister, Ian Thomas, Jenna Cavanaugh, and almost Spencer, too.

Surely these scattered thoughts were a side effect of the pill she'd swallowed an hour before. It was just kicking in, and her mind was speeding at a million miles a minute. Her eyes darted all over the place, and her hands twitched. *You got the Easy A shakes!* her friend Kelsey would say, if she and Spencer were in Kelsey's dorm room at Penn instead of locked in two separate interrogation cells in this dingy station. And Spencer would laugh, swat Kelsey with her notebook, and then return to cramming nine months' worth of AP Chemistry III information into her already jam-packed head.

When it was clear Spencer wasn't going to own up to the pills, the cop sighed and slipped the bottle back into his pocket. "Just so you know, your friend's been talking up a storm," he said, his voice hard. "She says it was all your idea—that she was just along for the ride."

Spencer gasped. "She said what?"

A knock sounded on the door. "Stay here," he growled. "I'll be back."

He exited the cell. Spencer looked around the tiny room. The cinder-block walls had been painted puke-green. Suspicious yellowish-brown stains marred the beige carpet, and the overhead lights gave off a high-pitched hum that made her teeth hurt. Footsteps sounded outside the door, and she sat very still, listening. Was the cop taking Kelsey's statement right now? And what exactly was Kelsey saying about Spencer? It wasn't like they'd rehearsed what they'd say if they got caught. They never thought they *would* get caught. That police car had come out of nowhere. . . .

Spencer shut her eyes, thinking about what had happened in the last hour. Picking up the pills from South Philly. Peeling out of that scary neighborhood. Hearing the sirens scream behind them. She dreaded what the next hours would bring. The calls to her parents. The disappointed looks and quiet tears. Rosewood Day would probably expel her, and Spencer would have to finish high school at Rosewood Public. Or else she'd go to juvie. After that, it would be a one-way trip to community college—or worse, working as a hoagie-maker at the local Wawa or as a sandwich board–wearer at the Rosewood Federal Credit Union, advertising the new mortgage rates to all the drivers on Lancaster Avenue.

Spencer touched the laminated ID card for the University of Pennsylvania Summer Program in her pocket. She thought of the graded papers and tests she'd received this week, the bright *98*s and *100*s at the top of each and every one. Things were going so well. She just needed to get through the rest of this summer program, ace the four APs she was taking, and she'd be at the top of the Rosewood Day pyramid again. She deserved a reprieve after her horrible ordeal with Real Ali. How much torment and bad luck did one girl have to endure?

Feeling for her iPhone in the pocket of her denim shorts, she pressed the PHONE button and dialed Aria's number. It rang once, twice . . .

Aria's own iPhone bleated in the peaceful Rosewood darkness. When she saw Spencer's name on the Caller ID, she flinched. "Hey," she answered cautiously. Aria hadn't heard from Spencer in a while, not since their fight at Noel Kahn's party.

"Aria." Spencer's voice was tremulous, like a violin

string stretched taut. "I need your help. I'm in trouble. It's serious."

Aria quickly slipped through the sliding glass door and padded up to her bedroom. "What happened? Are you okay?"

Spencer swallowed hard. "It's me and Kelsey. We got caught."

Aria paused on the stairs. "Because of the pills?"

Spencer whimpered.

Aria didn't say anything. *I warned you*, she thought. *And you lashed out at me.*

Spencer sighed, sensing the reason for Aria's silence. "Look, I'm sorry for what I said to you at Noel's party, okay? I . . . I wasn't in my right mind, and I didn't mean it." She glanced at the window in the door again. "But this is serious, Aria. My whole future could be ruined. My whole *life*."

Aria pinched the skin between her eyes. "There's nothing I can do. I'm not messing with the police—especially not after Jamaica. I'm sorry. I can't help." With a heavy heart, she hung up.

"Aria!" Spencer cried into the receiver, but the CALL ENDED message was already flashing.

Unbelievable. How could Aria do this to her, after all they'd been through?

Someone coughed outside Spencer's holding room. Spencer turned to her phone again and quickly dialed Emily's number. She pressed her ear to the receiver, listening to the *brrt-brrt-brrt* of the ringing line. "Pick up, pick *up*," she pleaded.

The lights in Carolyn's room were already off when Emily's phone started to beep. Emily glanced at Spencer's name on the screen and felt a wave of dread. Spencer probably wanted to invite her to a get-together at Penn. Emily always said she was too tired, but really it was because she hadn't told Spencer or any of her other friends that she was pregnant. The idea of explaining it to them terrified her.

But as the screen flashed, she felt an eerie premonition. What if Spencer was in trouble? The last time she'd seen Spencer, she'd seemed so scared and desperate. Maybe she needed Emily's help. Maybe they could help each other.

Emily's fingers inched toward the phone, but then Carolyn rolled over in bed and groaned. "You're not going to get that, are you? *Some* of us have class in the morning."

Emily pressed IGNORE and flopped back down to the mattress, biting back tears. She knew it was a burden for Carolyn to let her stay here—the futon took up nearly all the floor space, Emily constantly interrupted her sister's studying schedule, and she was asking Carolyn to keep a huge secret from their parents. But did she have to be so mean about it?

Spencer hung up without leaving Emily a message. There was one person left to call. Spencer pressed Hanna's name in her contacts list.

Hanna was zipping her suitcase closed when the phone

rang. "Mike?" she answered without looking at the screen. All day, her boyfriend had been calling her with random trivia about Iceland—*Did you know there's a museum about sex there? I am so taking you.*

"Hanna," Spencer blurted on the other end. "I need you."

Hanna sat back. "Are you okay?" She'd barely heard from Spencer all summer, not since she began an intensive summer program at Penn. The last time she'd seen her was at Noel Kahn's party, when Spencer's friend Kelsey came along, too. What a weird night *that* had been.

Spencer burst into tears. Her words came out in choppy bursts, and Hanna only caught bits of sentences: "The police . . . pills . . . I tried to get rid of them . . . I am *so* dead unless you . . ."

Hanna rose and paced around the room. "Slow down. Let me get this straight. So . . . you're in trouble? Because of the drugs?"

"Yes, and I need you to do something for me." Spencer clutched the phone with both hands.

"How can *I* help?" Hanna whispered. She thought about the times she'd been dragged to the police station— for stealing a bracelet from Tiffany, and later for wrecking her then-boyfriend Sean's car. Surely Spencer wasn't asking Hanna to cozy up to the cop that arrested her, as Hanna's mother had done.

"Do you still have those pills I gave you at Noel's party?" Spencer said.

"Uh, yeah." Hanna shifted uncomfortably.

"I need you to get them and drive them to Penn's campus. Go to the Friedman dorm. There's a door around the back that's always propped open—you can get in that way. Go to the fourth floor, room four-thirteen. There's a keypad combination to get into the room—five-nine-two-oh. When you get in, put the pills under the pillow. Or in the drawer. Somewhere kind of hidden but also kind of obvious."

"Wait, whose room is this?"

Spencer curled her toes. She was hoping Hanna wouldn't ask that. "It's . . . Kelsey's," she admitted. "*Please* don't judge me right now, Hanna. I don't think I can take it. She's going to ruin me, okay? I need you to put those pills in Kelsey's room and then call the cops and say that she's a known dealer at Penn. You also need to say she has a sketchy past—she's trouble. That will make the cops search her room."

"*Is* Kelsey really a dealer?" Hanna asked.

"Well, no. I don't think so."

"So basically you're asking me to frame Kelsey for something you both did?"

Spencer shut her eyes. "I guarantee you Kelsey's in the interrogation room right now, blaming me. I have to try to save myself."

"But I'm going to Iceland in two days!" Hanna protested. "I'd rather not go through customs with a warrant out for my arrest."

"You won't get caught," Spencer reassured her. "I

promise. And . . . think about Jamaica. Think about how we *all* would have been screwed if we hadn't stuck together."

Hanna's stomach swirled. She'd tried her hardest to erase the Jamaica incident from her mind, avoiding her friends for the rest of the school year so as not to relive or rehash the awful events. The same thing had happened to the four of them after their best friend, Alison DiLaurentis—really Courtney, Ali's secret twin sister—disappeared on the last day of seventh grade. Sometimes, a tragedy brought friends together. Other times, it tore them apart.

But Spencer needed her now, just like Hanna had needed her friends in Jamaica. They had saved her life. She stood up and slipped on a pair of Havaiana flip-flops. "Okay," she whispered. "I'll do it."

"*Thank* you," Spencer said. When she hung up, relief settled over her like a cool, misty rain.

The door burst open, and the phone almost slid from Spencer's hand. The same wiry cop strode into the room. When he noticed Spencer's phone, his cheeks reddened. "What are you doing with that?"

Spencer dropped it to the table. "No one asked me to hand it in."

The cop grabbed the phone and slipped it into his pocket. Then he gripped Spencer's hand and roughly pulled her to her feet. "Come on."

"Where are you taking me?"

The cop nudged Spencer into the hall. The odor of

rancid takeout burned her nostrils. "We're going to have a discussion."

"I told you, I don't know anything," Spencer protested. "What did Kelsey say?"

The cop smirked. "Let's see if your stories match."

Spencer stiffened. She pictured her new friend in the interrogation room, preserving her own future and wrecking Spencer's. Then she thought of Hanna getting into her car and setting the GPS to Penn's campus. The idea of blaming Kelsey made her stomach churn, but what other choice did she have?

The cop pushed open a second door, and pointed for Spencer to sit down in an office chair. "You have a lot of explaining to do, Miss Hastings."

That's what you think, Spencer thought, rolling back her shoulders. Her decision was a good one. She had to look out for herself. And with Hanna on her way, she'd get away with this scot-free.

It was only later, after Hanna had planted the drugs, after her call came into the central switchboard, and after Spencer overheard two cops talking about going to the Friedman dorm to search room 413, that Spencer found out the truth: Kelsey hadn't said a single word to implicate either herself or Spencer for the crimes they'd been accused of. Spencer wished she could undo everything, but it was too late—admitting she'd lied would get her into worse trouble. It was better to keep quiet. There was no way to trace what the cops had found back to her.

Shortly after that, the cops let Spencer go with a warn-ing. As she was leaving the holding room, two officers marched Kelsey through the hall, their meaty hands gripping her arm like she was in big, big trouble. Kelsey glanced at Spencer fearfully as she passed. *What's going on?* her eyes said. *What do they have on me?* Spencer had shrugged like she had absolutely no clue, then walked into the night, her future intact.

Her life went on. She took her APs and aced every single one. She returned to Rosewood Day at the top of her class. She got into Princeton early decision. As the weeks and months flew by, the nightmarish evening faded and she rested easy, knowing her secret was safe. Only Hanna knew the truth. No one else—not her parents, not the Princeton admissions board, not Kelsey—would ever find out.

Until the following winter. When someone discovered everything.

1

EVERY KILLER DESERVES
A NIGHT OUT

On a Wednesday evening in early March, Emily Fields lay on the carpet in the bedroom she used to share with her sister Carolyn. Swimming medals and a big poster of Michael Phelps hung on the walls. Her sister's bed was littered with Emily's warm-up jacket, tons of oversized T-shirts, and a pair of boyfriend jeans. Carolyn had left for Stanford in August, and Emily relished having a space all her own. Especially since she was spending almost all her time in her room these days.

Emily rolled over and stared at her laptop. A Facebook page blinked on the screen. *Tabitha Clark, RIP.*

She stared at Tabitha's profile picture. There were the pink lips that had smiled so seductively at Emily in Jamaica. There were the green eyes that had narrowed at all of them on the hotel's crow's-nest deck. Now Tabitha was nothing but bones, her flesh and innards eaten away by fishes and pounded clean by the tides.

We did that.

Emily slammed down the lid of her computer, feeling the urge to throw up. A year ago, on spring break in Jamaica, she and her friends had sworn that they'd come face-to-face with the real Alison DiLaurentis, back from the dead and ready to kill them once and for all, just like she'd meant to do at her family's house in the Poconos. After a series of bizarre encounters in which this new, enigmatic stranger had uttered secrets that *only* Ali had known, Aria had pushed her over the edge of the crow's nest. The girl had fallen several stories to the sandy beach, and her body had disappeared almost instantly, presumably carried out to sea by the tide. When the four of them saw the newscast on TV two weeks ago that this very same girl's remains had washed up on the shores of the resort, they thought the whole world would discover what they already knew: that Real Ali had survived the fire in the Poconos. But then, the bomb dropped: The girl Aria pushed wasn't Real Ali at all—her name was Tabitha Clark, just as she'd told them. They'd killed an innocent person.

As the newscast ended, Emily and her friends received a chilling note from an anonymous person known only as *A*, in the tradition of the two stalkers who'd tormented them before. This new A knew what they had done and was going to make them pay. Emily had been holding her breath ever since, waiting for A's next move.

The realization cascaded over Emily daily, startling her anew and making her feel horribly ashamed. Tabitha was dead because of her. A family was ruined because of her. It was all she could do to keep from calling the police and telling them what they had done. But that would ruin Aria, Hanna, and Spencer's lives, too.

Her phone bleated, and she reached for it on her pillow. ARIA MONTGOMERY, said the screen. "Hey," Emily said when she picked up.

"Hey," Aria said on the other end. "You okay?"

Emily shrugged. "You know."

"Yeah," Aria agreed softly.

They fell into a long silence. In the two weeks since a new A had emerged and Tabitha's body had been found, Emily and Aria had begun calling each other every evening, just to check in. Mostly, they didn't even talk. Sometimes, they watched TV together—shows like *Hoarders* or *Keeping Up with the Kardashians*. Last week, they'd both caught a rerun of *Pretty Little Killer*, the TV movie depicting Real Ali's return and killing spree. Neither Emily nor her friends had seen the movie the night it originally aired— they'd been too shell-shocked from the revelation about Tabitha to change the channel from CNN. But Emily and Aria had watched the rerun quietly, gasping at the actresses who played their roles and squirming at the over-dramatized moments where their doppelgangers found Ian Thomas's body or ran from the fire in Spencer's woods. When the movie hit its climax in the Poconos and the house exploded with Ali inside it, Emily shivered. The producers gave the show a definitive ending. They killed the villain and gave the girls their happily-ever-after. But they didn't know that Emily and her friends were once again being haunted by A.

As soon as they'd begun receiving notes from New A—on the anniversary of the horrible fire in the Poconos that had almost killed all of them—Emily was sure that Real Ali had survived the fire in the Poconos *and* the push off the balcony in Jamaica and was back for revenge. Her friends slowly began to believe that as well—until the news came out about Tabitha's true identity. But even that didn't rule out the possibility that Real Ali was still alive. She *still* could be New A and know everything.

Emily knew what her old friends would say if she voiced such a theory: *Get over it, Em. Ali's gone.* More than likely they'd reverted back to their old assumption that Ali had perished inside the burning house in the Poconos. But there was something all of them didn't know: Emily had left the front door unlatched and ajar for Ali before the house exploded. She could have easily escaped.

"Emily?" Mrs. Fields called out. "Can you come downstairs?"

Emily sat up fast. "I have to go," she told Aria. "I'll talk to you tomorrow, okay?"

She hung up the phone, crossed to the bedroom door, and looked over the railing. Her parents, still dressed in the matching gray sweat suits they wore for their evening power walks around the neighborhood, stood in the foyer. A tall, freckled girl with reddish-blond hair just like Emily's was next to them, a bulging duffel over her shoulder that said UNIVERSITY OF ARIZONA SWIMMING in big red letters.

"Beth?" Emily squinted.

Emily's older sister, Beth, craned her neck up and spread her arms wide. "Ta-da!"

Emily raced down the stairs. "What are you doing here?" she cried. Her sister rarely visited Rosewood. Her job as a teaching assistant at the University of Arizona, where she'd gone to college, kept her busy, and she was also assistant-coaching the U of A swim team, of which she'd been captain her senior year.

Beth dropped the duffel to the hardwood floor. "I had a couple days off, and Southwest was running a special. I thought I'd surprise you." She looked Emily up and down and made a face. "*That's* an interesting outfit."

Emily stared down at herself. She was wearing a stained T-shirt from a swimming relay carnival and a pair of too-small Victoria's Secret sweatpants with the word PINK written across the butt. The pants had been Ali's—*her* Ali's, the girl who was actually Courtney, whom Emily had confided in, giggled with, and adored in sixth and seventh grades. Even though the sweats were fraying at the hems and had long ago lost the string that cinched the waist, they'd become Emily's go-to after-school uniform in the past two weeks. For some reason, she felt that as long as she had them on, nothing bad would happen to her.

"Dinner's about ready." Mrs. Fields turned on her heel toward the kitchen. "Come on, girls."

Everyone followed her down the hall. Comforting smells of tomato sauce and garlic swirled through the air. The kitchen table had been set for four, and Emily's mother scuttled to the oven as the timer started to beep. Beth sat down next to Emily and took a long, slow sip of water from a Kermit the Frog tumbler that had been Beth's special glass since she was little. She had the same freckles across her cheeks and strong swimmer's body as Emily did, but her reddish-blondish hair was cut in a choppy bob below her ears, and she wore a small silver hoop earring at the top of her earlobe. Emily wondered if it had hurt to get it done. She also wondered what Mrs. Fields would say when she noticed it—she didn't like her children looking "inappropriate," piercing their noses or navels, dyeing their hair weird colors, or getting tattoos. But Beth was twenty-four; maybe she was beyond her mother's jurisdiction.

"So how are you?" Beth folded her hands on the table and looked at Emily. "It feels like ages since we've seen each other."

"You should come home more often," Mrs. Fields chirped pointedly from the counter.

Emily studied her chipped nails, most of which were bitten down to the quick. She couldn't think of a single innocuous thing to tell Beth—everything in her life was tainted with strife.

"I heard you spent the summer with Carolyn in Philly," Beth prompted.

"Uh, yeah," Emily answered, balling up a chicken-print napkin. The summer was the *last* thing she wanted to talk about right now.

"Yes, Emily's wild summer in the city," Mrs. Fields said in a half-touchy, half-joking voice as she placed a ceramic dish of lasagna on the table. "I don't remember *you* taking a summer off from swimming, Beth."

"Well, it's all water under the bridge." Mr. Fields sat down at his regular seat and grabbed a piece of garlic bread from the basket. "Emily's all set for next year."

"That's right, I heard!" Beth punched Emily playfully on the shoulder. "A swim scholarship to UNC! Are you psyched?"

Emily felt her family's gaze and swallowed a huge lump in her throat. "Really psyched."

She knew she should be happy about the swim scholarship, but she'd lost a friend, Chloe Roland, because of it—Chloe had assumed Emily was hooking up with her well-connected father in order to score a spot on UNC's squad, but the truth was that Mr. Roland had come on to her, and she'd done everything she could to avoid him. There was also a part of Emily that wondered if she'd even get to *go* to UNC next year. What if A told the police about what they did to Tabitha? Would she be in jail by the time freshman year started?

Everyone worked their way through the lasagna, their forks scraping against the plates. Beth started talking about a tree-planting charity group she was working with in Arizona.

Mr. Fields complimented his wife on the sautéed spinach. Mrs. Fields chattered about a new family she'd visited as part of the Rosewood Welcome Wagon committee. Emily smiled and nodded and asked her family questions, but she couldn't bring herself to contribute much to the conversation. She couldn't manage more than a few forkfuls of lasagna, either, even though it was one of her favorite dinners.

After dessert, Beth jumped up and insisted she'd do the dishes. "Wanna help, Em?"

Truthfully, Emily really wanted to go back to her room and burrow under her covers, but she didn't want to be rude to a sister she rarely saw. "Sure."

Together they stood at the sink, both of them staring out at the dark cornfield that bordered the backyard. As the basin filled with suds and the smell of lemon Dawn wafted around the room, Emily cleared her throat. "So what are you going to do while you're home?"

Beth glanced over her shoulder to make sure she and Emily were alone. "I have all kinds of fun things planned, actually," she whispered. "There's a costume party tomorrow that's supposed to be awesome."

"That sounds . . . nice." Emily couldn't conceal her surprise. The Beth she knew wasn't into partying. From what she remembered, Beth was a lot like Carolyn—she never broke curfew, never skipped a swim practice or class. Her senior year at Rosewood Day, when Emily was in sixth grade, Beth and her prom date, Chaz, a wiry swimmer with white-blond hair, hung out at the Fieldses' house after the dance instead of going to an after-party. Ali had been sleeping over that night, and they'd snuck down the stairs and spied on Beth and Chaz, hoping to catch them making out. But they'd been sitting on opposite sides of the couch, watching reruns of *24*. "No offense, Em, but your sister's really lame," Ali had whispered.

"Good, because you're coming, too." Beth splashed Emily with soapy water, getting some all over her U of A hoodie as well.

Emily quickly shook her head. Going to a party right now sounded about as fun as walking over hot coals.

Beth flipped the switch to the garbage disposal, and the water in the sink began to bubble. "What's up with you? Mom said you've been mopey, but you seem catatonic. When I asked you about your swim scholarship, you looked like you were about to burst into tears. Did you just break up with a girlfriend?"

A girlfriend. The chicken-silkscreened dish towel slipped from Emily's grasp. It always jolted her when one of her prim-and-proper family members mentioned Emily's sexual orientation. She knew they were trying to be understanding, but their chipper it's-okay-to-be-gay attitude sometimes made Emily feel embarrassed.

"I didn't break up with anyone," Emily mumbled.

"Is Mom still being really hard on you?" Beth rolled her eyes. "Who cares if you took a summer off from swimming? That was months ago! I don't know how you deal, living under this roof all by yourself."

Emily looked up. "I thought you liked Mom."

"I do, but I was dying to get out of here by the time senior year was over." Beth wiped her hands on a dish towel. "Now, c'mon. What's bugging you?"

Emily slowly dried a dish, looking into Beth's kind, patient face. She wished she could tell her sister the truth. About the pregnancy. About A. Even about Tabitha. But Beth would freak. And Emily had already alienated one sister.

"I've been stressed," she mumbled. "Senior year is harder than I thought it would be."

Beth pointed a fork at Emily. "That's why you need to come with me to this party. I'm not taking no for an answer."

Emily traced her fingers over a plate's scalloped edge. She desperately wanted to say no, but something deep inside her made her pause. She missed having a sister to talk to—the last time she'd seen Carolyn, over Christmas break, Carolyn had made every effort to avoid being alone with Emily. She'd even slept on the couch in the den, saying she'd gotten used to falling asleep in front of the TV, but Emily knew it was really to avoid their shared bedroom. Beth's attention and affection felt like a gift Emily shouldn't refuse.

"I guess I could go for a little bit," she mumbled.

Beth threw her arms around her. "I knew you'd be up for it."

"Up for what?"

They both turned. Mrs. Fields stood in the doorway, her hands on her hips. Beth stood up straighter. "Nothing, Mom."

Mrs. Fields padded back out of the room. Emily and her sister faced each other and burst into giggles. "We're going to have so much fun," Beth whispered.

For a moment, Emily almost believed her.

2

SPENCER HAS A DOPPELGANGER

"Move it a little bit to the left." Spencer Hastings's mother, Veronica, stood in the foyer of the family's grand house, one hand on her slim hip. Two professional picture-hangers were positioning a large painting of the Battle of Gettysburg under the curving double staircase. "Now it's a little too high on the right. What do you think, Spence?"

Spencer, who had just walked down the stairs, shrugged. "Tell me again why we took down the portrait of Great-great-grandpa Hastings?"

Mrs. Hastings gave Spencer a sharp look and then glanced worriedly at Nicholas Pennythistle, her fiancé, who had moved into the Hastingses' house a week and a half ago. But Mr. Pennythistle, still clad in his flawlessly fitting suit and shiny wingtips from work, was busy tapping away on his BlackBerry.

"Everyone needs to feel comfortable and welcome here, Spence," Spencer's mother answered quietly, pushing a lock of ash blond hair behind her ear. The four-carat diamond engagement ring Mr. Pennythistle had given her glinted under the overhead lights. "Besides, I thought Great-great-grandpa's portrait scared you."

"It scared Melissa, not me," Spencer mumbled. In truth, she liked the kooky family portrait—several sad-eyed spaniels perched on Great-great-grandpa Hastings's lap. Great-great-grandpa was also the spitting image of Spencer's father, who'd moved out of the Hastings abode after her parents' divorce and bought a loft in downtown Philadelphia. It had been Mr. Pennythistle's idea to swap out the portrait with the grisly Civil War tableau, surely wanting to expunge all evidence of Spencer's father from *his* new house. But who wanted to walk through the front door and be greeted by a bunch of rearing, angry steeds and bloodied Confederates? Just looking at the battle scene stressed Spencer out.

"Dinner is served!" a voice trilled from the kitchen.

Melissa, Spencer's older sister, popped her head into the hall. She'd offered to cook the family dinner tonight, and she wore a black apron that said GREEN GOURMET across the front and silver oven mitts on her hands. A thin black velvet headband held back her chin-length blond hair, a pearl necklace encircled her throat, and under-stated Chanel ballet flats adorned her feet. She looked like a younger, fresher version of Martha Stewart.

Melissa caught Spencer's eye. "I made your favorite, Spence. Lemon chicken with olives."

"Thanks." Spencer smiled gratefully, knowing this was a gesture of solidarity. The sisters had been rivals for a long time, but last year, they'd finally put aside their differences. Melissa knew Spencer wasn't adjusting well to the new family situation. But there were other things Spencer was having a hard time swallowing, too. Things Spencer didn't dare talk about with her sister—or with *anyone*.

Spencer followed her mother and Mr. Pennythistle—she still couldn't bring herself to call him *Nicholas*—into the kitchen just as Melissa was setting a baking dish in the center of the table. Their stepsister-to-be, Amelia, who was two years younger than Spencer, perched in the corner seat, napkin primly on her lap. She was wearing a pair of low-heeled booties Spencer had picked out for her on a recent shopping trip in New York, but her hair was still frizzy and her shiny cheeks were desperately in need of foundation.

Amelia scowled when she looked up and saw Spencer, and Spencer turned away, feeling a prickle of annoyance. It was clear Amelia still hadn't forgiven her for getting her brother, Zach, sent away to military school. Spencer hadn't meant to out Zach to his father. But when Mr. Pennythistle had walked in on Spencer and Zach in bed together, he'd assumed the worst and flown into a rage. Spencer had only announced that Zach was gay to get Mr. Pennythistle to stop hitting his son.

"Hey, Spencer," another voice said. Darren Wilden, Melissa's boyfriend, sat on the other side of Amelia, chewing on a piece of fresh-from-the-oven garlic bread. "What's new?"

A fist clenched in Spencer's chest. Though he now worked security at a museum in Philly, until recently Darren Wilden had been *Officer* Wilden, the chief investigator in the Alison DiLaurentis murder case, and it had been his job to sense when people were hiding something or lying. Could Wilden know about Spencer's new stalker, who—of course—went by *A*? Could he suspect what she and her friends had done to Tabitha in Jamaica?

"Uh, nothing," Spencer said haltingly, tugging on the collar of her blouse. She was being ridiculous. There was no way Wilden could know about A or Tabitha. He couldn't possibly know that every night, Spencer had bad dreams about the Tabitha incident, replaying the awful day in Jamaica over and over again. Nor could he know that Spencer read and reread articles about the aftershocks of Tabitha's death as often as she could—about how devastated Tabitha's parents were. How her friends in New Jersey held vigils in her honor. How several new nonprofits had sprung up to condemn teenage drinking, which was what everyone had assumed had killed her.

But it *wasn't* what killed her—and Spencer knew it. So did A.

Who could have seen them that night? Who hated them so much to torture them with the information and threaten to ruin their lives instead of going directly to the cops? Spencer couldn't believe that she and her friends were yet again faced with the task of figuring out who A might be. Even worse, she couldn't think of a single suspect. A hadn't written Spencer or the others another note since that harrowing newscast two weeks ago, but Spencer was sure A wasn't gone for good.

And what else did A know? A's last message said, *This is just the tip of the iceberg*, as if he or she was privy to other secrets. Unfortunately, Spencer had a few more skeletons locked in her closet. Like what had happened with Kelsey Pierce at Penn last summer—Kelsey had been sent to juvie because of what Spencer had done to her. But surely A couldn't know about *that*. Then again, A always seemed to know everything. . . .

"Seriously, nothing?" Wilden took another bite of crispy bread, his gray-green eyes on her. "That doesn't sound like the whirlwind schedule of a soon-to-be Princeton student."

Spencer pretended to wipe a spot off her water glass, wishing Wilden would stop staring at her as though she were a paramecium under a microscope. "I'm in the school play," she mumbled.

"Not just *in* the school play, you're the lead—as usual." Melissa rolled her eyes good-naturedly. She smiled at Mr. Pennythistle and Amelia. "Spence has starred in every production since preschool."

"And you're playing Lady Macbeth this year." Mr. Pennythistle sank ceremoniously into the heavy mahogany chair at the head of the table. "That's a challenging role. I can't wait to see the performance."

"You don't have to come," Spencer blurted, feeling heat rise to her cheeks.

"Of course Nicholas is coming!" Mrs. Hastings squeaked. "It's marked on our calendars!"

Spencer stared at her reflection in the back of her spoon. The last thing she wanted was a man she barely knew feigning interest in her life. Mr. Pennythistle was only coming to the play because Spencer's mom was making him.

Amelia speared a chicken breast from the platter that was being passed around. "I'm putting together an orchestra concert for charity," she announced. "A bunch of girls at St. Agnes are going to be rehearsing here for the next few weeks, and we're going to hold the concert at the Rosewood Abbey. Everyone can come to see my performance."

Spencer rolled her eyes. St. Agnes was the snooty private school Amelia attended, an institution even more obnoxiously exclusive than Rosewood Day. She'd have to figure out a way to get out of attending the performance; her old friend Kelsey attended St. Agnes—or at least she used to. Spencer didn't want to risk seeing her.

Mrs. Hastings clapped her hands together. "That sounds lovely, Amelia! Tell us the date, and we'll be there."

"I want to be available for *all* of you girls." Mr. Pennythistle glanced from Amelia to Spencer to Melissa, his gray-blue eyes crinkling. "We're a family now, and I'm really looking forward to us bonding."

Spencer sniffed. Where'd he get *that* line, Dr. Phil? "I already *have* a family, thank you very much," she said.

Melissa widened her eyes. Amelia had a smirk on her face like she'd just read a juicy piece of gossip in *Us Weekly*. Mrs. Hastings jumped to her feet. "You're being very rude, Spencer. Please leave the table."

Spencer let out a half laugh, but Mrs. Hastings nudged her chin toward the hall. "I'm serious. Go to your room."

"Mom," Melissa said gently. "This is Spencer's favorite meal. And—"

"We'll fix her a plate later." Mrs. Hastings's voice was strained, almost like she was about to cry. "Spencer, please. Just go."

"I'm sorry," Spencer mumbled as she stood, even though she wasn't. Fathers weren't interchangeable. She couldn't randomly bond with some guy she didn't even know. All of a sudden, she couldn't wait until next fall when she was at Princeton. Away from Rosewood, away from her new family, away from A, away from the secret about Tabitha—and all the other secrets A might know, too. It couldn't come fast enough.

Shoulders hunched, she stomped into the hall. A pile of mail was stacked neatly in the center of the hall table, a long, slender envelope from Princeton addressed to Spencer J. Hastings right on top. Spencer snatched it up, hoping for a fleeting second that perhaps the school was writing to tell her she could move in early—like now.

Soft, subdued voices sounded from the dining room.

Spencer's family's two Labradoodles, Rufus and Beatrice, bounded toward the window, probably smelling deer on the lawn. Spencer sliced open the envelope with her fingernail and removed a single sheet of paper. A logo for the Princeton admissions committee paraded across the top.

Dear Miss Hastings,

It appears there has been a misunderstanding. Apparently, two Spencer Hastingses applied to Princeton's incoming freshman class early decision—you, Spencer J. Hastings, and a male student, Spencer F. Hastings, from Darien, Connecticut. Unfortunately, our admissions board did not realize you were two separate individuals—some read your application, and others read the other Spencer's application, but we all voted as if you were one applicant. Now that we've realized our oversight, our committee needs to reread and review both of your applications thoroughly and decide which of you shall be admitted. Both of you are strong candidates, so it will most likely be a very tough decision. If there is anything you'd like to add to your application that might sway the admissions board, now would be an excellent time.

Sorry for the inconvenience, and good luck!
All the best,
Bettina Bloom
President, Princeton Admissions Board

Spencer read over the letter three times until the school's crest at the top of the page looked like a Rorschach blob. This couldn't be right. She had gotten *in* to Princeton. This was *done*.

Two minutes ago, her future was secure. Now she was poised to lose it all.

A lilting giggle snaked around the room. On instinct, Spencer shot up and glanced out the side window, which faced the old DiLaurentis house next door. Something shifted beyond the trees. She stared hard, waiting. But the shadow she thought she'd seen didn't reappear. Whoever had been there was gone.

3

PRETTY LITTLE LONER

"*Connect with the divine source of all life,*" a soothing voice chanted in Aria Montgomery's ears. "*With every exhale, let go of the tension in your body. First your arms, then your legs, then the muscles in your face, then . . .*"

Bang. Aria opened her eyes. It was Thursday morning at school. The door to the Rosewood Day auxiliary gym had flung open, and a bunch of freshman girls dressed in leotards and leg warmers pranced into the room for the first-period modern dance class.

Aria shot up quickly and pulled the headphones from her ears. She'd been lying on a yoga mat on the floor, thrusting her butt up and down in the air—the guru on the meditation tape said that the motion would cleanse her chakras and help her forget her past. But by the smirks on some of the freshman girls' faces, they probably thought she was doing some kind of weird sex stretch.

She scuttled into the busy Rosewood Day hall, tucking

the iPod back into her bag. All of the thoughts she'd tried so hard to forget swarmed back into her head like a knot of angry bees. Slipping into an alcove by the water fountains, she grabbed her cell phone from her jacket pocket. With one press of a button, she called up the page she'd been stalking obsessively on Google for two weeks now.

Tabitha Clark Memorial.

Tabitha's parents had set up the website to honor their daughter. On it were Twitter posts from friends, pictures of Tabitha from cheerleading practice and ballet recitals, details about a scholarship set up in her name, and links to Tabitha-related news stories. Aria couldn't stop looking at the page. She pounced on all of the news stories, always terrified that something—or some*one*—would connect Tabitha's death with her.

But everyone still thought Tabitha's death was a tragic accident. No one had even suggested that it might have been murder, and no one had made the connection that Aria and her friends had been in Jamaica the same time Tabitha was and at the same resort. Even Aria's brother, Mike, and her boyfriend, Noel, who had been there as well, didn't comment on the news story. Aria wasn't even sure if they'd seen it. To them, it was probably just another senseless death to tune out.

There was one person who knew the truth, though. A.

Someone giggled behind her. A bunch of sophomore girls stared at Aria from a bank of lockers across the hall. "Pretty Little Killer," one of them whispered, sending the rest into a fit of laughter. Aria winced. Ever since the made-for-TV movie of the same name had aired, kids walked down the hall quoting lines from the biopic of Real Ali's life to her face. *I thought we were best friends!* TV Aria said to Real Ali at the end, when Ali tried to burn down the Poconos house. *We were such losers before we met you!* Like Aria would have really *said* something like that.

Then a familiar figure swept into view. Noel Kahn, Aria's boyfriend, guided Klaudia Huusko, the blond Finnish exchange student who was living with his family, into an English classroom. Klaudia grimaced with every step, holding her Ace-bandaged ankle in the air and leaning heavily on Noel's muscled shoulder. Every guy in the hall stopped and stared at Klaudia's jiggling double-Ds.

Aria's heart started to bang. Two weeks ago, Noel, his two older brothers, Aria, and Klaudia took a trip to a ski resort in upstate New York. Once there, Klaudia told Aria that she was making a move on Noel and there was nothing Aria could do about it. Enraged, Aria had accidentally pushed Klaudia off the chair lift in retaliation. Aria told everyone Klaudia had slipped, and Klaudia played dumb like she couldn't remember what had happened, but Noel blamed Aria anyway. Since the trip, he had fawned over Klaudia's sprained ankle day and night, driving her to school, carrying her books between classes, and retrieving her coffees and sushi platters during lunch. It was a wonder he wasn't feeding her sashimi with Rosewood Day–embossed chopsticks.

Playing Florence Nightingale meant there was no time for Aria—not a hello in the halls, not even a phone call. He'd bagged on their standing Saturday date to Rive Gauche in the King James Mall for two weeks now. He'd also skipped out on the cooking class they were taking together at Hollis College, missing the class on grilling and marinades.

Noel emerged from the English classroom a minute later. When he spied Aria, instead of pretending she wasn't there and turning away, as he'd done the past two weeks, he strode straight toward her. Aria's spirits lifted. Maybe he was going to apologize for ignoring her. Maybe things would go back to normal.

She looked down at her trembling fingers. Her swirling nerves reminded her of the one and only time Noel had spoken to Aria in seventh grade at one of Their Ali's parties. They'd actually hit it off, and Aria had been on cloud nine until Ali sidled up to her later, telling Aria that she'd had a big wedge of cilantro between her teeth the entire time she and Noel had talked. "I really think Noel's out of your league," Ali—really Courtney—had told Aria in a gentle yet teasing voice. "And anyway, I think he likes someone else."

Yeah, like you? Aria had thought bitterly. What guy *didn't* have a thing for Ali?

Now, Noel stopped in front of a display case that featured this year's pieced-together and decorated Time Capsule game flag, the emblem of the yearly Rosewood

Day scavenger hunt. Printed copies of other years' flags hung in the case as well—the real ones were buried behind the soccer fields—including the one from when Aria was in sixth grade. A big chunk of flag was missing in the center—Real Ali had found that piece, Their Ali had stolen it, and then Jason DiLaurentis, their brother, had stolen it from *both* of them and given it to Aria. It was all because of that Time Capsule piece that Their Ali had been able to make the dangerous switch with her twin sister, sending Real Ali off to the mental hospital for four long years.

"Hey," Noel said. He smelled like orange soap and pepper, an unlikely combination Aria couldn't get enough of. When Aria glanced at his Manhattan Portage messenger bag, she noticed that the party hat–wearing rhinoceros button Aria had bought for him at a local craft show was still nestled between his pins for Rosewood Day lacrosse and the Philadelphia Phillies. Rhino pin had to be a good sign, right?

"Hey," Aria answered softly. "I've missed you."

"Oh." Noel pretended to be fascinated with the square face of his Omega watch. "Yeah, I've been really busy."

"Tending to Klaudia?" Aria couldn't help but snap.

Noel's features hardened, as though he was about to launch into his "She's in a foreign country and you should be more sensitive" speech again. But then he just shrugged. "Um, we need to talk."

A rock-sized lump formed in Aria's throat. "A-about

what?" she stammered, even though she had a horrible feeling she knew what Noel was about to say.

Noel pushed his yellow lacrosse bracelet, which all the players wore in some über-masculine show of brotherhood, around his wrist. He wouldn't look at Aria, not even at her feet. "I don't think it's working between us," he said. His voice cracked a little.

It felt like a karate kick to Aria's stomach. "W-why?"

Noel shrugged. His normally calm, easygoing face was all scrunched up, and his flawlessly smooth skin looked blotchy. "I don't know. I mean, we don't have that much in common, do we?"

The world suddenly went red. When Aria was pseudo-friends with Klaudia for a nanosecond, Klaudia had brought up how mismatched Aria and Noel were. Okay, so Aria wasn't like the lacrosse-playing, Ralph Lauren Polo–wearing clones Noel usually dated, but Noel said he *liked* that. Then again, how could she compare to an ice-blond Finnish sex goddess?

The all-natural cleanser the custodial staff used to mop the floors swirled in Aria's nose, making her queasy. A large guy on the basketball team bumped into her, knocking her into Noel, but Aria pulled away fast, suddenly uncomfortable with touching him. "So that's . . . *it*? All the time we spent together . . . it just doesn't matter?"

Noel shoved his hands in his pockets. "I'm sorry, Aria." He caught her eye, and for a split second, he really *did* look sorry. But there was something closed-off about him, too, like he'd already said good-bye to her long ago.

Tears wet the corners of Aria's eyes. She thought of all the weekends she'd spent with Noel. All the lacrosse games she'd watched, even though she didn't really understand the nuances of the game. All the secrets she'd confessed, like how she and Their Ali caught her father making out with his student, Meredith, near Hollis College in seventh grade. How when Real Ali returned last year and hit on Noel, Aria was sure Noel would dump her. How after Real Ali nearly killed them in the Poconos, she'd slept with the light on and kept a samurai knife her father had bought on a trip to Japan under her pillow. And how even though Aria had lost her virginity to a boy in Iceland in tenth grade, she'd wanted the second time she had sex to be really, truly special. Maybe it was a good thing she'd held out with Noel, considering what was happening now.

But there were some secrets Aria hadn't shared with Noel. Like what she'd done to Tabitha or what had really happened on their trip to Iceland. The Iceland incident alone would have made Noel dump Aria long ago. Maybe, in a twisted, karmic way, she deserved this.

She heard a snicker and peered into the open class-room door. Klaudia sat in the front row, her injured foot propped up on a spare chair. Kate Randall, Naomi Zeigler, and Riley Wolfe sat next to her—of course they'd all become fast friends with the equally devious and gossipy Klaudia. All four girls stared at her and Noel, big grins

on their faces. They had front-row seats to the breakup.
The news would be all over school in minutes. *Pretty Little
Loser was just Pretty Little Dumped!*

Aria spun on her heel and marched toward the bathroom before the tears started to fall. She peeked over her
shoulder, longing for Noel to call out her name, but he'd
turned and was walking in the opposite direction. When
he saw Mason Byers, one of his good friends, he stopped
and gave him a high five. Like he was carefree. Happy.
Thrilled to be rid of kooky Aria Montgomery once and
for all.

4

HANNA MARIN,
CAMPAIGN STRATEGIST

On Thursday evening, as the sun was sinking into the trees and dyeing the sky orange, Hanna Marin pressed her iPhone to her ear and waited for the voice mail message to beep. "Mike, it's me again. Are you ever going to pick up? How many times can I say I'm sorry?"

She pressed END. She'd left him sixteen voice mail messages, eleven texts, tons of Twitter posts, and a bunch of emails in the past two weeks, but her ex-boyfriend, Mike Montgomery, hadn't returned a single one. She knew how rash it had been to break up with him when he'd warned her about skeevy Patrick Lake, the photographer who told Hanna that she could be a model in New York. But how was she supposed to know Patrick would take compromising photos of Hanna and threaten to post them online if she didn't pay him off?

Hanna missed Mike. She missed watching *American Idol* with him and making fun of the singers. She'd heard he'd taken a small role in the school's production of *Macbeth*. When they were dating, they consulted one another before joining activities—Hanna would definitely have put the kibosh on the play.

And she especially missed Mike in light of what was happening with A and Tabitha. Hanna wouldn't have told Mike what she and the others had done, but to have someone around who cared about her would be so comforting right now. Instead, she felt alone and scared. She so wanted to believe that what they'd done to Tabitha was in self-defense. They'd *thought* Tabitha was Real Ali, who was hell-bent on murdering them. But no matter how many ways Hanna rationalized it, everything boiled down to one devastating fact: They had killed an innocent girl. They were all guilty. They knew it. And A knew it, too.

Hanna stepped out of her Toyota Prius and looked around. The circular driveway of her father's new house, a six-bedroom redbrick McMansion in Chesterbridge, two towns away from Rosewood, was edged with a few fledgling saplings, tethered by feeble-looking ropes. White Grecian columns supported the porch, a large fountain in the front yard burbled peacefully, and rows of perfectly manicured shrubs that looked like upside-down ice cream cones lined either side of the front entrance. Such a grand abode seemed excessive for three people—her father, his new wife, Isabel, and Isabel's daughter, Kate—but it *did* seem like a fitting house for a man who was running for United States senator. Mr. Marin's campaign had kicked off a few weeks ago, and he had a great shot at winning. Unless, of course, A spilled Hanna's secret about Tabitha.

Hanna rang the doorbell, and Isabel whipped the door open almost immediately. She was dressed in a Tiffany-blue cashmere sweater, a black pencil skirt, and sensible low heels. The perfect dowdy wife of a senator-to-be.

"Hello, Hanna." The pinched look on Isabel's face said that she didn't quite approve of Hanna's boho Anthropologie dress and gray suede boots. "Everyone's in Tom's office."

Hanna swished down the hall, which was adorned with silver-framed photos of Isabel and her father's wedding last summer. She scowled at the picture of herself dressed in the ugliest bridesmaid gown Isabel could have selected: a mint-green, floor-sweeping number that made Hanna's hips look huge and her skin look sickly. She turned the frame around so that it faced the wall.

Her father and his campaign staff were sitting around the walnut desk in his office. Her stepsister, Kate, was perched on a Victorian sofa, fiddling with her iPhone. Mr. Marin's eyes lit up when he saw Hanna. "There she is!"

Hanna smiled. A few weeks ago, when his campaign consultants told him that she'd tested well with the voting public, she'd suddenly become her dad's favorite daughter.

Isabel slipped into the room after Hanna and shut the French doors. "This is why I called you here." Mr. Marin pushed a series of flyers and website screen grabs across the table. The pages said things like *The Truth*

About Tom Marin and *Don't Believe the Lies* and *Not a Man You Can Trust*.

"These are all paid for by Tucker Wilkinson's committee," Mr. Marin explained.

Hanna clucked her tongue. Tucker Wilkinson was her father's biggest rival for the party nomination. He'd served as state senator for years and had oodles of campaign funds and tons of friends in high places.

She scootched forward to look at his photo. Tucker Wilkinson was a tall, handsome, dark-haired man who looked vaguely like Hugh Jackman. He had that slightly unnerving, ultra-white politician smile, the kind that tried so hard to say *Trust me.*

Sam, a senior staff member who had droopy eyes and a penchant for wearing bow ties, shook his head. "I heard Wilkinson bribed a Harvard admissions officer to let in his oldest son, even though he had a two-point-oh GPA."

Vincent, who managed Mr. Marin's website, stuffed a piece of Trident gum in his mouth before saying, "He does everything he can to dig up the skeletons in everyone's closets during campaigns, too."

"Luckily, he hasn't found anything on us." Mr. Marin looked around at his staff. "And he *won't*—unless there's something I need to know. What Jeremiah did was a shock. I don't want to be blindsided again."

Hanna flinched at the mention of Jeremiah, her father's aide who'd recently been dismissed for stealing $10,000 from the campaign's petty cash fund. The thing was, Jeremiah hadn't stolen the money . . . Hanna had. But she'd *had* to. It was the only way to keep Patrick quiet about the photos he'd taken.

Kate's phone chimed. She read the screen and giggled.

"Kate?" Mr. Marin sounded impatient. "Maybe you could put that away?"

"Sorry." Kate turned the iPhone facedown and glanced pointedly at Hanna. "Sean just texted me the *funniest* thing."

Hanna bristled inside, but she tried not to let it show. Kate had recently started dating Sean Ackard, Hanna's ex. Hanna didn't miss Sean in the slightest, but it did hurt that he'd chosen to date the girl she hated most.

Mr. Marin stacked the printouts in a neat pile. "So. Is there anything anyone would like to come clean with?"

Hanna's insides churned. Would Wilkinson's people find out about Tabitha? She glanced out the window. A car rolled slowly down the road. She squinted toward the silhouetted trees that served as a barrier between her dad's property and the neighbor's. For a split second, it looked like a shadow darted between the trees.

Her cell phone beeped.

Hanna pulled it out of the bag and hit the SILENT button, but then, glancing around to make sure her dad wasn't looking, she peeked at the screen. When she saw the garbled letters and numbers of the return center, a cold, rigid feeling seeped into her bones. She pressed READ.

What would Daddy say if he knew his new favorite daughter was a thief? —A

Hanna tried her hardest to keep a composed look on her face. Who could be doing this to her? How did A know where Hanna was right this second? She glanced at Kate—she *had* been fiddling on her own phone seconds ago. Kate gave her an annoyed glare back.

She shut her eyes and rifled through the other possibilities of who New A might be. At first, Real Ali had made so much sense. She must have somehow survived the fire *and* the fall from the crow's nest and come back to haunt them. But now that Hanna knew the girl they'd killed was Tabitha, she realized how crazy it was to think Ali had made it out of the Poconos house. But who else had they hurt? Who had seen what had happened in Jamaica, *and* the mess Hanna had made with Patrick, *and* God knows what else?

"Hanna?"

Hanna looked up dazedly. Everyone was standing and leaving the room. Her father stood over her, a concerned look on his face. "Are you okay? You look kind of . . . pale."

Hanna glanced out the French doors. Kate and Isabel wandered off toward the kitchen. The other staff members had vanished. "Actually, do you have a second?" Hanna asked.

"Sure. What's up?"

Hanna cleared her throat. She could never tell her dad about Tabitha, but there was one thing she could come clean about before A confessed for her. "Well, you know how you said we should come to you about skeletons in our closets?"

A crease formed on Mr. Marin's brow. "Yes . . ."

"Well, there's something I need to tell you."

Hanna turned away from her father and let the whole story spill out. About Patrick. How sure she'd been that he really believed in her. How he'd leered at her when he'd showed her the incriminating photos. "I was so afraid he was really going to post them online," she said, her eyes trained on a bunch of rolled-up campaign posters in the corner. "I was afraid he was going to ruin you. So I took the money from the safe. I didn't know what else to do. I didn't want to destroy your campaign."

After she finished, there was a punishingly long silence. Mr. Marin's cell phone beeped, but he didn't move to check it. Hanna didn't dare look at him. She felt filled with shame and hatred. This was even worse than the time Their Ali had caught Hanna vomiting at her dad's house in Annapolis after a massive binge.

All at once, the pain was just too much. She let out a pathetic puppy-whimper of a sob. Her shoulders shook silently. After a moment, she heard him sigh.

"Hey." He placed his hands on her shoulders. "Hanna. Don't cry. It's okay."

"No, it's not," Hanna blubbered. "I ruined everything. And now you hate me again."

"Again?" Mr. Marin drew back, frowning. "I never hated you."

Hanna sniffed loudly and raised her eyes to him. *Yeah, right.*

Her father stroked his chin. "I mean, I'm *surprised*. And a little shocked. But it was very brave to admit something you aren't proud of. Only, why would you go to some stranger's apartment to have photos taken in the first place? And why didn't you come to me when this was happening?"

Hanna hung her head. "I didn't want to upset you."

Her dad looked imploringly at her. "But I could have done something. I could have stopped this. You should know you can come to me with your problems."

Hanna inadvertently laughed. "Actually, Dad, I *can't*," she blurted. "I haven't been able to for years." Her father flinched, and Hanna's whole body sagged. "Sorry. That came out wrong. What I meant to say was . . ."

He held up his hand to cut her off, looking defensive. "I think you *did* mean it. But I've tried with you, Hanna. Don't forget you didn't want to speak to me for years, either. How do you think *I* felt?"

Hanna widened her eyes. For a long time, when her dad lived in Annapolis, she hadn't taken his calls, pretending she was busy. Really, she didn't want to hear about Kate and how wonderful she was compared to chubby, ugly, fat Hanna. It was something they'd never really talked about. Hanna hadn't realized her dad had even noticed.

"I'm sorry," Hanna mumbled.

"Well, I'm sorry, too," her father said gruffly.

This made tears spill down Hanna's cheeks even faster. After a moment, her father pulled her close, running his fingers up and down Hanna's arm. Finally, she wiped her eyes and looked up at her dad. "Do you want me to call Jeremiah? I could beg him to come back. Come clean about what I did." She could only imagine the satisfied smirk on Jeremiah's face when she told him *that*.

Mr. Marin shook his head. "Actually, Jeremiah is working for Tucker Wilkinson now."

Hanna gaped. "You're kidding."

"I wish I was. I guess we really *couldn't* trust him." Mr. Marin grabbed a TOM MARIN FOR SENATOR printed notepad from his desk. "I want you to give me any information you've got on this Patrick guy. Emails, phone numbers, anything you can think of. What he did to you is sick, Hanna. We need to find him and make him pay."

Hanna scrolled through her phone and gave him Patrick's details. "What about the money I stole? Do you want me to pay you back somehow?"

Mr. Marin twirled the pen between his fingers. "Just work extra hard on the campaign for me. I was going to mention this to you after the meeting anyway—we need to figure out ways to capture the youth vote. Kate's already on board. What about you?"

"Don't you have a paid staff to do that?"

"Of course I do. But I want you girls to be involved, too."

Hanna pressed her tongue into her cheek. The last thing

she wanted was to be on a committee with perfect Kate, but there was no way she could say no to her dad—not now. "Okay."

"I can't figure out how to reach young people," Mr. Marin said. "I assumed that you two would have some insight."

Hanna thought for a moment. "Do you have a Twitter account?"

"Yes, but I don't entirely *understand* Twitter." Mr. Marin looked sheepish. "Do you have to invite people to be your friends, like on Facebook?"

"People just follow you. I can take over your Twitter account if you want. And what if we use it to arrange a flash mob?"

Mr. Marin frowned. "Didn't a flash mob cause riots in Philly a few summers ago?"

"It would be a *controlled* flash mob," Hanna said with a small smile. "We could reach out to everyone on a local campus like Hollis or Hyde and have them gather for an impromptu rally. Maybe we could hire a band. The cooler we make it sound, the more kids will want to come even if they don't know what it is. You could appear and make a speech, and we could have people in the crowd registering them to vote, too."

Mr. Marin cocked his head. His eyes glimmered in the same way they did when he was about to say yes to a trip to Hershey Park, which Hanna used to beg for every weekend. "Let's try it," he said finally. "I think we should go with Hyde College—it's small and close to Philly. Can you make the arrangements?"

"Sure," Hanna said.

Mr. Marin leaned forward and touched Hanna's hand. "See? You're a natural at this. And what you said, earlier. About . . . well, about how things have changed between us." His voice was soft and tentative, almost nervous. "I don't *want* it to be that way."

"I don't, either." Hanna sniffed. "I don't know what to do about it, though."

Mr. Marin thought for a moment. "Why don't you stay here some nights?"

Hanna looked up. "Huh?"

"The new house is so big. There's a bedroom for you that's always open." He fiddled with the silver pen in his hand. "I miss you, Han. I miss having you around."

Hanna smiled shyly, feeling like she was going to cry again. She didn't want to live with Kate again, but things did seem different with her dad now. Maybe living with him would be better this time. Maybe they *could* start over.

"Okay," she said shyly. "I guess I could stay here a few nights next week."

"Great!" Mr. Marin looked thrilled. "Whenever you want." Then, his expression turned serious again. "So that's it, then? There isn't anything else you want to tell me?"

Tabitha's face swooped through her mind like a dive-bombing hawk, but Hanna shut her eyes and willed it out again. "Of course not."

He smiled at her and cuffed her softly on the arm. "Good girl."

Hanna rose, gave her father a kiss, and left. *That* had gone better than she planned. Probably better than A had planned, too.

But after she let herself out the front door, she noticed something wedged under her front tire. It was a crumpled-up flyer for *Pretty Little Killer*, the TV biopic that had aired the night the news had broken about Tabitha.

Ali's eyes were hauntingly blue, and her cruel smile seemed alive, like she could jump out from the page at any moment. A faint giggle sounded in Hanna's ears, and she spun around, checking the quiet neighborhood street. It was empty, but she still felt like someone was watching. Knowing her every secret. And ready to tell.

5

THE LITTLE MERMAID

"I don't understand why we're going to this party at midnight." Emily shifted her weight on the chicken-print cushioned barstool in the Fieldses' kitchen. "Didn't you say it started at nine?"

Beth dabbed eye shadow on Emily's upper lids. "No one goes to parties at nine. Midnight is the fashionable hour."

"And how would *you* know that, good girl?"

"'Good girl'?" Beth snorted. "Ha!"

"Not so loud!" Emily whispered.

It was a few minutes past eleven, and Emily's parents had already retired after a family dinner of pot roast, a game of Scattergories, and a boring TV program about the history of the railroad. They had no idea Emily and Beth were going out on a school night, much less to a loft in Philly full of college kids and booze.

Beth had spent the last hour slathering Emily in

makeup, using a curling iron to give her reddish-blondish hair bouncy, sexy waves, and even demanding Emily wear the black satin push-up bra in her drawer, which Emily had bought at Victoria's Secret with Maya St. Germain, a girl she'd dated last year.

"Looking different will get you out of your funk," Beth had advised. Emily wanted to tell her that she was pretty sure the only thing that would get her out of her funk would be if it turned out killing Tabitha had been a dream, but she appreciated Beth's effort.

"There. Your transformation is complete," Beth said now, swiping a bit of lipstick on Emily's lower lip. "Take a look."

She pushed a yellow hand mirror into Emily's hands. Emily stared at her reflection and gasped. Her eyelids looked smoky and sultry, her cheekbones were sharply defined, and her lips were full and downright kissable. It reminded her of the way Ali used to make her up during sleepovers. All her friends urged Emily to wear makeup to school, but she always felt embarrassed applying it herself, sure she'd somehow do it incorrectly.

Beth dangled a slinky black flapper dress and a black headband with a feather poking out the top under Emily's nose. "Now put these on. Then you'll be set."

Emily looked down at the good-luck Ali sweats she was still wearing. She wanted to ask Beth if she could keep them on, but even she knew that was going too far. "Can't I wear jeans?"

Beth's features settled into a scowl. "This is a costume party! And jeans are *not* fabulous. We want you hooking up with someone tonight."

Hooking up? Emily raised a newly plucked eyebrow. Beth had surprised Emily since she'd been home. Emily had heard L'il Kim floating out from Beth's old bedroom, and Beth had belted out all of the lyrics, even the dirty ones. And Beth had shown Emily a picture of Brian, her new boyfriend—who also happened to be the head swim coach.

"Who are you and what have you done with my sister?" Emily joked now, taking the dress from Beth's hands.

"Why, you don't remember me being such a risk-taker?" Beth teased back.

"I remember you being a lot like Carolyn." Emily made a pinched face.

Beth tilted forward. "Did something happen between you two?"

Emily fixed her eyes on the refrigerator. Her mother, organized to the core, had pinned up next week's dinner menu. Monday was tacos. Tuesday was spaghetti with meatballs. Tuesday was *always* spaghetti with meatballs.

Beth placed her chin in her hand, talk show host–style. "C'mon. Spill it."

Emily wished she could. *Carolyn never let me forget what a terrible daughter I was*, she could say. *All I wanted was for her to wrap her arms around me and tell me it would be all right, but she never did. She wasn't even there in the delivery room with me. She only found out afterward, when it was all over, and then she was just kind of like, "Oh."*

But she shrugged and turned away, the pain and the secret too great. "It doesn't matter. It was just stupid stuff."

Beth stared at Emily, like she knew Emily was hiding something. But then she turned away and glanced at the clock over the microwave. "Okay, Miss Fabulous. We're leaving in ten."

The party was in Old City—ironically, the neighborhood in Philly where Emily's obstetrician's office had been. After finding a parking spot in a garage across the street, Beth, who was wearing a Statue of Liberty crown, a long, green, Grecian-style dress, and gladiator sandals, strolled across the uneven cobblestones toward a freight elevator in an industrial-looking building. A bunch of other kids, all in elaborate costumes, jammed in with them, and instantly the small space smelled overpoweringly of deodorant and booze. A couple of guys in gangster pinstripes and porkpie hats glanced at Emily appreciatively. Beth nudged her excitedly, but Emily just adjusted her feather headband and stared at the elevator safety card on the wall, wondering when this thing had last been serviced. *If it doesn't break down while we're in it, I'll stay for an hour,* she wagered with herself.

Pounding music thudded through the walls as the elevator creaked up three stories. The doors opened into a dark loft crammed with votive candles, huge tapestries and paintings, and tons of people in costume. Cher writhed with Frankenstein on a makeshift dance floor. The evil queen from *Snow White* swing-danced with Barney the dinosaur. A zombie wriggled on top of a table, and two aliens waved at passing cars from the fire escape.

"Whose party is this again?" Emily yelled to Beth.

Her sister raised her palms to the sky. "I have no idea. I got the invite off Twitter. It's called 'March Monster Madness.'"

Floor-to-ceiling windows looked out at Penn's Landing and the Delaware River. Emily craned her neck and immediately spotted Poseidon's, the seafood restaurant where she'd worked last summer. It was the only job that offered health insurance—Emily could just imagine *prenatal checkup* showing up on her parents' insurance bill—and every day, she'd worked until her ankles ached, her voice was raw from saying *Yo ho ho!* in a gruff, pirate-ish tone, and her stomach heaved. She always crawled back to the dorm at Temple smelling like fried clams.

At the bar, Beth ordered four shots. "Bottoms up!" she said, handing two of the glasses to Emily.

Emily examined the dark liquid in the glass. It smelled like the gag-worthy Fisherman's Friend menthol lozenges her father insisted she suck on when she had a sore throat, but she swallowed it down anyway. Then, someone bumped Emily's shoulder. A girl in a green wig and a long mermaid dress complete with a fish tail practically fell into her.

"Sorry!" the girl yelled. Then she looked Emily up and down and started to smile. "Killer!"

Emily stepped back, her limbs suddenly stone. "Ex*cuse* me?"

"Your outfit." The girl felt the fabric of Emily's dress between her fingers. "*It's killer!*"

"Oh. Th-thanks." Emily's heart slowed. Of *course* she hadn't said Emily was a killer.

"It's my dress." Beth butted in between them and slung her arm around Emily's shoulders. "But doesn't she look amazing in it? I'm trying to get her to come out of her shell and be a little naughty tonight—dance on top of the table, make out with a stranger, flash Market Street . . ."

The mermaid's eyes brightened. She reminded Emily of a sexier, green-haired version of Ariel from *The Little Mermaid.* "Ooh, I like it. A bad-girl bucket list."

Beth gave the girl a high five. "What do you want to start with, Em?"

"How about kissing a stranger?" the mermaid suggested.

"Or stealing someone's underwear," Beth said.

"Ew!" Emily wrinkled her nose.

Beth put her hands on her hips. "Okay, then. Come up with something better."

Emily turned away from her sister and surveyed the crowd, not loving the idea of a bad-girl bucket list. The music was something fast and galvanizing, nothing like the trite stuff DJs always played at Rosewood Day dances.

Two girls dressed as hippies held hands in the corner. A couple in *Star Wars* Stormtrooper uniforms fed each other shots on the couch by the window.

Then the mermaid grabbed her hand, leaned into Emily, and kissed her on the mouth. Emily froze. She hadn't kissed anyone since Real Ali last year, and this girl's lips felt soft and warm.

The mermaid pulled away, grinning. "There. Now you can cross off one item on your bucket list. You kissed a stranger."

"That only half counted!" Beth cried. "She kissed you! Now *you* have to go kiss someone!"

"Yeah, pick someone!" The mermaid clapped her hands. "Or even better yet, close your eyes, spin around, and point!"

Emily tried to catch her breath, her lips still tingling. That kiss had felt *amazing*, and it flipped a switch inside her. Suddenly she wanted to show the new girl she was brazen and unafraid—worthy of kissing again. She whirled around the room and pointed. When she opened her eyes again, she was pointing at a tall, cute girl in dark-framed glasses and a Superman suit and cape.

"Supergirl!" Beth pushed Emily forward. "Go for her!"

Fueled with adrenaline, Emily knocked back the second shot and marched over, hoping the mermaid was watching. Supergirl was talking to a group of guys. Emily grabbed her hand and blurted, "Excuse me?" When Supergirl whirled around with a questioning look, Emily stood on her tiptoes and planted a big kiss on her lips. At first, the girl seemed shocked, her lips firm, but after a moment she softened and kissed her back. She tasted like blueberry-flavored lip gloss.

Emily pulled away, winked, and ran back to her sister. "Well?" Beth asked. "How was it?"

"Fun!" Emily admitted, feeling flushed and exhilarated. She looked around for the mermaid, but she had vanished. She tried not to feel disappointed.

"*Good*," Beth said. She took Emily's hands and swung them back and forth. "What do you want to do next?"

Emily spun around the room, then pointed at the couch. "Bounce on the cushions?"

"Do it!"

Beth pushed her forward, and Emily tentatively climbed on the couch and bounced lightly. She was about to get back down, but a guy nearby dressed in a sombrero and an ornate Mexican vest grinned at her. *Go for it!* he mouthed, giving her a thumbs-up. So Emily jumped higher and grinned, suddenly feeling like she was back in her living room, bouncing on the couch when her mom's head was turned. With every leap, she felt just a little bit freer and lighter. When Beth helped her off, she was even giggling.

The next dares came fast and furious. She bummed a cigarette from a big Asian guy with a piratelike bandana on his head. She raced across the dance floor, pinching girls' butts. Beth told her to go up to the big floor-to-ceiling window and moon Market Street, and Emily *almost* did it, until she remembered that Beth might see her C-section scar if she pulled up her dress. She danced wildly in front of the window instead, giving the traffic below a show. After indulging each and every impulse, she felt lighter and lighter, shedding her normally scared self in a crumpled, discarded heap on the floor.

After goading the DJ to show her how to spin records, Emily sloppily engulfed Beth in a hug. "This is amazing. Thanks so much."

"Told ya you needed to get out," Beth teased. "And how about Miss Goddess of the Sea?" She pointed at the mermaid, who was gyrating on the dance floor. "She's totally into you. You should go for her."

"She's not *into* me." Emily swatted her. She snuck a peek at the mermaid anyway. Her shimmery green dress hugged her every curve. When she noticed Emily watching, she blew her a kiss.

When Emily and Beth stood in line at the bar to get more drinks, the mermaid danced back over to them. Emily leaned into her. "So do you know who's throwing this party?"

The girl patted her green wig. "I'm not sure *anyone* here does. Rumor has it this is a big record exec's loft. I found out about it online."

A couple of girls swished past in a cloud of pot smoke. Emily ducked out of their way. "Are you from around here?"

"The suburbs." The girl made a scrunched-up face. "*Boring.*"

"Me too. Rosewood." As soon as Emily said it she flinched, sure the girl would probably look at Emily carefully and realize that she was one of the *Pretty Little Killer* girls.

But the girl just shrugged. "I go to a private school close to there. I'm almost out though, thank God."

"Do you know what college you're going to yet?" Emily glanced at the University of Pennsylvania keychain swinging from the girl's expensive-looking gold handbag. "Penn?"

An undefined expression moved across the girl's features. "I don't think any colleges would want someone like me." Then she grabbed Emily's arm, her face brightening again. "I've got a dare for you, badass." She pointed at a girl across the room who was wearing a fringed, Pocahontas-like jumpsuit and a large Native American headdress. "Steal that from her. Put it on. I bet you'd look hot in it."

Emily's stomach swooped. Maybe Beth had been right about this girl's crush. "You're on."

Giggling, she darted across the floor until she was a few feet away from Pocahontas. Then, with a quick, brave, light swipe, she grabbed the headdress from the girl's head. Emily's arms were suddenly full of feathers. Pocahontas's hands flew to her hair. She whipped around in time to see Emily plopping the headdress on her own head and running wildly through the loft.

"You *rock!*" the mermaid cried when Emily returned.

"When can I hang out with you again? I'll die if we don't become friends."

Emily almost blurted that she hoped they'd become *more* than friends. "Give me your information," she said instead, pulling out her cell phone. "God. I just realized. I don't even know your *name*."

"Where are my manners?" The girl slowly traced her finger over the label of her handbag. "I'm Kay."

"I'm Emily." She gave the girl a big smile and handed over her unlisted phone number. She'd vowed not to give it out to anyone besides family and very close friends, but all of a sudden, that felt like something scared Old Emily would do.

And tonight, she'd left Old Emily behind.

6

A FALLEN STAR

The following morning, Spencer perched on the edge of a green velvet chair in the auditorium at Rosewood Day. In her hands was a ragged copy of William Shakespeare's *Macbeth* with all of the lines for Lady Macbeth, the character she was playing in the Honors Drama production, highlighted in pink marker. As she thumbed nervously through the first scene, Pierre Castle, the brand-new Honors Drama teacher and director, clapped his hands.

"Okay! Lady M, up on the stage!" Pierre, who insisted that students use his first name, refused to utter the name *Macbeth* in fear of the centuries-old curse—apparently, those who dared speak it aloud had succumbed to deadly fevers, suffered severe burns, endured stabbings, and gotten mugged. Today was Pierre's first rehearsal as director, and he'd started off by calling the production "The Scottish Play" and addressing Macbeth and Lady Macbeth by their initials, which confused most of the freshmen. Pierre had been called in to pinch-hit when Christophe, the school's venerable old teacher-director, moved to Italy with his boyfriend. Everyone said Pierre had been a score, though. He'd been a dramaturge for a production of *Cymbeline* in Philly and quite a few Shakespeare in the Park seasons in New York City.

Tucking the script under her arm, Spencer climbed the risers, her knees wobbling. Last night, she'd tossed and turned until the wee hours of the morning, trying to figure out how the horrible Princeton admissions mix-up had happened. At 2 A.M., she'd thrown the covers back and looked at the letter again, hoping it wasn't real. But when she'd looked up Bettina Bloom on Princeton's website, there she was, head of the admissions board, looking smug in her photo.

It was preposterous that there was another high-achieving Spencer Hastings in this world. Spencer had also Google-stalked Spencer F., as she'd begun to call him. Apparently, Spencer Francis Hastings had run for mayor in Darien, Connecticut, as a sixteen-year-old and almost won. On his Facebook profile, he bragged about sailing around the world with his dad last summer and that he'd been a runner-up for the Westinghouse science prize in tenth grade. All of the pictures on his page showed a scrubbed, handsome guy who looked like he was exceedingly polite to old ladies but had six girlfriends at any given time. When Spencer F. received the same Princeton letter Spencer had, he'd probably shrugged and contacted some foreign dignitary or Hollywood director he was BFFs with and asked them to make one convincingly worded phone call to admissions.

This wasn't fair. Spencer had worked much, *much* too hard to get into Princeton. She'd also done horrible things in order to secure her spot, including ruining Kelsey's future last summer. She *had* to be the Spencer who was admitted.

But while Spencer may not have run for mayor, she did have acting. She had starred as the lead in every play the school put on, starting with her title role in *The Little Red Hen* in first grade. From there, she'd beat out Ali—really Courtney—for the role of Laura in the seventh grade's production of *The Glass Menagerie*, impressing even the seniors with her maturity and fragility. In eighth grade, after Ali vanished—or, rather, after the Real Ali killed her—she'd played Mary in *Long Day's Journey into Night*, receiving a standing ovation. Last year's *Hamlet* was the only production she hadn't starred in, and that was because she'd been banned from all school activities because she'd plagiarized her sister's Golden Orchid essay. It was actually a godsend that Rosewood Day was putting on *Macbeth* this year and that Spencer was cast as Lady Macbeth—it was a challenging role, one that the Princeton admissions board would be very impressed with. It could be enough to give her an edge over Spencer F.

The floorboards on the stage squeaked under Spencer's battleship-gray J. Crew ballet flats. Pierre, who was clad in all-black garb and wore what looked suspiciously like guy-liner, tapped a silver Mont Blanc pen against his lips. "We're going to try your sleepwalking scene, Lady M. Did you run through that with Christophe?"

"Of course," Spencer lied. Actually, Christophe had been so busy with his relocation plans that he'd assumed Spencer knew her lines and didn't need to practice.

Pierre's gaze dropped to the script in Spencer's hands. "Are you still using that? The performance is in less than two weeks!"

"I've almost got all my lines down," Spencer protested, even though it wasn't exactly true.

She heard a snicker off to the left. "She would *so* not get into Yale Drama," someone said in a low voice.

Spencer whipped around. The voice belonged to Beau Braswell, another new transplant to Rosewood Day and Spencer's costar as Macbeth. "Pardon?" Spencer demanded.

Beau clamped his lips together. "Nothing."

Ugh. Spencer turned back around and pushed up the sleeves of her Rosewood Day blazer. Beau had moved here from Los Angeles, and with his high cheekbones, longish dark hair, intentional bad-boy scruff, and beat-up Indian motorcycle, he'd quickly become the It Boy of Honors Drama. To every girl except Spencer, that is. Last month, when all the early college acceptances rolled in, he'd casually mentioned that he'd gotten into Yale's drama program. If "casually mentioning" was pompously talking about it Every. Single. Day. The Yale reference especially stung today, now that Spencer's future was so precarious.

"All right." Pierre tapped his pen against his script, and Spencer jumped. "Let's take it from the start of the scene. Doctor? Gentlewoman?" He looked at Mike Montgomery and Colleen Lowry, who were in the scene, too. "You're watching Lady M's predicament from the sidelines. And . . . *action!*"

Mike, playing Lady Macbeth's doctor, turned to Colleen, Lady Macbeth's maid, and asked how long it had been since Lady Macbeth first walked in her sleep. Colleen answered that apparently Lady Macbeth got up in the middle of the night, wrote something on a piece of paper, then sealed up the secrets tight.

Then Pierre motioned to Spencer, and she stumbled into the scene and started feverishly rubbing her hands. "*Yes, here's the spot,*" she said passionately, trying to sound like a madwoman who was wracked with guilt for killing the king.

"*Hark, she speaks!*" Mike recited.

"*Out, damned spot! Out, I say!*" Spencer bellowed. She glanced down at the script and said a few more lines. When she got to the part about how she could still smell the king's blood on her skin, Pierre let out a long sigh.

"Cut!" he yelled. "I need more emotion from you, Spencer. More guilt. All of your evil deeds are catching up to you, making you have nightmares and see blood on your hands. Try to picture what it *really* feels like to murder someone."

You don't know the half of it, Spencer thought with a shiver, instantly thinking of Tabitha. What if the Princeton admissions board somehow got wind of that? What if A told them? She winced and shut her eyes as the scene continued.

"Spencer?" Pierre prompted.

Spencer blinked. A few lines had gone by that she'd completely missed, and now the director was staring at her. "Um, sorry, where were we?"

Pierre looked annoyed. "Mike, can you repeat your line?"

"*This disease is beyond my practice, yet I have known those which have walked in their sleep and died holily in their beds,*" Mike said.

Spencer glanced at the script. "*Wash your hands, put on your nightgown . . .*"

But as she was saying the words, her thoughts drifted again. What if Princeton somehow knew about what had happened with Kelsey last summer? The police said they wouldn't put the bust on Spencer's permanent record, but maybe Princeton had found out another way.

The summery June night when she'd first met Kelsey swirled in her mind. It had been at a bar called McGillicuddy's on the University of Pennsylvania campus. The floors were sticky with beer, there was a Phillies game on the flat-screen, and the bartenders were lining up neon-colored shots on the counter. The room was stuffed with summer students, most of them underage. Spencer stood next to a guy named Phineas O'Connell, who sat behind her in AP Chem III.

"You're taking four APs in six weeks?" Phineas asked her over a pint of Guinness. He was cute in a layered-haired, vintage-T-wearing, Justin-Bieber-goes-emo way. "Are you insane?"

Spencer shrugged nonchalantly, pretending she wasn't freaked out by the brutal course load. When she'd received her end-of-year grades at Rosewood Day, she'd gotten three Bs for the year—*and* had slipped to twenty-seventh in the class ranking. That simply would not do. Taking—and acing—four APs was the only thing that would save her GPA and get her into an Ivy.

"I'm taking four APs, too," said a voice.

Behind them was a petite girl with cinnamon-red hair and sparkling green eyes Spencer had seen around the Penn dorms. She wore a faded T-shirt from St. Agnes, a snotty private school near Rosewood, and a pair of oat-colored Marc Jacobs espadrille sandals that had just come out in stores. Spencer was wearing the same exact shoes, except in blue.

Spencer smiled in commiseration. "It's nice to know someone's as crazy as I am."

"I think I need to clone myself to get all the work done." The girl laughed. "*And* murder the girl who lives next to me. She listens to *Glee* songs nonstop—and sings along." She put her finger to her temple and made a *pow* noise, simulating a gun.

"You don't need to clone yourself—*or* switch rooms." Phineas spun a green class ring around his finger. "If you girls are serious about acing four APs, I know something that can help."

Spencer placed her hands on her hips. "*I'm* serious. I'll do whatever it takes."

Phineas looked at the other girl. "I'm serious, too," she said after a pause.

"Well, then, come on."

Phineas took Spencer and the second girl's arm and led them toward the back of the bar. As they walked, the girl turned to Spencer. "Do I know you? You look really familiar."

Spencer gritted her teeth. That was probably because she'd been all over the news and *People* magazine as one of the girls who'd been tormented by their old, presumably dead best friend. "Spencer Hastings," she said in a clipped voice.

The girl paused, then gave a quick nod. "I'm Kelsey. By the way, I *love* your shoes. Are you on the Saks Secret Shopper list, too?"

"Of course," Spencer said.

Kelsey bumped Spencer's hip. And that was all she said about that. Spencer wanted to kiss her for not bringing up Alison DiLaurentis, twin-switching, or a certain text-messager named A.

"Lady M?" a sharp voice called. Pierre looked like his head was about to explode.

"Uh . . ." Spencer glanced around. Mike and Colleen had left the stage. Had the scene ended?

Pierre shooed Spencer toward the seats. "Witches? You're up next!"

The witches, who were played by Hanna's stepsister, Kate Randall, Naomi Zeigler, and Riley Wolfe, jumped up from an impromptu manicure session at the back of the auditorium.

"Hey, Beau," Riley said as they climbed on the stage, batting her pale, stubby eyelashes at him.

"Hey," Beau said, shooting each of the girls a winning grin. "Ready to cackle and cast magic spells, witches?"

"Of course," Naomi giggled, tucking a piece of blond hair behind her ear.

"I wish I could *really* cast a magic spell," Riley said. "I'd have Pierre put *me* in the role of your wife and kick Spencer to the curb."

All three of them shot Spencer daggers. Spencer didn't interact with Naomi or Riley very often, but she always felt wary of them. Once upon a time, they'd been Real Ali's BFFs. Then, when the switch happened, Their Ali—Courtney—dumped them abruptly, and they were no longer popular. They'd had it in for Spencer and her old friends ever since.

Spencer turned back to Pierre, who was assiduously making marks in his script, probably about how poor her performance had been.

"I'm really sorry about my scene," she said. "I was distracted. I'll get it together tomorrow."

Pierre pursed his thin lips. "I expect my actresses to give one hundred and ten percent every day. Was *that* your one hundred and ten percent?"

"Of course not," Spencer squeaked. "But I'll be better! I promise!"

Pierre didn't look convinced. "If you don't start taking this part more seriously, I'll have to give the part of Lady M to Phi instead."

He gestured to Spencer's understudy, Phi Templeton, who was sitting in the middle of the aisle, her nose buried in the *Macbeth* text. Her legs, which were clad in black-and-white striped stockings, extended into the aisle like those of the house-flattened Wicked Witch in *The Wizard of Oz*. A piece of toilet paper was stuck to her Doc Marten shoe.

"Please don't do that!" Spencer cried. "I need a good grade in this class."

"Then get your head into this play and *focus*." Pierre slapped his script shut. A red velvet bookmark covered with kissing lips floated out, but he made no motion to grab for it. "If you nail this role, I'll give you an A for the year. But if you don't . . ." He trailed off and raised his eyebrows ominously.

A cough sounded from the left. Naomi, Riley, and Kate snickered from the witches' cauldron. Everyone stared at her from the audience, too.

"I've got it under control," Spencer said, marching off the stage and up the aisle as confidently as she could, pointedly stepping on the strap of Phi's backpack.

Pushing open the auditorium's double doors, she emerged into the windowed lobby, which was filled with *Macbeth* posters and smelled like spearmint gum. Suddenly, a faint whisper swirled in her ear.

Murderer.

Spencer shot up and looked around. The lobby was empty. She walked quickly to the stairwell, but there was no one there, either.

A creak sounded, and Spencer jumped again. When she turned, Beau was standing behind her.

"I can help you practice, if you want," he said.

Spencer stiffened. "I don't need your help, thank you very much."

Beau pushed back a lock of silky brown hair that hung in his face. "Actually, I think you do. If you look bad, I look bad, and Yale wants all my performance tapes. It will impact what classes I'll get into in the fall."

Spencer let out an indignant squeak. She was about to turn away, but the letter from Princeton whooshed back to her. Beau *had* gotten into Yale Drama. Pompous ass or not, he probably knew a thing or two about acting. She needed all the help she could get.

"Okay," she said frostily. "If you really want, we can rehearse together."

"Great." Beau pushed against the auditorium door. "Sunday. At my place."

"Wait!" she called. "How am I supposed to know where you live?"

Beau gave her a strange look. "My address is on the drama club call sheet, just like everyone else's. You can find it there."

He pivoted into the auditorium and swaggered down the rows of seats. Naomi, Riley, Kate, and all the other drama club fangirls nudged each other and gawked at him appreciatively. Even though Spencer would have died if Beau had caught her, she couldn't help but ogle his cute butt as he moved down the aisle, too.

7

THANK GOODNESS FOR
CELL PHONE ADDRESS BOOKS

Before the last period on Friday afternoon, Aria lingered
outside her art history class with her phone open, stalking
the Tabitha Clark Memorial website. There were a few
new postings, mostly from friends and family offering
condolences. She also noticed a mention of a CNN special
about spring break alcohol abuse that would air next
week; apparently, Tabitha's story would be mentioned.
Aria swallowed a huge lump in her throat. It felt so weird
and terrible to just let the world think that Tabitha had
perished because of drinking.

She looked up just in time to see Mike stop at his locker.
He was talking to Colleen Lowry, a pretty cheerleader in
his grade; rumor had it they were in a scene in the school
play together. As he slammed the locker shut and turned
a corner, Mike placed his hand on Colleen's butt. He'd
spent the last few weeks moping over his breakup with
Hanna, but it looked like he was moving on.

Despair filled her. Would there come a time when Aria was over Noel, too? Would she eventually be able to look at random items around her room—an empty plastic cup from an outdoor concert on the Camden waterfront she and Noel had attended this past summer, a large temporary tattoo template of Robert Pattinson, who Noel teased Aria about loving, the schedule of the cooking class they were taking together at Hollis—and not burst into tears? She couldn't stop thinking about what she'd done wrong in the relationship. Dragged him to too many poetry readings, probably. Acted bored at the many Typical Rosewood parties he threw. And then there was what happened in Iceland. But only Hanna knew about that, and she was sworn to secrecy.

"Aria."

Aria turned and saw Hanna striding toward her with purpose. Even though her auburn hair was pulled back into a sleek ponytail, her makeup looked like it had been professionally applied, and the pinstriped tunic under her blue Rosewood Day blazer was perfectly pressed, she still seemed frazzled. "Hey." She sounded out of breath.

"What's up?" Aria asked.

Hanna fingered the leaf-green leather satchel on her shoulder. Her eyes shifted back and forth. "Have you gotten any notes from . . . *you* know?"

Aria toyed with a hemp bracelet she'd bought at a head shop in Philly. "Not since the one two weeks ago." The newscast of Tabitha's remains washing up on shore flashed through Aria's mind. "Why, have you?"

The between-classes classical music, which the Rosewood Day administration thought was mentally stimulating, stopped abruptly, signaling that the next period was about to begin. Hanna twisted her mouth and looked across the hall at the trophy case.

Aria grabbed Hanna's wrist. "What did it say?"

A fresh crop of kids scampered past. "I-I have to go," Hanna stammered. Then she scuttled down the hall and ducked into a French classroom.

"Hanna!" Aria cried out.

Hanna's French classroom door slammed shut. After a moment, Aria dropped her shoulders, let out a pent-up sigh, and walked into her own class before the final bell rang.

Twenty minutes later, Mrs. Kittinger, the art history teacher, dimmed the lights and switched on the old-school slide projector, which always made a rattling noise and smelled slightly of burnt hair. A dusty yellow beam flickered down the center of the classroom and projected an image of *Salon at the Rue des Moulins* by Henri de Toulouse-Lautrec onto the white screen in front of the blackboard. French prostitutes sat around a Parisian brothel, killing time.

"Everyone keeps secrets, especially artists," Mrs. Kittinger said in her deep, gravelly voice, which matched her slicked-back, boyish haircut and her elegantly tailored men's suit. Everyone at Rosewood gossiped that Mrs. Kittinger was a lesbian, but Aria's mother knew her from the art gallery where she worked and said she was happily married to a sculptor named Dave.

"And by looking at Mr. Toulouse-Lautrec's paintings," Mrs. Kittinger went on, "you might think his secret had something to do with matters of the flesh, but in fact his problems were quite the opposite. Any guesses?"

Bored silence reigned. Art history was Aria's favorite subject, but most of the other kids weren't taking it seriously. They'd probably elected to take it because it sounded like *art*, which didn't require much thought. On the first day of class, when Mrs. Kittinger handed out the thick textbooks, a lot of the students stared at the pages like they were written in Morse code.

Finally, James Freed raised his hand. "Was he born a woman?"

Mason Byers snickered, and Aria rolled her eyes.

"Actually, that's pretty close," Mrs. Kittinger said. "Toulouse-Lautrec was born with congenital defects, mostly because his parents were first cousins."

"Hot," James Freed said under his breath.

"He had a growth disease that gave him the legs of a child and the torso of an adult," Mrs. Kittinger added. "Rumor had it that he also had deformed genitalia."

"*Ew*," a girl said. Aria had a feeling it was Naomi Zeigler. Someone else giggled next to Naomi, and Aria was pretty sure she knew who that was, too. Klaudia. She'd unfortunately joined the class at the end of last week.

Mrs. Kittinger flipped to the next slide. It was a self-portrait of a red-haired artist, done with swirling brush strokes. "Who's this?"

"Vincent Van Gogh," Aria answered.

"Correct," Mrs. Kittinger said. "Now, Mr. Van Gogh seems like such a happy fellow, right? Always painting sunflowers or beautiful starry nights?"

"That's not true," Kirsten Cullen piped up. "He was severely depressed and in lots of pain. And he took painkillers, which might have altered his visual perception, which could be why his paintings are so vibrant and hypnotic."

"Very good," Mrs. Kittinger said.

Aria shot Kirsten a smile. She was the only person besides Aria who actually tried in this class.

Mrs. Kittinger shut off the projector, turned the lights back on, and walked to the blackboard, her oxfords clacking loudly on the wood floor. "Our next project is going to be about psychology. I'm going to assign you an artist, and you're going to investigate his mental state and link it to his work. The paper is due not this coming Monday, but next."

Mason groaned. "But I have an indoor soccer tournament all next week."

Mrs. Kittinger gave him an exasperated look. "Luckily for you, we're working in pairs."

Aria instantly turned to Kirsten, wanting to work with her. Other kids silently paired up, too. "Not so fast." Mrs. Kittinger lifted a piece of chalk in the air. "*I'm* doing the pairing, not you."

She pointed to Mason Byers and matched him with Delia Hopkins, who hadn't said a word all semester. She paired Naomi Zeigler and Imogen Smith, a tall girl with large boobs who'd never shaken her reputation as the class slut.

Then Mrs. Kittinger pointed to Aria. "And Aria, you'll report on Caravaggio. And you'll work with . . ." She pointed at someone in the back. "What did you say your name was again, dear?"

"Is Klaudia Huusko," chirruped a voice.

Aria's blood went cold. *No. Please, please, no.*

"Perfect." Mrs. Kittinger wrote Aria's and Klaudia's names on the board. "You two are a team."

Mason turned around and stared at Aria. Naomi let out a *mrow*. Even Chassey Bledsoe giggled. Clearly everyone knew that Noel had dumped Aria and was with Klaudia now.

Aria swiveled around and looked at Klaudia. Her uniform skirt barely skimmed her thighs, showing off every curve of her impossibly perfect Finnish legs. Her ankle was propped up against the back of Delia's chair, but Delia was too much of a wuss to tell her to move it. A beat-up leather bomber jacket hung over her shoulders. Aria squinted at it, recognizing the eagle military patch on the arm. It was Noel's jacket, a beloved hand-me-down from his great-grandfather, who'd fought in World War II. Once, Aria had asked to try it on, but Noel had refused— he didn't let anyone wear it, he said. It was too special.

Guess the rules didn't apply to his new Finnish girl-friend.

Klaudia met Aria's gaze and smiled triumphantly. Then she turned to Naomi. "Guess what I plan for this weekend? I go with Noel to romantic dinner! We going to have wine, feed each other bites of meal, is going to be sexy time!"

"That sounds amazing." Naomi smirked at Aria.

Aria faced front again, her cheeks on fire. She *hated* Klaudia. How could Noel fall for her ridiculous act? Everything about her was fake, even her choppy, I-don't-know-English accent—when Klaudia had threatened Aria on the chair lift, all traces of it had vanished. It seemed the bimbos of the world always got the guys. Where did that leave Aria?

She looked around the classroom. Both art history and English classes met here, so there was a motley mix of Cézanne and Picasso prints and black-and-white photos of Walt Whitman, F. Scott Fitzgerald, and Virginia Woolf. Tacked up in the corner was a poster labeled GREAT SHAKE-SPEAREAN SAYINGS. That poster had hung in Aria's English classroom last year, too, the class that had briefly been taught by Ezra Fitz, with whom Aria had had a fling until A got him fired.

Ezra. Now *there* was someone who would have enjoyed going to an art gallery and commiserating about all the Typical Rosewoods. The first time Aria and Ezra had met, they'd had a real connection. Ezra understood what it was like to be part of a family that was falling apart. He got what it was like to be different.

Aria surreptitiously pulled out her phone and looked at her contacts list. Ezra's name was still there. *Just wondering what you're up to*, she typed in a new email. *Going through a hard time right now. Feeling lonely and in need of a good convo about poetry writing and the ridiculousness of the suburbs. Ciao, Aria.*

And then, before she lost her nerve, she pressed SEND.

8

THE STARS ALIGN

Later that Friday, Hanna and Kate pulled into a space next to Mr. Marin's car on the Hyde campus, an old Jesuit college in the leafy suburbs a few miles outside Philadelphia. It was unseasonably warm, and kids walked across the street sans coats. Boys played Frisbee on the dry, greenish-yellow lawn, and preppy girls sipped lattes underneath the clock tower, which chimed out the hour in six deafening *bongs*. It was the perfect night for a flash mob.

"So is the band definitely coming?" Hanna said to Kate, scanning the parking lot. After Mr. Marin informed Kate about the flash mob plan, Kate had offered to hire some band called Eggplant Supercar from Hollis College. Apparently they drove an Astro van with flames painted on the sides, but Hanna didn't see it anywhere.

Kate rolled her eyes. "Yeh-*hes*. That's like the twentieth time you've asked."

"Is someone nervous?" Naomi cackled from the backseat.

"Maybe someone realizes that a flash mob is a stupid idea," Riley chimed in.

"Seriously," Kate mumbled. "When I heard about it, I thought Tom was joking."

Riley and Naomi snickered. Klaudia, who was squeezed in the bitch seat, barked out a horsey, slutty laugh.

Hanna glanced at her dad's car to her left, wishing he'd overheard, but Mr. Marin was talking animatedly on his cell phone. When Kate told her she'd recruited her friends to help with the flash mob today, Hanna should've put her foot down. Now that Mona Vanderwaal, Hanna's old BFF, was dead, and Hanna wasn't hanging out with Emily, Aria, or Spencer anymore, she felt Kate, Naomi, and Riley's insults much more acutely. It was like she was back where she started in sixth grade: a loser. Except thinner. And a lot prettier.

"There they are," Kate said, pointing triumphantly. A van rolled into the parking space on the other side of them, and a bunch of ragged guys spilled out, carrying music equipment. One had a patchy beard and greasy skin. Another had an elongated head and a prominent chin. The others looked like they could be in a police lineup. Hanna sniffed. Couldn't Kate have hired a cuter band?

Mr. Marin finally climbed out of the car and strode up to the band. "Thanks for helping us out tonight," he said, shaking each of their hands.

"Okay, let's get them set up, ladies," Kate said to her friends, grabbing a bunch of neon-green TOM MARIN FOR SENATE flyers from the backseat. "You do your Twitter thing, Hanna."

Naomi sniffed. "Like it's really going to work," she said under her breath. The four girls whirled around and led the guys toward a band shell to the left of the clock tower. Everyone moved deferentially out of their way.

Mr. Marin clapped his hand on Hanna's shoulder as she climbed out of the car, too. "You all set?"

"Of course," Hanna answered. She grabbed her phone, opened her email, and sent Gregory, a computer science major at Hyde who claimed to know how to tap into everyone's Twitter and email accounts on campus, a message. *I'm ready.* Seconds later, Gregory replied that the flash mob tweet had been posted. Hanna had crafted it last night: *Something huge is happening in the band shell. Be there or be a nobody.* Short and sweet. Elusive yet intriguing.

"I sent the tweet," Hanna told her dad. "You should probably head up to the stage and wait. I'll watch from below."

Mr. Marin kissed the top of Hanna's head. "Thank you so much."

Don't thank me quite yet, Hanna thought uneasily. She walked into the square, looking around. Kids were still playing Frisbee. Girls giggled over a magazine, not even glancing at their phones. What if Kate was right? What if nothing *did* happen? She could picture it: Kate, her evil cronies, and the band standing on the pavilion, staring out at an empty courtyard. Her father looking disappointedly at Hanna, losing all faith in her. Tomorrow Hanna would be the laughingstock of Rosewood Day—and her dad's campaign.

When she was almost to the band shell, three girls wandered into the square, holding their phones and looking around. A couple of the guys slammed their textbooks shut and meandered over, curious looks on their faces. Two kids rolled up on skateboards. Hanna caught snippets of their conversation: *Is something happening? Did you see that on Twitter? Who posted it? Someone get Sebastian. He'll know.*

Suddenly it was like a stampede. Kids poured out of the dining hall, emerged from the dorms, streamed in from late classes. A group of girls in sorority sweatshirts gathered under a big oak tree plastered with carvings. Some guys chugging beers from inside paper bags shoved one another by a board covered in advertisements for roommates, yoga lessons, and free tutoring services. Everyone was staring at their phones, their fingers moving over the keyboards. Retweeting. Asking what was up. Gathering more people.

Yes.

Kate turned around on the stage. When she saw the crowd, her mouth settled into a straight, annoyed line. Hanna gave her a triumphant three-fingered wave, then sent out a text telling her dad's aides that they could start circulating with voter registration forms and flyers. A few minutes later, the band began to play. Thankfully, despite their ugliness, they were pretty good, and everyone started to bounce to the music. A green banner that advertised Mr. Marin's campaign rose in the air. When Eggplant Supercar—they *seriously* needed a new name—finished a song, the lead singer roared into the microphone: "Let's hear it for Tom Marin!" and Mr. Marin walked onto the stage and waved, the crowd actually *cheered*.

Hanna let the sound wash over her body. Maybe this would win her dad the election. Maybe Hanna had a future in campaign management. She pictured herself on the cover of *Vanity Fair* in a sleek Armani suit. Visiting the White House. Riding on Air Force One, wearing big Jackie O sunglasses . . .

"This band is decent," said a voice.

Hanna jumped. A tall, lanky guy with wavy brown hair, dark eyebrows that framed kind, sparkling brown eyes, and a square, superhero-esque jaw stood beside her. He wore a faded navy T-shirt that said HYDE across the chest, slim-cut jeans, and a beat-up pair of Sperry Top-Siders. He was also standing close enough to Hanna that she could smell his Tom Ford Azure Lime cologne, her absolute favorite. He looked familiar for some reason, but she wasn't sure why. Maybe she'd had a dream about him or something. He was definitely hot.

"Do you know the band's name?" the guy asked, his eyes still fixed on Hanna.

"Um, Eggplant Supercar," Hanna answered, absently

twirling a piece of auburn hair around her finger. Thank God she'd recently had it highlighted at Henri Flaubert at the King James.

"I like them." The guy pushed his hands into his pockets. "Hyde doesn't usually do cool stuff like this. I think we've been voted Most Boring Campus in a bunch of magazines, actually."

Hanna took a breath, about to tell him that he could thank her for setting the whole thing up, when suddenly three burly guys holding beer cans cut between them. After they passed, the boy pushed around a couple of bodies to stand next to Hanna again. "Doesn't the singer look exactly like Bert from *Sesame Street*?" he asked, pointing to the guy with the elongated head. He was fondling the microphone like he was in love with it.

"Totally." Hanna giggled. "I was thinking the same thing."

"Of course, I shouldn't talk," the boy said sheepishly. "People used to call me Harry Potter when I was growing up."

"Really?" Hanna cocked her head and inspected him. He was tall but not too tall, and his limbs were long and lanky without being too skinny. "I don't really see a resemblance."

"I used to wear these goofy wire-rimmed glasses when I was younger. I picked them out at the eye doctor myself. You would've thought my mom would have been a little smarter, but instead she was like, *Get them!*"

Hanna giggled. "When I wore glasses, I chose fuchsia plastic frames and pink lenses. I looked like I had a disease. My third-grade school picture was horrific."

"Don't even get me *started* on school pictures." The guy winced. "In my fifth-grade photo, I had black rubber bands on my braces. It looked like there was tar oozing from my mouth."

"I had pink and green rubber bands on my braces. Disaster." The words were out of Hanna's mouth before she could stop them, and her confession surprised even her. Never had she willingly volunteered information about what a loser she used to be, especially to someone so good-looking. But there was something warm and inviting about this guy that actually made it fun to commiserate.

He straightened up and gave her a challenging look. "Well, I was way too skinny as a kid. Concave chest, knobby knees, picked last for every team in gym class. Top that."

"*I* was chubby." Hanna laughed self-consciously. "More like fat, actually. I looked like a beast next to my friends. My dad even called me a piggie once—like it was funny." She shut her eyes.

"I got called scarecrow. Anorexic boy. Freak."

"So? I was Chubby Couture. Hanna Fat-Assa." Hanna felt a hurtful twinge. Actually, Their Ali had made up those nicknames when they were friends.

The guy reached out and touched the inside of Hanna's

wrist. It felt electrifying. "I bet no one calls you a loser anymore, huh?"

She swallowed hard, meeting his eyes. "Or you."

The crowd moved again, this time pushing them into each other. Hanna tipped sideways, and the guy slipped his arm around her waist. When the mob shifted again, they didn't break apart. Hanna breathed in his spicy, soapy smell, her pulse in her throat. He rested his chin in her hair. His hipbone pressed against her waist. She could feel his smooth, hard chest beneath his thin T-shirt. Something stirred deep inside her, filling her with heat. When he leaned down to kiss her, Hanna was struck with shock. But the kiss felt so good, so *right*, that she couldn't help kissing him back.

They pulled away, staring into each other's eyes. The guy looked as shocked as Hanna felt. He cleared his throat. "Do you want to—"

"I think we should—" Hanna said at the same time.

They both stopped and chuckled. He grabbed her hand and pulled her through the crowd until they turned into a dark alley between one of the classroom buildings and an internet café called Networks. They ran down it crookedly, hand in hand, tripping over empty cardboard boxes and abandoned Coke and beer cans. The guy stopped, pulled Hanna to the wall, and started kissing her fervently. Hanna kissed him back, tasting his slightly salty skin, touching the sinewy muscles in his arms, burrowing her hands under his T-shirt. Never before had she felt so swept away.

Finally, they pulled away, panting hard. "Wow," the guy whispered, out of breath. "This is . . . crazy."

"I know," Hanna said.

He gripped Hanna's hands. "What's your name?"

"Hanna."

"I'm Liam," he said.

"That's the most beautiful name I've ever heard," Hanna murmured dreamily, barely aware of what she was saying. She didn't know what her body was doing. Her father was up on the stage now, giving a speech about voting and change for the better and all kinds of other optimistic political promises. Hanna knew she should be out there, being the good little campaign strategist, but she couldn't tear herself away from Liam's embrace. She wanted to stay here in this dingy alley for the rest of her life, with Liam.

9

EMILY'S GOT A TYPE

"Smile!" Kay pulled Emily close and aimed her camera phone at both of them as they stood under the marquee at the Electric Factory, a music club in downtown Philly—the Chambermaids, Kay's favorite band, was going on in an hour. Emily smiled as the flash went off, and then Kay inspected the screen. "You look super-cute! Your sister will love it."

Kay pressed a few buttons, sending the image off to Beth, who was out with a friend tonight. She'd insisted Emily go alone, though. "You're the one Kay wants," she'd urged. "I guarantee you guys are going to hook up by the end of the night."

Truthfully, Emily had been ecstatic when Kay had called her this morning asking if she wanted to hang out. All she could think of was the quick but electrically charged kiss at the party, of Kay dancing, unfettered, and of what Kay said at the end of the night: *I'll die if we don't become friends.* There was something dangerous and unpredictable about Kay. Hanging out with her gave Emily the same deliciously illicit feeling she used to get when watching an R-rated movie at Ali's when she was younger: R movies were banned at the Fields house, which made Emily even more curious to see what they were all about.

When she'd met Kay in the lobby earlier, she'd been pleasantly surprised: Out of her mermaid dress and wig, Kay was even hotter than Emily imagined. She had long reddish hair that fell almost to the small of her back. Her gray vintage T-shirt pulled across her torso, hinting at perky boobs and a flat stomach. Kay's eyes had lit up when she saw Emily emerge through the throng, as if she liked what she was seeing, too.

Now, a doorman ripped their tickets, and the girls pushed through the front door. "Drinks," Kay said with purpose, weaving around a bunch of kids milling by the stage. They got into the line behind two girls in matching T-shirts with photos of the Chambermaids. It was funny to see that the band members were all guys—and hot ones, too. Emily had envisioned girls in cleaning lady uniforms.

"How do you know this band?" Emily asked.

"I heard them on Pandora last summer." Kay twisted a piece of hair around her finger. "They got me through a rough patch."

Emily touched the feather earrings that hung from her ears. "What kind of rough patch?"

Kay stared off at the stack of amps that lined the wall.

"I spent some time away from home. It's a boring story, though."

"I know all about rough patches," Emily admitted, looking down at her toes. "My parents sent me away, too. I went to Iowa to live with my cousins. It was a disaster, and I ran away."

Kay widened her eyes. "Are you okay?"

Emily shrugged. "Yeah. But I've been through other things, too. If my parents ever found out they'd do a lot more than send me away." She shut her eyes for a moment and tried to imagine what her mother's reaction would be if she learned Emily had been pregnant, but she simply couldn't come up with anything extreme enough, save for her mother's head literally exploding. She didn't even dare consider what her mother would do if she found out about Tabitha.

"I've kept tons of things from my parents, too," Kay said, almost with relief. "I used to be so much wilder than I am now. These days, my parents don't trust me at all. Most of the time, if I want to go anywhere, I have to sneak out." She smiled slyly and bumped Emily's hip. "I doubt they would've let me out with you tonight, Miss Bad-Girl Bucket List."

Emily struck a pose, channeling devilish New Emily. "Don't think I'm done with the bad-girl bucket list. There might be a few things to cross off on the list tonight."

"I was hoping you'd say that," Kay said, her green eyes on Emily's. A tingle sizzled up Emily's backbone.

It was Kay's turn to order, and she asked the bartender for two Captain Morgan and Cokes. When he slid the glasses across the bar, she raised hers in the air. "To a checkered past, and a brighter future."

Emily snorted. "That sounds like a valedictorian speech."

An uncomfortable expression slid across Kay's face, and she gazed up at the overhead lights. After a moment, she turned back to Emily, the look gone. "Do you kiss strange girls at parties often? You looked like you had some experience with it."

Emily blushed. "No, kissing a stranger—well, *two* strangers—was a first for me." But then she paused, feeling a surge of honesty. "I did have a girlfriend last year, though."

Kay looked intrigued. "What was that like?"

Emily felt her cheeks burn even brighter. She ducked her head. "Actually, it's pretty awesome."

Kay stirred her drink with the little red straw. "Guys suck. And girls are so much cuter."

"They are," Emily said in a half whisper. She stared at Kay, entranced by the smooth, freckly skin on her bare shoulders and neck. Kay stared back.

Then Kay lifted her glass again. "Another toast. This time to girl-on-girl action."

"Cheers," Emily said, clinking her glass to Kay's once more.

Kay took a long, almost grateful sip. "So. I think sneaking backstage and meeting the band should be on your bad-girl bucket list."

Emily raised an eyebrow. "Okay. But how are we going to do that?"

Kay pointed to a bouncer who was manning a door near the stage. "Tell that guy you're Rob Martin's girlfriend and you want to see him for a sec before he performs. And slip him this." She pressed something in Emily's hand. Emily opened her palm and saw it was a twenty.

"He'll know I'm lying!" Emily whispered.

Kay sank into her hip. "I'll back you up. C'mon. This is an easy one."

The crowd shifted, creating a clear path to the bouncer. The few sips of rum Emily had taken burned in her chest. Adrenaline pumped through her body, making her feel tingly and *alive*.

Rolling her shoulders back, Emily snaked through the crowd and stopped at the dingy black door next to a stack of Marshall amps. The bored-looking bouncer, who could have been a body double for Vin Diesel, leafed through a motorcycle magazine. Emily glanced over her shoulder, and Kay gave her an encouraging nod.

"Excuse me," Emily said sweetly, touching the guy's elbow. "Do you mind if we go in for a sec? I'm Rob Martin's girlfriend, and I want to see him before he goes on."

The guy lowered the magazine and squinted at her. His eyes scanned Emily's reddish-blondish hair, her toned swimmer's shoulders, and her thin waist. Emily was glad she'd snagged a pair of skinny jeans from Beth's suitcase and paired them with one of the few snug-fitting T-shirts her parents hadn't banned. Her fingers curled around the bill Kay had handed her. After a moment, she pushed it into the bouncer's palm. Then she slid her fingers up his wrist and squeezed his bicep. "Strong," she said in a voice that she couldn't believe belonged to her. "I bet you can bench a ton."

Miraculously, the bouncer smirked, stepped aside, and unlocked the door for them. Emily slipped through the door, and Kay followed her. The door slammed shut again, muffling the sound from the crowd. The dark hallway smelled like stale beer and sweat.

"Oh my God." Emily clapped her hands over her mouth. "I can't believe I did that."

"You rock." Kay grabbed her shoulders and shook them excitedly. "I couldn't have done that better myself. And the bicep-squeeze? *Priceless!*" Then she clutched Emily's wrist. "Come on. Let's go crash their party."

Their footsteps rang out on the concrete floor. They reached a heavy, sticker-plastered door next to a glowing red EXIT sign. "I bet this is it," Kay whispered. She pushed on it gently. "Hello?"

"Yeah?" called a guy's voice from the other side.

Kay nudged the door open with her foot. Four tall, youngish guys blinked at them from ratty folding chairs and lumpy couches. One of them wore a slim-fitted suit, and the others had on vintage T-shirts and jeans. They all held open cans of beer, and they were watching *Flight of the Conchords* on a tiny computer screen propped up on an overturned milk crate. There were posters all over the walls for other bands that had played here—John Mayer, Iron & Wine—and a bizarre collection of Benjamin Franklin memorabilia, bobble heads and figurines and a life-sized Ben Franklin cardboard cut-out.

"Who are you?" Fitted Suit stared at Kay and Emily.

"I'm Kay." Kay sauntered into the room. "And this is Emily. We thought you boys could use some fun."

Fitted Suit nudged the other band members. All of them canvassed Kay appreciatively. "I'm Rob," Fitted Suit said, holding out his hand.

"I know," Kay said. She pointed to the others. "And you're Yuri, Steve, and Jamie."

"So you guys are fans?" the guy named Steve asked.

"*Clearly.*" Kay breezed over to a small table in the corner, which held several bottles of liquor and some mixers. Without asking, she poured herself a drink. "Why doesn't someone turn up the music? Doesn't dancing help you loosen up before a show?"

The band members exchanged a glance, then Rob leapt up and put an Adele song on the stereo. Instantly, Kay started swaying back and forth to the music, beckoning the guys to dance, too. For a while, they just grinned at Kay, but then Rob got up and twirled her around. The guy named Jamie sat on the couch next to Emily. "Do you two sneak backstage often?"

Emily felt suddenly shy, like she used to when Her Ali

dragged her to Rosewood Day parties and made her talk to guys. "Not really. But I hope you don't mind."

Jamie waved his hand dismissively. "Our manager keeps us locked in here. It gets so boring. Your friend's something, huh? Totally . . . *infectious.*"

Emily turned and watched Kay spinning around the room. If Kay were an infection, Emily hoped she'd catch it. Kay's body moved so gracefully and fluidly that it was hard for Emily to tear her gaze away. She'd always wanted to be someone like Kay, a girl who could charm absolutely anyone, even if she didn't know them. She tried to picture Kay at Rosewood Day. She'd probably have everyone in her back pocket, just like Their Ali.

"Em!" Kay called from the makeshift dance floor. "Come dance! This is my favorite song!"

Emily stood, pulling Jamie up with her, too. Both of them moved into the circle and let Kay swing them around. Soon enough, everyone was singing the words to Adele. Kay lifted her cell phone above the group and snapped picture after picture, pausing to type in captions or send a text. Kay caught Emily's eye across the group and winked, and Emily winked back. And as the song hit its third refrain, Kay shot Emily a covert smile.

"You're amazing," Emily whispered to her as they passed mid-spin.

"You are, too," Kay whispered back.

A faint giggle echoed in Emily's ears. Emily whipped

around, suddenly on high alert. For a second she was certain she'd see someone peering through the window in the door that led to the stage. A blond someone, perhaps.

But to her great relief, no one was there.

10

OH, *AMOUR* . . .

As the fifties-era bubble-shaped clock in her bedroom clicked from 3:59 to 4:00 P.M. on Saturday afternoon, Aria rolled over on her bed and leafed through yet another copy of French *Vogue*, pretending she was in a hotel suite on the Left Bank of Paris instead of in her father's house in Rosewood. She had cotton balls wedged between each bare toe from the pedicure she'd given herself, and next she was going to soak in a long, hot bubble bath. She had six other activities planned, too, all to fill the weekend hours without Noel.

Eyeing her laptop on her desk, she sat up and listened for the sounds in the house. Byron and Meredith had taken baby Lola to an infant swim class, and Mike was most likely at one of his friend's houses. Satisfied that no one was around to randomly burst into her room and see what she was doing, she dragged the laptop to her bed, touched the click wheel to wake up the screen, and typed in the web address for the Tabitha Clark Memorial page.

As usual, Tabitha's pretty smiling face popped up. A few new pictures had appeared on the site: one of Tabitha when she was in about seventh or eighth grade, sitting on a beach, the burns apparent on her arms and legs. Another was a shot of her a few years later, standing in what looked like a sleek hotel lobby next to a giant potted cactus someone had adorned with two plastic eyes, a nose, and a mouth. There were dark circles under her eyes, but her smile looked happy.

Aria felt a wave of nausea and looked away. *You killed her*, a voice needled her from deep inside her brain.

Her cell phone, sitting next to the bottle of blue-black Essie nail polish on her bed, buzzed. NEW TEXT MESSAGE. Aria's insides twisted. When she rose and looked at the screen, the text was from a number with a 917 area code, not A's usual CALLER UNKNOWN or jumble of letters and numbers. She opened it up.

Look out your window.

A shiver snaked up her spine. All at once, the house felt *too* empty and silent. She crept toward her large bedroom window, parted the curtains, and prepared to peek into the front yard.

A dark-haired figure stood on the lawn, a cell phone in his hand. Aria blinked hard, taking in the familiar rumpled jacket, pointed chin, and pink lips. Surely it was a cruel trick of the light. But then, the figure looked up, noticed Aria's face at the window, and grinned broadly. He held a poster board over his head. Printed on it, in sloppy red letters, was I MISSED YOU, ARIA!

"Holy shit," Aria whispered.

It was Ezra Fitz.

"Brie, arugula, and sun-dried tomato for you." Ezra pulled a wax paper–wrapped sandwich out of a picnic basket. "And"–he paused bashfully–"McDonald's chicken nuggets for me." He glanced at Aria. "Old habits die hard, I guess."

Heat rose to Aria's cheeks. She'd once happened upon Ezra eating chicken nuggets in his office at Rosewood Day, but she wondered if he meant the statement in more ways than one.

Ezra removed the rest of the basket's contents one by one: a container of ripe, juicy green grapes, a bag of salt-and-vinegar chips—Aria's favorite—and a bottle of champagne with two plastic glasses. He arranged everything on the large boulder they were sitting on and craned his neck up at the bright blue sky poking through the trees. "I was hoping we could eat during sunset, but I guess I'm a little off."

"No, this is *amazing*," Aria gushed, hiding her trembling hands under her thighs. She still couldn't believe this was happening. Twenty minutes ago, after ripping the cotton balls from between her toes and changing from her stained Hollis sweatshirt into a vintage silk blouse she'd gotten in Amsterdam, she'd sprinted down the stairs and flung open the front door. There was Ezra, the guy she'd pined after for so long, the guy she was sure was her soul mate even after he turned out to be her teacher, standing with his arms outstretched. "I've missed you so much," he had said. "When you wrote to me, I had to come right away."

"But I wrote to you for months," Aria had replied, remaining rooted to her spot on the porch.

Ezra had looked stricken, saying he'd never received any correspondence from her. He added that his email account had been hacked a year ago, and it had taken him a while to get things sorted out—maybe some of his emails had gotten lost in the ether. Normally, Aria would have thought it was a lame guy excuse, but Ezra looked so apologetic that she believed him.

Then, Ezra had scooped her up in his arms, carried her off to his beat-up Volkswagen Beetle, which was parked at the curb, and told her he wanted to take her out on a date—right then and there—to make up for lost time. Of course Aria agreed.

Now, they were at St. Mary's Creek, a beautiful old park along a glittering stream with lots of jutting boulders, mini waterfalls, and a quaint bed-and-breakfast that served the best pancakes in all of the Main Line. Even though the weather was a pleasant fifty-something degrees, ideal for rock climbing or a hike, there wasn't a single other person around.

Ezra popped the champagne cork and poured two glasses. "You look amazing." His wolfish blue eyes rose to hers. "I've been thinking about you so much—I should have never left so abruptly without making plans for us to see each other again. Especially after all that happened with your friend. I wanted to reach out to you, but I didn't know if you wanted to hear from me."

"I would have loved to hear from you," Aria whispered, meaning it with all her heart. "And you look amazing, too." She took in Ezra's appearance. His gray checked blazer had a hole in the elbow, the white button-down was wrinkled, and his chinos were frayed at the hems. His hair was long and ragged, too, and there were hollows in his cheeks. He was still adorable, but he looked like he'd spent hours in the car. "You didn't drive all the way from Rhode Island just to see me, did you?"

"Oh, I didn't end up settling in Rhode Island, though I *would* have driven from there to see you." Ezra dipped a nugget in barbecue sauce and popped it in his mouth. "I stayed there for a little while, but then I moved to New York City."

"Oh!" Aria couldn't temper her excitement. "Do you like it there? I applied to a bunch of schools in New York."

"I love it." Ezra got a dreamy look on his face. "I have this tiny apartment in the West Village. Every night

I watch the cars stream up Sixth Avenue. I love the energy. The creativity. Being around so many different people at once."

"That's exactly how I feel about New York, too," Aria gushed, loving how she and Ezra were always on the same wavelength.

"I could absolutely see you living there." Ezra took Aria's hands. Touching him felt like walking into an old, cozy house. "Maybe you could come and visit me sometime. Look at those colleges you applied to."

Aria stared down at his big hands in hers, utterly speechless. She half expected to hear the far-off giggle she associated with A, but all she heard were tweeting birds and the rushing stream.

She must have been silent for a beat or so too long, because Ezra pulled his hands away. "God. I'm an idiot. You don't have a boyfriend, do you?"

"No!" Aria shook her head emphatically. "Well, I mean, I don't *now*. I did, though, while you were gone. It's not like I knew you were coming back." She let out a self-conscious laugh.

"Let me guess. Noel Kahn?"

Aria's mouth dropped open. "How did you know?"

Ezra chuckled. "He had it bad for you in English class."

"We didn't have that much in common, though," Aria said quietly, staring at a silvery fish swimming below them in the stream. "And . . . you don't have a girlfriend, right?"

A smile spread across Ezra's face. He cupped Aria's chin in his hands. "Of course I don't. Why else would I come to see you?"

Aria smiled shyly. "How long are you staying?"

"How long do you *want* me to stay?"

Forever, Aria wanted to say.

"I'm bunking with a friend outside town. He says I can stay as long as I like." Ezra pushed a piece of Aria's hair behind her ears. "Tell me everything about what's going on with you. How's your family? They split up, right? How's that going? And what did you mean in your email when you said you felt lonely? Are you okay?"

Aria pressed her hand to her chest, touched by his interest and concern. "I'm fine," she said, suddenly meaning it. "Actually, I'd rather hear about you first. What are you doing in New York? Going to grad school? Do you have a job? I bet it's something fabulous."

Ezra's throat bobbed. "Well, I did have a job at a nonprofit for a while, but then I was laid off. So after that . . ." A bloom of red appeared on his cheeks. "I did some writing. And, well, I wrote a novel."

"A *novel*?" Aria's jaw dropped. "As in a complete, start-to-finish *book*?"

Ezra laughed bashfully. "That's right. But I don't know how good it is."

"I'm sure it's amazing!" Aria clapped. "What's it about? When's it going to be published?"

"Let's not get ahead of ourselves." Ezra glanced at his

backpack, which sat behind them on the rock. "But if you're interested, I have the manuscript. . . ."

"Of course I'm interested!" Aria said. "I'd love to see it!"

Ezra pressed his lips together, as if weighing the decision. "No agents are representing me yet. It might never even get published. The book industry is a little harder to crack than I thought." He let out a bitter laugh Aria had never heard before.

"Am I going to have to tackle you to see this thing?" Aria teased.

"Okay, okay." Ezra undid the straps on his backpack and pulled out a sheaf of dog-eared papers held together by a blue rubber band. The front page said *See Me After Class, by Ezra Fitz* in boldface.

"I can't believe you wrote this," Aria whispered reverently. "Is it about a teacher?"

Ezra grinned mysteriously. "Maybe." He pushed the pages toward her. "Do you want to read it?"

"Yes!" Aria flipped through the ruffled pages. "I know I'm going to love it. And . . . thank you." She looked up at him, feeling a rush of emotion. "For everything. Coming back. This picnic . . ."

Aria trailed off, and they stared at each other for a few long beats. Then, Ezra inched forward on the rock until their bodies were touching. As soon as he wrapped his arms around Aria's waist and touched his lips to hers, she felt a whoosh of pleasure. The kiss deepened, and Ezra shrugged out of his jacket, tossing it on a rock next to them. Aria slithered out of her pea coat.

"Ahem," someone whispered.

Ezra and Aria pulled apart, breathing hard. A group of old women, clad in hiking gear and fanny packs and carrying walking sticks, had emerged from around the bend and were staring at them with disgusted looks on their faces.

"Sorry!" Ezra called out, quickly buttoning up his shirt.

The women sniffed and headed toward the B&B, balancing expertly on the rocks. Ezra shot Aria a mortified look and covered his mouth with his hand. "That was like being caught by my grandma," he whispered.

"Or the school librarian," Aria giggled.

Ezra gathered her in his arms and looked deep into her eyes. "Let's hope we get caught lots more times."

Aria felt a swirl of complete and utter happiness. Then, she leaned forward and kissed Ezra softly on the lips. "I couldn't agree more."

11

SUMMER SCHOOL REUNION

Later that same afternoon, Spencer pulled her Mercedes coupe into her family's driveway after a long study session at the Rosewood Public Library. "*But screw your courage to the sticking place, and we'll not fail,*" she recited. It was from the speech where Lady Macbeth convinces her husband to kill Duncan, the king. "*When Duncan is asleep, whereto the rather shall his day's hard journey . . .*"

Then her mind went blank. What came after that?

She shifted into park. This was infuriating. She'd mastered all the lines of *The Taming of the Shrew* in tenth grade when she was studying for the PSATs, volunteering for the Rosewood soup kitchen, playing field hockey, *and* juggling six honors classes. As much as she loathed giving Beau the satisfaction of coaching her tomorrow, maybe she needed it.

Inhaling a chakra-cleansing, yoga-fire breath, she pulled her Madewell duffel coat around her and grabbed her gold Dior handbag from the passenger seat, a gift she'd gotten herself for getting into Princeton. When she slipped out of the car, she nearly collided with a black Range Rover parked off to the left. She scowled at its shiny chrome wheels, souped-up navigation console, and cheery bumper sticker on the back that proclaimed PROUD PARENT OF A ST. AGNES HONOR STUDENT. Mr. Pennythistle owned a fleet of vehicles, but a Range Rover wasn't one of them. Which meant there were visitors.

When she opened the front door, a soft voice floated out from the den, followed by a girlish peal of laughter. Spencer suppressed a groan. Amelia had certainly taken Mrs. Hastings's "Make yourself at home" directive very seriously. She'd had friends over almost every single day, each of the guests geekier than the last.

Spencer stomped down the hall, making as much noise as she could so that Amelia would know she was coming. Sure enough, when she passed the large room, which held a giant-screen TV and comfy wraparound couches, Amelia glanced up. She was holding a shiny black flute on her lap—the ultimate dork accessory. Ten other girls sat around the room, instruments in each of their hands, too. *Losers.*

"What's going on?" Spencer asked irritably.

"The St. Agnes Charity Chamber Music Group," Amelia shot back in an equally huffy voice. "Remember how I said we're giving a concert? Veronica said it was fine to rehearse here."

Spencer hated how Amelia called her mother *Veronica*, like they were all peers at a cocktail party. She was about to make a snarky reply, but then her gaze fell on a red-haired girl on one of the couches. At first, she did a double take. Then a triple take. It was like seeing a ghost.

"K-Kelsey?" Spencer stammered.

"Spencer." The girl placed a violin back in its hard plastic case and blinked hard, like she couldn't believe what she was seeing either. "Wow. Long time no see."

The room began to spin. It was Kelsey Pierce, Spencer's old friend from the Penn summer program. The one she'd ruined.

Her thoughts drifted back to the bar where she and Kelsey had met. Phineas had led Spencer and Kelsey into the tiny bathroom at the back. There was graffiti all over the walls, and a dingy toilet and pedestal sink stood in the corner. The room smelled heavily of puke and stale beer.

Phineas reached into his pockets and handed each of the girls a smooth white pill. "This is how you score fives on all your exams."

"What is it?" Spencer turned her head away. Pills weren't her thing. She didn't even like taking aspirin for headaches.

"It's called Easy A," Phineas explained. "It's totally amazing. Keeps you focused for hours. It's the only way I got through junior year."

"Where did you get it?" Kelsey's voice cracked.

"Does it matter?" Phineas leaned against the sink. "I'm willing to let you girls try it out. Share the wealth, right?"

He thrust the pills toward them again. Spencer licked her lips. Of course she'd heard of Easy A, but only through those stupid public service announcements on TV and the gloom-and-doom flyers on the inside doors of the bathroom stalls at Rosewood Day. But Phineas's words gripped her hard. *It'll keep you focused for hours.* Spencer had no idea how she was going to get through four AP classes in six weeks. Maybe desperate times called for desperate measures.

Taking a deep breath, she reached out, snatched the pill from Phineas's palm, and placed it under her tongue. "You won't regret it." Phineas turned to Kelsey. "What about you?"

Kelsey picked at her thumbnail. "I don't know. I was busted for drugs when I was younger. I'm trying to stay away from stuff like this."

"You won't get in trouble," Phineas said.

"No one will know," Spencer urged.

Kelsey continued to rock back and forth on her heels. There was a trapped-kitten expression on her face, the same look Emily, Aria, Hanna, and Spencer herself got when Their Ali dared them to swim in Peck's Pond, where the police had once found a dead body.

Finally, Kelsey held out her hands. "I guess I should live a little, huh?" Phineas dropped it into her palm. Her throat bobbed as she swallowed it. "Here's to fives on our exams!"

Six weeks later, Spencer got all fives. And Kelsey, thanks to Spencer, was behind bars.

"Let's take a break," Amelia said now. Spencer snapped back to the moment, looking up as all the musicians were standing. Some stretched their arms above their heads. Others pulled out their phones and started to text.

Kelsey crossed the room until she was next to Spencer. "We're twinsies," she said, picking up a gold purse near the doorway. It was the same exact Dior tote Spencer was carrying. "So . . . long time no see."

"Um, yeah," Spencer answered warily, fiddling with one of the brass buttons on her blazer sleeve.

The grandfather clock in the foyer banged out the hour. Kelsey stared at Spencer, her gaze seemingly boring straight through Spencer's skin. Spencer's stomach swirled. Spencer hadn't seen or heard from Kelsey since that day in the police precinct.

Someone cleared her throat, and Spencer turned to see Amelia's curious gaze on both of them. Spencer padded down the hall and into the kitchen, motioning for Kelsey to follow—the last thing she wanted was for Amelia to eavesdrop. The kitchen smelled of fresh-cut rosemary, which Spencer's mother had started steeping in water ever since she found out it was Mr. Pennythistle's favorite scent.

"I didn't know you played." Spencer gestured at

the bow Kelsey was still clutching tightly, almost like a weapon.

Kelsey stared at it. "I've played since I was little. Amelia's orchestra group puts on concerts for charity, and my probation officer counts charity stuff as community service."

"Probation officer?" Spencer blurted before she could stop herself.

Kelsey's expression turned guarded. "You know. For what happened at Penn."

Spencer cut her eyes away.

"I mean, you heard, right?" Kelsey's posture was rigid and her left fist, the one that wasn't holding the violin bow, was clenched tight. "I had to go to juvie for two months. You're lucky they let you off with a warning." She raised an eyebrow. "How'd you get away with *that*?"

It felt as if the temperature in the room had suddenly shot up twenty degrees. Spencer was too afraid to meet Kelsey's gaze. She felt confused, too—she'd always assumed Kelsey knew, deep down, that she'd planted those drugs in her dorm room and told the cops about her checkered past. But what if she *didn't*?

When Spencer looked up again, Kelsey was still staring at her. "Anyway, I heard you got into Princeton. Congrats."

Spencer flinched. "H-how did you know I got into Princeton?"

"A little birdie told me," Kelsey said lightly.

Amelia? Spencer wanted to ask, but she couldn't make her mouth work. Kelsey had set her sights on Princeton, too, but it was doubtful the school had sent her a congratulatory early admission letter to cellblock D in juvenile hall. Then again, it seemed like they'd only sent one to Spencer by mistake.

"Kelsey?" Amelia's nasal voice called from the den. "We need you! We're going to run through the Schubert piece again!"

"Okay," Kelsey yelled. Then she turned back to Spencer. Her mouth opened, as if she was going to say something, but then she seemed to change her mind and shut it again. "Good luck with Princeton, Spencer. I hope that all works out for you." Then she walked stiffly away, the bow at her side.

Spencer sank into a kitchen chair, her heart pounding so hard it drowned out the sounds of the musicians.

Beep.

Spencer jumped. It was her cell phone, which was in the front pocket of her Dior bag that now sat on one of the chairs at the island. Swallowing hard, she paced over and pulled it out. There was a new text from an unknown sender. But before she read it, something caught her attention in the hall. Kelsey stood in the doorway to the den. She turned her head away as soon as Spencer looked up, but Spencer could tell she'd been watching. There was now a slim cell phone in the same hand that held the violin bow, too.

Stomach roiling, Spencer glanced down at the phone and pressed READ.

Think your summer bestie forgives you for being such a pill? Somehow I doubt it . . . Mwah! —A

12

SOMEONE IS WATCHING

Later that night, Emily rolled her family's Volvo station wagon into the Rosewood Day teacher's lot and turned off the engine. As it was eight on a Saturday, the campus was empty, and all of the Gothic-style arched windows were dark. She stared at the school's stone façade, a flurry of memories flooding her mind: walking single-file into school in fifth grade, watching enviously as Real Ali, Naomi Zeigler, and Riley Wolfe stood at the front of the line; running to get to class and accidentally bumping Real Ali's shoulder. "Watch it, Oscar the Grouch!" Ali teased. People used to call Emily that because of her chlorine-green, swim-damaged hair, but it hurt the most when Ali said it.

And then there was the day when Real Ali stood on this very strip of concrete, bragging about how her brother, Jason, had told her where a Time Capsule flag piece was hidden. She'd been so infuriatingly confident that day, filling Emily both with longing and frustration. *I could steal her the piece*, Emily had thought brazenly. What unfolded next led to the most wonderful, bizarre, and scary years of Emily's life.

Usually, thinking about Real Ali filled Emily with ambivalence. How could she both fear and feel for someone at the same time? How could she have let a psychopath go free? And why did she find herself looking around for Real Ali everywhere, desperate to prove that she was still here, even though that would mean certain death for her and her friends?

But today, she felt too dazed and tired to dwell on it for long. She couldn't stop thinking about Kay. At the end of the show last night, both of them a little more than tipsy, they'd set up a time to hang out next week. This morning, Kay had already sent a couple of steamy IMs. *Can't wait to see you again, hot stuff.* And, *Hope you got your cute butt out of bed this morning!* Emily hadn't received such provocative notes since Maya. But maybe Kay was flirty in general.

Now, she glanced at her cell phone again. About an hour ago, Spencer had sent a group text to Emily, Aria, and Hanna. *We need to talk. Come to the swings. Eight P.M.* Emily had texted her back, wanting details, but Spencer hadn't answered. She wondered if this was about A.

Shivering, she climbed out of the car and trudged over to the swings by the elementary school, the spot where Emily and her friends had regularly met through the years—long ago to gossip, but more recently to talk about A's chilling notes. The climbing dome towered in the distance, looking like a many-legged giant spider. The large avant-garde shark a local artist had created for the school loomed in the field beyond, the moonlight reflecting eerily off its smooth planes. Spencer was sitting on the middle swing, bundled up in a blue duffel coat and Ugg boots. Hanna leaned against the slide, arms crossed over her slender chest. And Aria, who had a faraway, dreamy expression on her face, huddled by the infamous spinning disc kids called the Hurl Wheel.

Spencer cleared her throat when Emily approached. "I got another note from A."

Emily's stomach twisted. Aria swallowed audibly. Hanna kicked a boot against the slide, making a hollow sound.

"Has anyone else?" Spencer went on.

"I did," Hanna said in a quavering voice. "On Wednesday. But I took care of it."

Spencer's eyes bulged. "What do you mean, 'took care of it'?"

Hanna wrapped her arms around her body. "It's personal."

"Was your note about Kelsey?" Spencer demanded.

"Who's Kelsey?" Hanna squinted.

Spencer settled back on the swing. "*Kelsey*, Hanna. The girl you . . . *you* know . . . this summer. At Penn. The one you . . ."

Hanna flinched. "My note wasn't about *her*. It was about . . . something else."

"Well, my note *was* about Kelsey," Spencer said.

Aria frowned. "Kelsey, your friend from the summer program?"

"Uh huh," Spencer said. "A knows what I did to her."

Emily shifted her weight, vaguely remembering Spencer mentioning Kelsey. Spencer had called Emily a few times last summer, since they'd both been in the city, but Emily hadn't hung out with her at all. And as June dragged into July, there was something . . . *off* about Spencer's tone of voice on the phone. She spoke so fast, like she was trying to set a world record for the most number of words said in a minute. Once, Emily had been sitting outside Poseidon's on Penn's Landing with her friend Derrick, who worked at the restaurant as a line cook. Derrick was the only person Emily had told her secrets to—well, *some* of her secrets, anyway. She'd been pouring her heart out about how she was going to have this baby without her parents knowing when Spencer's name flashed on her cell phone screen. Emily answered, and Spencer instantly launched into a story about how her new friend, Kelsey, did the funniest impression of Snooki from *Jersey Shore*. She was talking so quickly her words all ran together.

"Are you okay, Spence?" Emily asked.

"Of course I'm okay," Spencer answered breathlessly. "I'm better than okay. Why wouldn't I be okay?"

"You sound weird, that's all. Like you're on some-thing."

Spencer snickered. "Well, I mean, I took a little something, Em. But it's no biggie."

"You took *drugs*?" Emily whispered, awkwardly leaping to her feet. A few passersby stared at her giant *16 and Pregnant* stomach.

"Chill," Spencer answered. "It's just these pills called Easy A."

"*Just?* Are they safe?"

"God, Emily, don't freak out, okay? It's a study drug. This guy I get it from, Phineas, took it for a year with no side effects. And he's doing better here at Penn than I am."

Emily didn't answer. She watched as people boarded the Moshulu restaurant clipper ship in the harbor, looking happy and problem-free.

Finally, Spencer sighed. "I'm fine, Em. I promise. You don't have to worry about me, *Killer*." It was the nickname Their Ali had given Emily long ago when she thought Emily was too protective. Then Spencer hung up without saying good-bye.

Emily looked at Derrick, who was sitting quietly on the bench next to her. "Is everything okay?" he asked in a heartbreakingly sweet voice.

All of a sudden, Emily felt like she was going to cry. What was happening to her friends? Spencer wasn't the kind of girl who turned to drugs. Emily wasn't the type of girl who got pregnant. "What do you know about a drug called Easy A?" she asked Derrick.

He frowned. "It's not something *I* would try."

Now, Aria wrapped her fingers around the pole that supported the swings, and Emily came back to the present. "What did you do to Kelsey?" Aria asked.

Hanna's head shot up. "You don't know?"

"I don't, either," Emily said, looking back and forth at both of them.

Spencer stared off into the trees. "It was that night when I called you from the police station, Aria. The cops had caught Kelsey and me with drugs. They questioned us separately, and I was *sure* Kelsey was placing all the blame on me. That's what the police told me, at least. So I called all of you. Emily didn't pick up, and you . . ." She trailed off, staring down at the ground.

"I didn't think it was right to help," Aria filled in, sounding defensive.

"Right." Spencer's voice was tight. "So I called Hanna next. I had her plant pills in Kelsey's room and then call the cops and say she was a known dealer."

Emily stepped back, feeling her shoes sink into a muddy patch of grass. "*Seriously?*"

"I didn't know what else to do!" Spencer raised her hands in protest. "I panicked."

"Don't forget the part about finding out that Kelsey *didn't* tell on you after all," Hanna said nervously, casting her eyes around the empty playground.

"I only found out after it was too late," Spencer said.

"So you did it for no reason?" Aria squeaked, her tone a tad sanctimonious.

"Look, I'm not proud of it," Spencer said, her cheeks reddening. "But Kelsey *showed up* at my house today to hang out with my stepsister, and she was acting all cagey and weird. At first, I wasn't sure if she knew I sent her to juvie, but this note pretty much proves it." She held her phone screen up. *Think your summer bestie forgives you for being such a pill?*

Hanna picked nervously at her bottom lip. "How would Kelsey know you sent her to juvie? You said there was no way for the cops to trace it back to us."

"I have no idea." Spencer sounded exasperated. "Maybe Kelsey figured it out. Maybe she's A. She had her phone out when I got my text!"

Aria spun the Hurl Wheel with the tips of her fingers. "But Kelsey wasn't in Jamaica, was she?"

"And I don't know why Kelsey would be after *all* of us," Emily added. "Aria and I didn't do anything to her."

"Maybe she thinks we were all in on what I did to her," Spencer said.

"That would make sense." Hanna gave an empty swing a slight push. "Think of that *People* article. It said we were best friends. Told each other everything. Kelsey could have assumed all of us had a hand in framing her and protecting Spencer."

Emily's stomach swirled. Could that be possible?

"I'm still not sure," Aria said. "Maybe A is one of Tabitha's friends. Or someone who knew Mona Vanderwaal or Jenna Cavanaugh."

"Jenna's friends would be after *Ali*, not us," Spencer argued.

"Maybe A *is* Ali," Emily suggested hesitantly.

Everyone swung around and glared at Emily. "What?"

Emily lifted her hands in surrender. "Two weeks ago, we thought Ali survived the fire. Who's to say Ali wasn't in Jamaica, feeding Tabitha those crazy lines about all of us? We still don't know how Tabitha knew our secrets or had Ali's string bracelet. Maybe Ali followed us back here after Tabitha died and watched us all summer."

Spencer slapped her arms to her sides. "Em, Ali died in the Poconos. There's no way she made it out of that house."

"Why didn't the cops ever find her body?"

"Haven't we been over this?" Spencer said through her teeth.

Hanna leaned against the slide. "I really think she's gone, Em."

Aria nodded. "When we ran out of the house, the door slammed shut. Even if Ali made it to the door, it's unlikely she could've pushed it open after inhaling all that smoke. Remember how heavy it was? And seconds later, the house exploded. Even the DiLaurentises' fireproof safe burned up."

Emily rocked back and forth on her heels, thinking of the moment in the Poconos when she'd left the door ajar so Ali could escape. "What if the door was open? Maybe the wind blew it open or something."

Hanna put her hands on her hips. "Why are you so sure Ali's alive? Do you know something we don't?"

The trees swished in the distance. A car drove slowly past the school, its high beams on. The secret pulsed inside Emily. If she told her friends, they'd never trust her again.

"No, no reason," she mumbled.

Suddenly, a *snap* sounded from the woods. All of the girls turned and squinted into the distance. It was so dark out that Emily could barely see the outlines of the trees.

"Maybe we should go to the cops," Emily whispered.

Hanna sighed. "And say what? That we're killers?"

"We can't go through this again!" Emily's breath came out in billowing white puffs. "Maybe the cops will understand about Tabitha. Maybe they'll . . ."

Suddenly, she felt so exhausted. Of course the cops wouldn't understand about Tabitha. They'd lock Emily and her friends up for the rest of their lives.

"Look," Spencer said after a moment. "Let's not do anything rash, okay? There's way too much at stake here. We need to figure out who A is and what A plans to do next *before* it happens—without help from the cops. My money's on Kelsey." She pressed a button on her phone. "She's the only person with a real motive. I'll try and find out what she's up to the next time she shows up at my house. You never know, she might be watching you guys, too. Do you remember what she looks like?"

Aria raised one shoulder. "Vaguely."

"She was at that party at the Kahns'," Hanna murmured.

"I've never seen her," Emily pointed out.

Spencer pulled her finger across her phone and then turned it toward the others. "This is from last summer, but she looks exactly the same."

Everyone leaned in to look at the picture on the screen. A petite redheaded girl wearing a tight-fitting St. Agnes School T-shirt grinned back at them. Emily blinked hard at the girl's familiar upturned nose, arched eyebrows, and mysterious smile, the kind that said *I've got a secret, and I dare you to get it out of me.* Her thoughts scattered in a thousand directions. She did know Kelsey after all.

She was Kay.

13

KISSING WITHOUT A LICENSE

Later that night, Hanna strode into Rue Noir, a swanky lounge bar off the Hyde campus. There was a long, curved bar at the back of the room, a small dance floor to the left, and dozens of comfy couches and dark, private nooks in which a couple could cuddle for hours. She couldn't think of a better place for her first official date with Liam.

He wasn't here yet, so Hanna scoped out an empty couch farthest away from a group of fraternity guys and their skanky-looking dates and surreptitiously checked her reflection in the hand mirror she kept in her purse. She looked even more perfect than she had at the flash mob, with no indication she'd had a stressful meeting with Spencer and the others two hours earlier, strategizing about who the new A might be.

She shut her eyes. Spencer's Kelsey theory worried her. It wasn't just Spencer who had ruined Kelsey's life—

Hanna was guilty, too. She'd helped frame Kelsey to set Spencer free.

Hanna had met Kelsey last summer at one of the Kahns' legendary summer parties. They had invited all the neighbors and set up beer kegs, an inflatable jumping castle, and an old-school photo booth in their backyard. Spencer and Kelsey had breezed onto the Kahns' patio, talking a little too loudly and assertively. Usually, Spencer was demure and impeccably behaved at parties, but that night she seemed obnoxiously drunk. She chatted up Eric Kahn, flirting with him in front of his college girlfriend. She told Cassie Buckley, Ali's older field hockey friend—who was now sporting a tough, goth-chic look—that she'd always thought she was a bitch. She seemed unhinged and scarily unpredictable.

It didn't take long for people to start whispering about her. *I never took* her *for the type*, Naomi Zeigler said. *Not hot*, complained Mason Byers, who once got so drunk at a Kahn bash that he streaked naked through the woods behind the Kahns' property. And Mike, with whom Hanna had attended the party, squeezed Hanna's hand. "Those two are flying high, huh?"

The clouds had parted in Hanna's mind. *Of course.* Spencer and Kelsey weren't drunk: They were *on* something. At that, she marched over to Spencer, who was telling a rambling story to Kirsten Cullen. When Spencer saw her, she brightened. "Hey!" she said, punching Hanna's arm hard. "Where have you been, bitch? I've been looking all over for you!"

Hanna clamped down on Spencer's wrist and pulled her away from Kirsten. "Spence, what are you on?"

Spencer's shoulders stiffened. Her smile was wide and dangerous, nothing like the poised and perfect girl who ran practically every club at Rosewood Day. "Why, do you want some?" She reached into her bag and pressed something into Hanna's hand. "Take the whole bottle. There's plenty more where that came from. I have this amazing dealer."

Hanna stared at what Spencer had given her. It was a large prescription bottle with a bright orange cap. She slipped the bottle in her pocket, hoping that if she held onto the pills, Spencer would sober up and not take any more. "Are you taking this stuff a lot?"

Spencer rocked coyly from side to side. "Just to study. And it's fun at parties."

"Aren't you worried about getting caught?"

"I've got it under control, Hanna. Promise." Spencer rolled her eyes.

Hanna was about to say more, when suddenly she got a prickly feeling that someone was watching her. Kelsey stood a few paces away, her eyes fixed on Hanna.

"Uh, hey," Hanna said awkwardly, waving.

Kelsey didn't say hello back. She stared as though she could see right through her.

Slowly, Hanna backed away, unnerved by both of them. As soon as she did, Kelsey rushed to Spencer's side and started whispering. Spencer glanced at Hanna and laughed. It wasn't even her normal laugh, but something that sounded harsh and ugly and mean.

Maybe that was why, a month later, Hanna hadn't felt so bad about framing Kelsey. Surely Kelsey had been the one who'd introduced Spencer to drugs, meaning Hanna was saving the next girl Kelsey tried to get hooked. It was exactly how she'd rationalized it when they thought they'd killed Ali in Jamaica: If they hadn't killed her, Ali would have gone on to kill again.

But Tabitha *wasn't* Ali. And now someone might know what she had done to Kelsey, too.

A figure appeared over her, and Hanna looked up. There, also looking more gorgeous than he had at the flash mob, was Liam. He wore a pinstriped shirt and jeans that fit him perfectly. His wavy hair was pushed back from his face, showing off his amazing bone structure. Just looking at him sent ripples of pleasure across the surface of Hanna's skin.

"Hey," he said, grinning a bright, excited smile at her. "You look incredible."

"Thanks," Hanna said, feeling bashful. "So do you."

She slid over on the couch so that Liam could sit right next to her. He put his arms around her, pulling her into his side for a hug, but it quickly turned into a kiss. The background music, some electronic song, thumped a few measures. A few fraternity guys in the corner laughed raucously and downed shots.

Finally, Liam pulled back from Hanna and let out an embarrassed laugh, running his hand through his hair. "Just so you know, I'm not usually the kind of guy who drags girls into alleys to make out with them."

"I'm *so* glad you said that," Hanna breathed out. "I'm not that girl, either."

"It's just, when I saw you, and when we talked . . ." Liam grabbed Hanna's hands. "I don't know. Something magical happened."

If any other guy had said it, Hanna would have rolled her eyes, thinking it was a cheesy pickup line. But Liam seemed so earnest and vulnerable.

"I don't even know what made me go to the quad yesterday," Liam went on, his eyes squarely on Hanna, even when a group of three very pretty, very thin coeds in barely there dresses swept through the revolving door and shimmied up to the bar. "I had to get out of my dorm. I'd been holed up there for days, getting over an ex-girlfriend."

"I recently broke up with someone, too," Hanna said quietly, thinking of Mike, although now when she tried to imagine his face, all she could see was a big crayon scribble.

"Then we can get over them together," Liam said.

"Have you had lots of girlfriends?" Hanna asked.

Liam shrugged. "A few. What about you? I bet guys *love* you."

Hanna wanted to snort. She wasn't about to tell him about her disaster with Sean Ackard or how she and Mike had crashed and burned. "I've done okay," she admitted.

"But no one's as special as me, right?" Liam grinned.

Hanna touched the end of his nose playfully. "I think I need to know a few more things about you before I can be the judge of that."

"What do you want to know? I'm an open book." Liam thought for a moment. "I'm like a girl with PMS when it comes to Dairy Queen brownie blizzards. I cry at romantic comedies and when the Phillies won the World Series. The saddest thing in the world was when I had to put my twelve-year-old mastiff to sleep, and I'm really, really afraid of spiders."

"Spiders?" Hanna giggled. "Aw, poor baby."

Liam traced a swirl on the inside of Hanna's wrist. "What are *you* really afraid of?"

All at once, every light in the bar seemed to dim. Hanna felt someone's gaze on her from across the room, but when she raised her head, no one was looking. *A*, she wanted to say to Liam. *The feeling I got when Tabitha was about to push me over the roof. The fact that I actually killed someone . . . and someone knows.* But instead she shrugged. "Um, I don't like enclosed spaces."

"What if someone you really, really like is in the enclosed space with you?" Liam snuggled up to her, gazing into her eyes.

"I guess that's okay," Hanna whispered.

They started to kiss. Hanna wasn't sure how many minutes had passed, and she almost didn't hear Liam's phone bleating in his pocket. Finally, he pulled away, checked the screen, and winced. "It's my mom."

"Do you have to take it?"

Liam looked conflicted, but let the call go to voice mail. "She's going through some stuff right now. It's pretty intense."

Hanna scooted closer to him. "Do you want to talk about it?"

She figured Liam would say no, but he swallowed hard and looked at her. "Promise me you won't tell anyone this?" Hanna nodded. "My mom caught my dad having an affair last year. He got the woman pregnant, and he bribed her to have an abortion and go away."

A sour taste welled in Hanna's mouth.

Liam closed his eyes. "I'm sorry to unload that on you. I just don't have anyone else to talk to about it."

"It's okay." Hanna touched his leg. "I'm glad you told me."

"They hate each other now. It's a horrible thing to watch. I remember when they only had eyes for each other. I learned all of my lessons about love from them . . . and now I feel like they were all lies."

"People fall out of love," Hanna said sadly.

Liam looked at his phone, then tossed it back into his pocket and took Hanna's hands. "I have an idea. Let's get away from all this for a while. How about South Beach? I bet you look gorgeous in a bikini."

Hanna was surprised at the abrupt change of subject, but did her best to play along. She ran her hands over Liam's shoulders. He had the strong, taut body of a swimmer or a tennis player. "Sounds great. I love the ocean."

"I could book us our own private bungalow right on the water. We could have a private butler who serves us all of our meals in bed."

Hanna blushed and giggled self-consciously at the word *bed*. But even though it was crazy, she was half tempted to take Liam up on the offer. Not only was he gorgeous, Miami was a zillion miles away from A.

Suddenly, as if on cue, her cell phone beeped loudly in her bag. Irritated, she reached into the pocket to silence it, but then she noticed the alert on the screen. ONE NEW TEXT MESSAGE. Her heart began to pound. She glanced around the bar to see if anyone was watching. A bunch of girls giggled in a nearby banquette. The bartender handed a guy a drink and some change. And then she noticed a figure slipping behind the curtains at the back of the room. Whoever it was wasn't very tall, but Hanna could sense that he or she had been watching.

"Just a sec," Hanna murmured, tilting away from Liam and opening the text. Her stomach sank when she realized it was from the person she dreaded most.

Hannakins: Before you two get too comfy, better ask to see his driver's license. –A

Hanna frowned. *Driver's license?* What the hell would that tell her? That he wore corrective lenses to drive? That he was a resident of New Jersey, not Pennsylvania?

She slipped the phone back into her bag and turned to Liam again. "Anyway, you were talking about South Beach?"

Liam nodded, sliding closer to her. "I want to have you all to myself."

He bent to kiss her. Hanna kissed back, but A's message needled her. A was horrific and scary, but Hanna knew better than anyone that A's information was usually right on. What if Liam had herpes sores all over his mouth in his picture? What if he had a different nose? Or what if—horrors—Liam was freakishly young-looking for his age and was actually in his forties?

She pulled away. "You know, I technically have a rule," she said shakily. "Before I go on vacay with a guy, I have to see his license first."

A bemused smile appeared on Liam's face. "Luckily my license picture is awesome." He reached into his wallet. "I'll show you mine if you show me yours."

"Deal." Hanna grabbed her Louis Vuitton wallet from her bag and handed him the new license she'd gotten only a few months ago. Liam handed Hanna his license in exchange. When Hanna studied his image, relief flooded her. He looked gorgeous. No herpes sores. No altered nose. And he was two years older than she was, not in his forties. Her gaze traveled over the rest of the license. When she noticed the name, her eyes skimmed right past it. But then she stopped and looked again.

Liam Wilkinson.

Hanna's heart leapt to her throat. *No.* It couldn't be.

But when she looked at Liam, the evidence was all there. He had the same brown eyes as Tucker Wilkinson. The same lazy, people-love-me smile. Even his thick eyebrows were identical.

Liam's head shot up, Hanna's license in his hands. His face went pale. Hanna could see the connections forming in his mind. "You're related to Tom Marin," he said slowly. "That's why you were at Hyde last night."

Hanna lowered her eyes, feeling like she was going to vomit all over the velvet couch. "He's . . . my father," she admitted, each word filling her with pain as it spilled out of her mouth. "And your father is . . ."

"Tucker Wilkinson," Liam finished dolefully.

They stared at each other in horror. And then, over the sounds of the frat boys chanting *Chug chug chug*, the music, and the ice clacking together in the martini shaker, Hanna heard a far-off giggle. She turned and stared at the long glass window that faced the street. There, plastered on the window, was a ripped, neon-green piece of paper. It didn't take Hanna long to realize it was a piece of a Tom Marin flyer her dad's aides had passed out at the flash mob last night. The edges were raggedly torn so that only her father's face and a single letter from his name remained.

A lone, bold *A*.

14

SPENCER FREES HER MIND

The following afternoon, which was gray and cold, Spencer pulled a plaid scarf around her neck, stepped onto the curb on a side street in Old Hollis, and stared at the rambling Victorian house in front of her. Frowning, she checked the address on the drama club call sheet one more time. She was standing in front of the Purple House, aptly named because of the brilliant purple paint that covered every inch of its siding. The house was an institution in Rosewood—when Spencer was in sixth grade, she, Ali, and others used to ride bikes up and down this street, whispering the rumors they'd heard about the people who owned the place. "Someone told me they never bathe," Ali said. "The place is crawling with bed bugs."

"Well, *I* heard they host orgies," Hanna added. Everyone let out a collective *Ew*, but then a face had appeared at the window of the Purple House and they'd all quickly biked away.

Murderer.

Spencer paused from climbing up the front steps, her heart shooting into her throat. She stared at the quiet, almost vacant-looking houses on the street. A shadow slipped behind a pair of metal garbage cans in the alley.

She shivered and thought of her most recent note from A. Maybe her friends weren't convinced that Kelsey could be their new evil text-messager, but it was the most logical answer. Spencer had ruined Kelsey's life. Now Spencer had to stop her before Kelsey ruined hers—and her friends', too.

Over the summer, Spencer and Kelsey had become fast friends. Kelsey had confessed that after her parents had gotten divorced, she started acting out and fell in with a wild group of girls. She'd gotten into pot, and then started selling it. During a locker search at school, security found her stash. The only reason she wasn't expelled from St. Agnes was because her dad had recently donated a science wing, but her parents threatened to send her to a super-strict Catholic school in Canada if she stepped out of line again.

"I decided to turn things around," Kelsey said one night as she and Spencer lay together on her bed after a night of studying. "My parents refused to pay for it, saying it would be a waste after all the trouble I'd gotten into, but amazingly, a nonprofit I'd never heard of swooped in at the last minute and gave me a scholarship to go to the Penn program. I want to show my parents it was all worth it."

In turn, Spencer told Kelsey about her troubles, too—well, *some* of them. Like how she'd been tortured by A. How she'd stolen her sister's paper and passed it off as her own for the Golden Orchid prize. How she wanted to be the very best all the time.

They'd both been the perfect candidates for Easy A. At first, the pills hadn't had much effect other than making them both feel really awake even when they'd pulled all-nighters. But as time went on, they both began to notice when they *hadn't* taken it. "I can't keep my eyes open," Spencer would say during class. "I feel like a zombie," Kelsey would groan. They watched Phineas across the room, covertly slipping yet another pill under his tongue. If *he* was okay taking more, maybe they would be, too.

A car with a rattling muffler drove past, breaking Spencer from her thoughts. Straightening up, she climbed the steps to Beau's front porch, checked herself out in the front sidelight window—she'd dressed in skinny jeans, a soft cashmere sweater, and tall boots, which she thought looked appropriately cute but *not* like she was trying to impress Beau—and rang the bell.

No one answered. She rang it again. Still no one.

"Hel-*lo*?" Spencer said impatiently, rapping hard on the door.

Finally, a light snapped on, and Beau appeared at the window. He whipped open the door. His eyes were sleepy, his dark hair was tousled, and he was shirtless. Spencer nearly swallowed the piece of Trident she was chewing. Where had he been hiding *those* abs?

"Sorry," Beau said drowsily. "I was meditating."

"Of course you were," Spencer mumbled, trying not to stare at his thousand-sit-ups-a-day torso. This was like the time she and Aria had taken a life-drawing class at Hollis that had nude male models. The models seemed so nonchalant, but Spencer kept wanting to burst into giggles.

She strode into the foyer, noting that the inside of the Purple House was as chaotic-looking as the outside. The hallway walls were filled with an eclectic mix of hand-woven tapestries, oil paintings, and metal signs advertising brands of cigarettes and long-defunct diners. Shabby mid-century modern furniture adorned the large living room off to the left, and a rustic maple table covered in hardcover books of all shapes and sizes took up most of the dining room. At the end of the hall was an unrolled blue yoga mat. A small boombox sat nearby playing a soothing harp song, and an incense holder bearing a single lit stick wafted smoke into the air from an end table.

"So is your family renting this place?" Spencer asked.

Beau strolled over to the mat, scooped up a white T-shirt from the floor, and pulled it over his head. Spencer was both relieved and oddly disappointed that he was covering up. "No, we've owned it for almost twenty years. My parents rented it out to professors, but then my dad got a job in Philly and we decided to move back in."

"Did your parents paint it purple?"

Beau grinned. "Yep, back in the seventies. It was so everyone knew where the orgies were."

"Oh, I heard something about that," Spencer said, trying to sound nonchalant.

Beau snorted. "I'm messing with you. They were both literature professors at Hollis. Their idea of a thrill was reading *The Canterbury Tales* in Old English. But I heard all the rumors." He glanced at her knowingly. "Rosewood people love to talk, don't they? I heard some rumors about you, too, Pretty Little Liar."

Spencer turned away, pretending to be fascinated with a folk art sculpture of a large black rooster. Even though surely everyone in town—in the *country*—had heard about her ordeal with Real Ali, it was strange that someone like Beau had paid attention. "Most of the rumors aren't true," she said quietly.

"Of course they aren't." Beau strolled toward her. "But it sucks, doesn't it? Everyone talking. Everyone looking at you."

"It does suck," she said, surprised Beau had nailed her struggle so succinctly.

When she looked up, he was staring at her with an enigmatic look on his face. It was almost like he was trying to memorize every inch of her features. Spencer stared back. She hadn't noticed how green his eyes were before. Or the cute little dimple on his left cheek.

"So, um, should we get started?" she asked after an awkward beat.

Beau broke his gaze, walked across the room, and settled into a leather chair. "Sure. If you want."

Spencer felt a stab of exasperation. "You told me to come here so you could teach me. So . . . teach me."

Beau tilted the chair back and pressed a hand to his lips. "Well, I think your problem is that you don't understand Lady Macbeth. You're just a high school girl regurgitating her lines."

Spencer straightened her spine. "Of course I understand her. She's determined. She's ambitious. She gets in over her head. And then she's plagued by guilt for what she did."

"Where'd you get that from, SparkNotes?" Beau scoffed. "Knowing facts isn't the same as getting into the character. You have to experience what she experiences and really *feel* her. *That's* Method acting."

Spencer resisted the urge to laugh. "That's bullshit."

Beau's eyes flashed. "Maybe you're scared to really go for it. Method acting can dredge up some demons."

"I'm not scared." Spencer crossed her arms over her chest.

Beau rose from the chair and moved a few steps closer to her. "Okay, so you're not scared. But you *are* doing this to get a four-point-oh, aren't you? Not because you care about acting. Not because you care about the integrity of the play."

Heat rushed to Spencer's face. "You know what, I don't need this." She spun on her heel and started out of the room. *Arrogant jerk.*

"Wait." Beau clamped his hand on hers and spun her around. "I'm challenging you. I think you're good, better than you realize. But I also think you can step it up to the next level."

The sudden scent of sandalwood incense tickled Spencer's nose. She looked down at Beau's large, warm fingers tightly entwined around hers. "Y-you think I'm good?" she asked in a voice barely over a whisper.

"I think you're very good," Beau said in a suddenly tender voice. "But you also have to let go of a lot of things first."

"Let go of what?"

"You need to *become* Lady Macbeth. Go to a special place inside of you to understand her motivations. Feel what she feels. Know what *you* would do, if faced with her predicament."

"Why does it matter what *I* would do?" Spencer protested. "*She's* the character Shakespeare wrote about. Her lines are there on the page. She helps kill the king and sits silently by while her husband kills off everyone else in his way. Then she freaks."

"Well, wouldn't *you* freak if you killed someone and kept terrible secrets?"

Spencer looked away, a lump rising in her throat. This was a little too close for comfort. "Of course I would. But I'd never *do* that."

Beau sighed. "You're taking this too literally. You're not Spencer Hastings, good girl, straight-A student, teacher's pet. You're Lady Macbeth. Sinister. Conniving. Ambitious. You convinced your husband to murder an innocent man. If it hadn't been for you, he might not have gone off his rocker. What does it *feel* like to be responsible for so much damage?"

Spencer picked at a loose thread on her cashmere sweater, uncomfortable with Beau's scrutiny. "How do you become one with Macbeth? Where's the special place you go to?"

Beau looked away. "It doesn't matter."

Spencer placed her hands on her hips.

Beau pressed his lips together. "Fine. If you must know, I was bullied a lot when I was younger." His voice was pinched. "I thought a lot about getting revenge. That's where I go. I think about . . . them."

Spencer's hands went slack at her sides. The words hung heavily in the air. "Do you want to talk about it?"

Beau shrugged. "It was these assholes in my eighth-grade homeroom. I wanted to hurt them so badly. It's not the same as Macbeth's ambition, but it gets me in the right head space."

He walked across the living room and spun a large old globe around and around. With his hunched shoulders and heavy head, he almost looked vulnerable. Spencer shifted her weight. "I'm really sorry that happened to you."

The corners of Beau's mouth pulled up in a wry smile. "I guess we have something in common, huh? You were bullied, too."

Spencer frowned. She'd never thought of A as a bully, exactly, but it wasn't far off the mark. And come to think of it, Their Ali bullied them, too . . . even though she was their best friend.

She looked up at Beau and was surprised to see he was staring at her again. They held each other's gaze for a few long beats. Then, with one swift movement, Beau sprang across the room and pulled Spencer to him. His breath was minty on her cheek. Spencer was certain they were going to kiss. And even crazier, she *wanted* to.

Beau's face loomed teasingly close. He slid his arms along Spencer's back and ran his fingers through her hair, which gave her shivers. Then he stepped away. "That's *one* way of letting go," he said softly. "Now, c'mon. We have a lot of work to do."

He turned and strolled back into the hall. Spencer stared after him, her skin slightly sweaty and her emotions a jumble. She might have let go for a moment, but could she really let go in the way she needed to and connect with Lady Macbeth? It would mean facing what she did to Tabitha. Confronting the guilt.

She worried, suddenly, what on earth she'd just gotten herself into.

15

WHAT YOU SEE ISN'T WHAT YOU GET

On Sunday morning, Emily did all her laundry, cleaned her bathroom, read a chapter of history homework, and even voluntarily went to church with her mother, all to avoid a certain phone call. But by 2 P.M., after she'd driven Beth to the airport for her flight to Tucson, walked her to security, and driven home again, she knew she'd procrastinated for too long.

Finally, she dialed Spencer's number, nerves jangling. She needed to set Spencer straight. She'd gone over it in her head a million times, and there was no reason someone as awesome as Kay, someone whom Emily had connected with instantly, someone who seemed totally guileless and fragile and vulnerable, could be A.

"Emily," Spencer answered on the third ring, sounding like her typical tightly wound self.

"Hey." Emily bit down hard on her pinkie nail, her

heart suddenly racing. "Um, there's something I need to tell you. It's about Kelsey."

Spencer paused. "What about her?"

"Well, this is going to sound weird, but I actually met her the other day. At a party. Completely randomly. She introduced herself as Kay, but when you showed me that picture yesterday, it was definitely her."

Spencer gasped. "She sometimes went by that—the letter *K*, for Kelsey. Why didn't you say anything last night? This is proof that she's stalking us!"

Emily glanced at her expression in the mirror. There were big furrows in her forehead, and her cheeks were red, the way she always looked when she felt conflicted. It seemed like Spencer was accusing her of withholding important information—or maybe Emily was just interpreting her tone of voice that way because she felt guilty of that very thing. "I-I don't know why I didn't say anything," she said. "I guess because she seemed really sweet—her meeting me didn't seem premeditated at all. And I don't think she has a clue who I am or that I'm friends with you. There's no way she can be A."

"Of *course* she's A!" Spencer cried with such volume that Emily moved the phone away from her ear. "Emily, she knows exactly who you are. She's out to get all of us. Can't you see that?"

"I think you're being paranoid," Emily protested, pausing by the window to watch a spider build a silken web. "And honestly, I can't believe you framed her. I wouldn't have supported you on that." She thought about the remorseful look that had crossed Kay's—Kelsey's—face when they'd talked about how no colleges wanted her, and the undercurrent of shame in her voice when she'd talked about how her parents didn't trust her.

Spencer sighed. "Like I said, it's not like I'm *proud* of what I did. I mean, are you proud of what *you* did last summer?"

Emily winced. *That* was low. "You're not thinking straight," she said after a moment, trying to push her own trouble from last summer out of her mind. "A is someone else. Someone who was in Jamaica."

"Who, Ali?" Spencer laughed mirthlessly. "She's dead, Em. She really is. Look, I get that Kelsey might have seemed really nice—I liked her, too, once. But she's dangerous. Stay away from her. I don't want you getting hurt."

"But—"

"Do this for me, please? Kelsey's trouble. She wants revenge." There was a voice in the background on Spencer's end. "I have to go," she said after a pause and then hung up.

Emily stared at the phone's screen, her thoughts whirling.

Almost immediately, her phone beeped again. She turned it over, wondering if it was Spencer sending a text, perhaps thinking more rationally. But it was an email from Kay—Kelsey. *We're hanging out this afternoon, right?*

Sinking onto her bed, Emily thought about every moment she'd spent with Kay so far. Not for one second had she seemed anything less than fun, sweet, and amaz-ing. She *wasn't* A. There was no way. Real Ali was. Emily could feel it in her bones.

Emily opened a reply. *Absolutely*, she wrote. *See you soon.*

A few hours later, Emily walked toward the Rosewood Lanes, the old bowling-alley-slash-cocktail-lounge that had a large neon sign of a ball striking ten pins above the entrance. She spied Kelsey—Emily felt foolish for thinking her name had been *Kay* when really it had just been her first initial, and now she couldn't think of her by anything other than her full name—waiting by the door, dressed in jeans, a long yellow tunic sweater, and a green anorak with a furry hood. She was taking a big swig from a Poland Spring water bottle. When Kelsey saw Emily, she jumped, quickly stuffed something back into her gold purse, and shot Emily a huge but slightly off-kilter smile. "Ready to bowl?"

Emily snickered. "We're not *really* bowling, are we?"

"If the Chambermaids guys want to, I'm all for it." The band members from the Chambermaids had challenged Kelsey and Emily to a friendly game of bowling.

The two of them walked into the darkly lit bowling alley. It smelled like old shoes and fried mozzarella sticks and was filled with the sounds of heavy balls crashing into pins. Both of them scanned the crowd, which was a mix of old guys in satin bowling league jackets, Hollis students swilling cocktails, and high-school kids drawing porno-graphic pictures on the big scorecards that were reflected on the ceiling. They were early, though, and the guys from the band were nowhere to be seen.

"Let's grab some snacks." Kelsey headed to the bar. They settled on two plush red stools. The bartender, a stout guy with a bushy beard and several large tattoos on his biceps, strolled over and gave them a dirty look. He didn't seem the type who'd tolerate underage drinkers. Emily asked for water. Kelsey ordered a Diet Coke and some fries.

When the bartender trundled away, silence fell between them. All Emily could think of was her conversation with Spencer. On one hand, she felt like a traitor for defying Spencer's wishes. On the other, she was certain Spencer was wrong about Kelsey being A.

"I think we know someone in common," Emily blurted out, not able to hold it in any longer. "Spencer Hastings. We used to be best friends, actually. Spencer said she met you at the Penn summer program."

Kelsey flinched. "Oh," she said quietly, peering down to inspect her strawberry-colored split ends. "Yeah. I knew Spencer."

Emily turned over an old coaster for Pabst Blue Ribbon beer, its corners chipped away. "Actually, I'm surprised you haven't recognized me. I was one of Alison DiLaurentis's best friends, too. One of the Pretty Little Liars."

Kelsey's lips made a small *O*. After a moment, she

smacked the side of her head. "God, *right*. Spencer told me about all of that. You must think I'm a huge idiot. I knew you looked familiar . . . I just didn't know from where."

"I'm sorry I didn't tell you before," Emily said quickly, noting that Kelsey genuinely seemed surprised about who she was. "I didn't feel like talking about it. I hate people defining me by what happened."

"Of course." Kelsey nodded like she was absolutely tuned in to the conversation, but her eyes darted distractedly all over the bar area. Her hands were shaking a little, too, as if she'd drunk a hundred cups of espresso.

The bartender returned and plunked down their drinks and a large plate of fries. Kelsey busied herself with dousing them in ketchup and salt. After taking a sip of her Diet Coke and eating a fry, she raised her eyes to Emily again. "Spencer and I lost touch last summer. It was because I . . ." A muscle at her temple twitched. "I was sent away to juvie."

Emily blinked. "Oh my God. I'm so sorry." She hoped she sounded surprised.

Kelsey shrugged. "I haven't told that many people—a lot of kids at school think I did an exchange program. But the cops found drugs in my dorm room at Penn, and it was my second strike. I don't even know if Spencer knew about it, even though she was with me the night it went down. I saw her the other day and told her, but she reacted really strangely. Maybe it's because she . . ." She was talking very quickly, so it was jarring when she trailed off. "I'm sorry. She's your friend. I shouldn't talk about her."

"We're not as close as we used to be." Emily pushed her straw around her water glass, making a mini whirlpool with the ice cubes.

Kelsey's hands shook faster. When she reached for the fries, she could barely hold one without it wobbling all over the place. "Are you okay?" Emily asked worriedly.

"I'm fine." Kelsey shot Emily a tight smile and tucked her hands in her lap. "Just a little overwhelmed, I guess."

Emily touched Kelsey's shoulder. "I'm not judging you, you know. We've all made mistakes. I'm really flattered you told me about juvie. It must have been really rough."

"It was."

Kelsey's quavering voice made Emily's heart break. She felt terrible that Kelsey had been sent to juvie for something she wasn't entirely guilty of. How could Spencer have done such a thing? And it appeared that Kelsey had no idea, either. Should *Emily* tell her?

Kelsey leaned into Emily. "Going to juvie was horrible, but probably not as awful as losing a best friend. And you were stalked, too, right? By her twin?" Her eyes widened.

The sound of bowling balls striking pins thundered behind them, and a group of bowlers burst into applause. "I can hardly think about it," Emily whispered. "Especially because . . ." Now it was her turn to trail off. She'd been about to say, *Especially because I think the Real Ali is still alive.*

Suddenly, a scrawny older woman in a baggy wife-beater and child-sized acid-washed jeans clonked by in rented bowling shoes. "Oh my God," Kelsey blurted. "Velma!"

Emily craned her neck to look, then burst out laughing. "You know her, too?" Velma was an institution at this place—Emily had noticed her ever since she started coming here as a second grader with her Brownie troop. She always bowled by herself, got some insane score, and then sat at the bar and smoked a zillion cigarettes. Everyone was afraid to talk to her. Now, when Velma passed a greasy-haired guy with a huge beer gut, he actually cowered.

"Of course I know her," Kelsey said. "She's *always* here." Then she touched Emily's arm. "I have a challenge for you, bad girl. Steal one of her Marlboros." She pointed to a pack of Marlboro Lights in Velma's back pocket.

Emily thought about it for a moment, then slid off the bar stool. "That's easy."

Velma had paused at the end of the bar to study a scorecard. Emily crept up behind her, giggling with every few steps. When she was almost behind Velma, the cigarettes within reach, the old woman turned around and peered at Emily with lined, rheumy-blue eyes. "May I help you, darlin'?"

Emily's mouth dropped open. She'd never actually heard Velma speak before, and was surprised by her clear, songbirdlike voice and oozing-with-sweetness southern accent. It was so disarming that she took a few big steps backward, waving her arms in front of her body and blurting, "Never mind. Sorry to bother you."

When she returned to her seat, Kelsey was doubled over. "You totally choked!"

"I know," Emily said between gulps of laughter. "I didn't expect her to be nice!"

"Sometimes people aren't what they seem." Kelsey swallowed a chuckle. "Like you. You look all sweet and sporty, but deep down you're a wild child." And then, before Emily knew what was happening, she leaned forward and gave Emily a little peck on the cheek. "And I *love* it," she whispered in Emily's ear.

"Thanks," Emily said back. Kelsey was definitely right about that—people *weren't* what they seemed. Kelsey wasn't a crazy, duplicitous stalker, as Spencer had implied. She was just a normal girl, much like Emily was.

She was also the coolest friend Emily had made in a long time. A girl Emily didn't have any intention of dropping anytime soon.

16

ARIA'S FAVORITE BOOK EVER

On Monday morning, Aria sat at a long study table in the Rosewood Library. The room was full of kids browsing for books, working at the computer stations in the corner, and secretly playing games on their phones. After making sure no one was looking, Aria pulled out the thick manuscript Ezra had given her and opened to the last page she'd read. Instantly, a blush rose to her cheeks. Ezra's novel was utterly romantic, exceptionally vivid, and all about *her*.

Ezra had given her a different name—Anita—and they lived in a different town—somewhere in northern California—but the girl in the book had long, blue-black hair, a willowy ballerina frame, and startling blue eyes, which was exactly what Aria saw when she looked in a mirror. The novel had started out with an account of Anita and Jack, Ezra's alias, meeting in Snookers, a college bar. On page two was a conversation about how shitty American beer was. On page four was their shared nostalgia about Iceland. On page seven, they snuck off to the bathroom and kissed. In reading, Aria got to see the situation from Ezra's perspective. He wrote that Anita was "fresh" and "nubile" and "the stuff of dreams." Her hair was "like spun silk," and her lips "tasted like petals." Not that Aria thought petals really *had* a taste, but it was still awesome.

The similarities didn't stop there. When Jack and Anita discovered they were teacher and student, they got all weird and embarrassed about it, just like they had in real life. Only, in Ezra's novel, they figured out a way to make it work. They met in secret after school at Jack's apartment. They snuck off to the city to attend art openings. They confessed their love to one another by night and acted completely professional by day. There were some strange missteps, like how Anita was way clingier than Aria had ever been in real life, and how Jack could be droning and pedantic at times, subjecting Anita to diatribes about philosophy and literature. But those things were easy to adjust in the next draft.

As Aria read, all worries that Ezra had forgotten about her in the year he'd been away flew out the window. Writing this novel had surely taken many long, arduous, thoughtful months—Aria must have been on his mind *all the time.*

"Hey, can I talk to you?"

Aria looked up and saw Hanna pulling back a chair

beside her. She covered the manuscript with her hand. "Sure. What's up?"

Hanna bit her glossy bottom lip. "Do you really think"—she glanced around nervously—"*you know who* is Kelsey?"

Aria twisted her mouth, her heart jumping. "I don't know. Maybe."

Hanna looked worried, maybe for good reason. Aria had been surprised when she heard that Hanna had helped get Spencer out of jail. She remembered Spencer's frantic phone call, saying she'd gotten caught with drugs. She'd felt terrible for hanging up on Spencer, but she would have felt wrong helping her, too. And anyway, she had still been smarting from the last time she'd seen Spencer, at one of Noel's parties a few weeks before.

Spencer had come to the party with Kelsey, and it was obvious the two of them were on something. Halfway through the bash, at about the time the boys were starting to play beer pong, Aria had pulled Spencer around the side of the Kahns' house, where it was quieter. "I realize we all need to blow off some steam sometimes," she whispered, "but drugs, Spence? Really?"

Spencer rolled her eyes. "You and Hanna are worse than parents. It's safe—I swear. And actually, Aria, if you ever break up with Noel, you should go for my dealer—he's hot and totally your type."

"Is this because of your friend?" Aria spotted Kelsey across the Kahns' expansive lawn. She was sitting in

James Freed's lap, and her blouse had fallen off her shoulder, revealing the lacy cup of her bra. "Did she get you into this?"

"Why do you care?" Spencer's features were cold and closed.

Aria stared at her. *Because we're friends? Because we share all kinds of awful secrets together? Because you saw me push Alison DiLaurentis to her death, and I trust you with not telling anyone, ever?* "I don't want to see you get hurt," Aria said aloud. "We could find you a rehab program. I'd sit with you while you detox—whatever it takes. You don't *need* drugs, Spence. You're awesome without them."

"You are *so* one to talk." Spencer gave Aria a half-playful, half-rough shove. "Like you didn't do crazy drugs when you were in Iceland? You definitely *acted* like you were stoned when you came back. And you *had* to have been stoned to go after that English teacher. I mean, he's hot, Aria, but seriously? A *teacher*?"

Aria's mouth fell open. "I'm trying to help you," she said stiffly.

Spencer crossed her arms over her chest. "You know, you act like you're all open-minded and cool, but deep down, you're afraid of everything." Then she wheeled around and marched across the lawn to Kelsey. Kelsey unwound herself from James, and she and Spencer glanced at Aria and started whispering.

Several Typical Rosewood Girls carrying dog-eared copies of *Teen Vogue* brushed past, yanking Aria back to the present. Hanna fiddled with a snap on her bag. "I got another note," she admitted, her eyes darting around the room. "Whoever A is—Kelsey or someone else—A is watching our every move."

And then, abruptly, Hanna slung her purse over her shoulder, slid from the chair, and disappeared through the library turnstiles. Aria watched the double doors slam shut, feeling a sudden chill. Maybe A *was* Kelsey—she certainly seemed like a girl heading off the rails. But how did Kelsey know so much about them? Could she know about Jamaica—and that Aria was a cold-blooded killer?

There was a faint cough behind her, and Aria had the distinct feeling someone was staring. When she whipped around, she nearly collided with Klaudia. "Jesus!"

"*Shhhh!*" Mrs. Norton, the librarian, called from her post at the front of the room, giving Aria a sharp look.

Aria blinked at Klaudia, whose Rosewood Day blazer looked at least two sizes too small and was pulled taut across her perky boobs. Klaudia stared back at Aria, then down at the contents on the desk. A curious eyebrow rose. Aria looked down and saw that the title page of Ezra's manuscript was clearly visible. So was the dedication page: *To Aria, for making this all possible. Yours, Ezra.* She quickly covered the pages with her yak-fur bag. "What do you want?" she asked Klaudia.

"We need to talk about the art history project," Klaudia whispered.

"Let's meet at Wordsmith's on Wednesday at six," Aria answered, just wanting Klaudia to go away. "We'll talk about it then."

"Fine," Klaudia said at normal volume, then turned and flounced to the back corner, where Naomi, Riley, and Kate were waiting. As soon as Klaudia reached them, the four girls started to quietly giggle. Naomi pulled out her phone and showed the girls something on the screen. They all glanced at Aria and snickered once more.

Aria gathered up Ezra's manuscript and stuffed it back into her bag, feeling like she was on display. When her own phone rang, three loud chimes piercing the sacred library silence, Mrs. Norton's head looked like it was going to pop off her neck. "Miss Montgomery, turn that phone off *now!*"

"Sorry," Aria murmured, fumbling for her phone, which had fallen to the bottom of her bag. When she saw the screen, her heart froze in her chest. ONE NEW TEXT FROM ANONYMOUS. Taking a deep breath, she pressed the button to open the text.

What novel would Ezra have written if he knew the truth about what you did? —A

Aria let her phone fall back into her bag and gazed around the room. Kirsten Cullen glanced at her from the computer card catalogue. Naomi, Riley, Klaudia, and

Kate were still giggling in the corner. Someone slipped into the stacks before Aria could see who it was.

Hanna was right. Whoever A was, he or she was watching them closely, tracking their every move.

17

KISSING IN THE CHURCHYARD

That night, Hanna tramped down a steep slope toward the darkened windows of the old Huntley Rectory, an imposing stone building on twelve acres in southern Rosewood. The church had once been a mansion that housed an older, wealthy railroad baron and his Olympic-team-in-training of male fencers. The railroad baron had gone crazy, murdered several of the fencers, and escaped to South America. His mansion had been converted into a monastery shortly thereafter, but people were always saying they heard swordfight sounds and ghostly, tormented wails from the tallest towers.

The heels of her booties sank into the muddy soil. A twig snapped against her face. A couple of fat raindrops splattered on her forehead, making her skin prickle, and Hanna kept thinking she saw two huge eyes watching her from the trees. What was she thinking, agreeing to meet Liam here? What was she thinking, agreeing to meet Liam at *all*?

She was such an idiot. How could she fall so madly and crazily for a guy she knew nothing about, just because he paid her a couple of compliments and was an amazing kisser? It was as bad as her crush on Patrick, and look where *that* had gotten her. When she'd left Rue Noir last night, she'd vowed to put all this behind her— there was no way she could fraternize with the son of her dad's biggest enemy. And when she'd met her father at Starbucks this morning to discuss how well the flash mob had gone, he'd been scowling at something in the paper. Hanna peeked over his shoulder; it was an article about Tucker Wilkinson and how much money he gave to charities. "As if he actually cares about multiple sclerosis," Mr. Marin said under his breath. "That whole family has poison for blood."

"Not his kids," Hanna squeaked before she could stop herself.

Her father gave her a sharp look. "Everyone in that family is the same."

But between then and now, an achy longing had bloomed inside of her. She kept thinking of the way Liam looked at her, like there was no other girl in the universe. How he confessed that damaging secret about his dad, seeming so broken and sad. How he wanted to take her to Miami so he could have her all to himself. How the unbearable loneliness she'd felt since she broke up with Mike vanished when she was with him, and how she forgot all about A, Tabitha, and Kelsey when they were together. So when Liam texted her earlier this afternoon, asking if she'd meet him here—sufficiently secluded, she noted, so that no one would see them—Hanna couldn't help but text him back that she would.

The old mansion-turned-church rose up before her, a huge structure of stonework, turrets, and antique stained glass. The saints etched into the windows seemed to glare at Hanna in judgment. Something scuttled around the corner, and Hanna froze.

"*Psst.*"

Hanna jumped and spun around. Liam stood in shadows under an old, blown-out lamppost. Hanna could make out the shy smile on his face. A huge part of her wanted to run to him, but instead she stood where she was, giving him an uncertain look.

"You came." Liam sounded surprised.

"I'm not staying long," Hanna answered quickly.

Liam's feet made squishy noises in the mud as he walked closer. He took her hands, but she quickly pulled away. "This isn't right," she said.

"Then why does it *feel* right?"

She crossed her arms over her chest. "My dad would kill me if he knew I was with you. Wouldn't your dad kill you, too? This isn't some kind of setup, is it?"

"Of course not." Liam touched her chin. "My dad has no idea I'm here. Really, I should ask *you* if this is a setup. I told you a huge secret, before I knew who you were."

"I'm not going to tell anyone about that," Hanna

muttered. "That's your business, not mine. And my father doesn't play dirty." *Like yours does*, she almost added, but didn't.

Liam looked relieved. "*Thank* you. And, Hanna, who cares about a political campaign?"

Hanna twisted her mouth. All of a sudden, she didn't know how she felt about *anything*.

"I couldn't go another day without seeing you." Liam ran his fingers through her hair. "I've never felt such a strong connection with anyone else before. I don't care whose daughter you are. I wouldn't trade this for anything."

Hanna's heart melted, and when Liam began to kiss her, she no longer felt the drizzle on her cheeks. Slowly, her body sank into him, and she breathed into his neck, his soft, shampoo-smelling hair.

"Let's run away together," Liam whispered in Hanna's ear. "Not to Miami. Somewhere farther. Where have you always wanted to go?"

"Umm . . . Paris?" Hanna whispered.

"Paris is awesome." Liam slipped his hands under Hanna's shirt. She jumped a little at his cold palms on the small of her back. "I could rent us an apartment on the Left Bank. We wouldn't have to deal with any of this election bullshit. We could disappear."

"Let's do it," Hanna decided, swept up in the moment.

Liam drew away, reached into his jacket pocket, and took out his cell phone. He pressed a button and then held the phone to his ear. Hanna frowned. "Who are you calling?"

"My travel agent." The cell phone's screen glowed green. "I can get us on a flight tomorrow, I bet."

Hanna giggled, flattered. "I wasn't actually *serious*."

Liam pressed END. "Well, you say the word, Hanna, and we'll go."

"I want to know absolutely everything about you first," Hanna said. "Like . . . what are you majoring in?"

"English lit," Liam answered.

"Really? Not political science?"

Liam scrunched up his face in disgust. "I have no interest in politics."

"And how is it that you have a travel agent on call?"

"He's an old family friend," Liam said.

Hanna wondered if the Wilkinson family had lots of *old family friends*—probably on the political payroll. "So you've been to Paris before?"

"Once, with my parents and brothers, when I was nine. We did the tourist crap, but I just wanted to sit at a café and watch people."

Hanna leaned against the damp stone wall, not caring if it made wet prints on her butt. "I went to Spain once with my parents. All they did was fight, so I stuffed my face and felt miserable." Liam chuckled, and Hanna lowered her head, mortified. Why had she blurted all that out? "I shouldn't have told you that."

"Hey, it's okay." Liam stroked her arm. "My parents

fought like crazy, too. But now they just . . . don't speak."
He got a faraway look on his face, and Hanna knew he
was thinking about the trouble his parents were in. She
touched his arm gently, not sure how to comfort him.

Suddenly, the doors to the church banged open. Liam
grabbed Hanna's hand and pulled her into the shadows.
A bunch of teenagers sauntered out, followed by a familiar ash-blond woman in a knockoff Burberry jacket, but
Hanna couldn't quite place her.

"I'm so sorry," Liam said in Hanna's ear. "I wanted to
meet you here because I didn't think anyone would be
around tonight."

More people streamed out of the church. Then, Hanna
saw a head of chestnut hair and flinched. It was Kate, arm-
in-arm with Sean Ackard. Sean walked stiffly, like he was
a little afraid of Kate's touch. He held a flyer in his hand
that said V CLUB across the top in big capital letters.

That was why ugly Knockoff Burberry Jacket was familiar—
it was Candace, the head of the Virginity Club meeting
Hanna had crashed long ago in hopes of getting back together
with Sean. They must have moved the support group from
the Rosewood YMCA, where it had been held last year, to
here. So Sean was still a devout virgin! Hanna was dying to
ask Kate how she'd liked her first V Club meeting. Had they
sworn off touching? Had Sean bought her a no-sex promise
ring yet? A mirthful laugh slipped from her lips.

Kate froze and Sean came to a halt next to her. She
looked around. "Is someone there?"

Hanna clamped her mouth shut. Liam stood very still beside her.

"It was probably a raccoon," Sean said finally, guiding her to the parking lot.

"Did you know her?" Liam whispered once they were out of earshot.

"She's my *stepsister*," Hanna said. "If she saw me with you, I'd be dead."

Liam stiffened. "I'd be dead, too. My dad would probably stop paying my tuition at Hyde. Take away my car. Kick me out of the house."

"That makes two of us." She leaned her head on Liam's shoulder. "We'd be homeless together."

"I can think of much worse punishments," Liam said.

Hanna ducked her head. "You probably say that to all the girls."

"No, I don't." He looked so sincere that Hanna leaned in and kissed him forcefully on the mouth. He kissed her back, and then moved to her cheeks, her eyes, her forehead. His hands caressed her waist. Who cared if she'd only met him a few days ago? Who cared if this was wrong? Who cared if their families hated each other? Liam was right: This kind of connection shouldn't be ignored. It was like one of those rare comets—it only came around once every thousand years.

Two hours and a million kisses later, Hanna climbed back into her car and sank against the seat. She felt blissed-out and exhausted. It was only then that she noticed the little blinking green light on the top of her cell phone. She pulled it from the pocket of her bag and touched the screen. ONE NEW TEXT, it said.

She glanced up, gazing around the parking lot. The streetlights cast golden, uninterrupted circles of light on the pavement. The wind rattled the handicapped parking signs and blew an empty gum wrapper into the grass. No one was here. With shaking hands, she touched the screen to read the message.

> Hannakins: I know you guys are living out your own private Romeo and Juliet love story, but remember: Both of them die in Act V. —A

18

ALL GREAT ACTRESSES HALLUCINATE!

"*Double, double, toil and trouble*," Naomi, Riley, and Kate screeched as they circled a cauldron on the Rosewood Day stage on Monday afternoon. "*Fire burn and cauldron bubble.*"

The three girls beckoned Beau-as-Macbeth toward them, shaking their boobs and making kissy-faces, which definitely wasn't called for in the script. All of them had changed out of their Rosewood Day uniforms into skinny jeans, low-cut tunics, and Halloween-esque witches' hats.

One row in front of Spencer, Jasmine Bryer, a brunette sophomore who was playing Lady Macduff, nudged Scott Chin, her on-stage husband. "They look like hookers, not witches."

"You're just pissed because they blew you off when you asked to sit with them at Steam yesterday," Scott said knowingly, snapping his gum.

Spencer sunk down lower in her seat and picked

absently at a tiny hole in her knee socks. The auditorium smelled like old shoes, the salami hoagies the crew advisor always brought in for an after-school snack, and patchouli oil. There was a commotion on the stage, and when Spencer looked up, Kate, Naomi, and Riley were daintily stepping off the risers, their witch hats in their hands. "Oh, everyone?" Naomi called out. "We want to remind you about the cast party after the performance on Friday. It's going to be at Otto. We hope you *all* can come." She looked directly at Beau as she said this.

Spencer rolled her eyes. Only Naomi, Riley, and Kate would hold the cast party at Otto, a fancy bistro down the street. Usually, the cast fetes were held in the auditorium or the gym. Two years ago, they'd thrown it in the cafeteria.

"We also suggest you all dress *nicely,* as the *Philadelphia Sentinel* is going to be there," Riley added nasally, now glowering at the other actors, who usually looked as though they were going to a Renaissance Faire—even when they *weren't* rehearsing Shakespeare. "Hopefully, they'll interview all of us."

Pierre snorted. "We'd better work our asses off, then." He spied Spencer in the back row. "Speaking of which, Mr. M? Lady M? Are you ready?"

Spencer jumped up. "Definitely." Beau rose, too.

Naomi and Riley gazed longingly at Beau as he sauntered up the aisle. "Good luck," Naomi said, fluttering her eyelashes. Beau shot her a dismissive smile.

Then the girls turned to Spencer and snickered. "There's something really *off* about her, don't you think?" Naomi whispered loud enough for Spencer to hear, her buttery blond hair falling into her face. "Maybe someone's lost her dramatic touch."

"Personally, I think the girl who played her on *Pretty Little Killer* was a much better actress than she is," Kate said. The others tittered.

Spencer stepped onto the stage, ignoring them. Pierre narrowed his eyes at Spencer. "We're going to rehearse the scene where you tell Mr. M to kill the king. I hope *you've* got it a bit more together today."

"Absolutely," Spencer chirped, pushing a lock of blond hair over her shoulder. At Beau's house yesterday, they'd rehearsed dozens of scenes, and she felt prepared and connected. She kept repeating a mantra in her head: *I'm going to nail this, and Princeton is going to want me.* She exchanged a glance with Beau, who had walked onto the stage as well. He shot her a kind, encouraging smile, and she smiled back.

"Okay." Pierre prowled around the stage. "Let's take it from the top, then."

He gestured to Beau, who began the monologue about how Macbeth wasn't sure whether he should commit murder. When it was Spencer's cue to enter, she repeated the mantra in her head again. *I'm going to nail this, Princeton is going to want me.*

"*How now, what news?*" she said.

Beau spun around and looked at her. "*Hath he asked for me?*"

Spencer gave him an annoyed look, as though he were actually her husband and yet again hadn't listened to one word she'd said. "*Know you not he has?*"

Beau lowered his eyes and said that they must not discuss the murder any further—he couldn't go through with it. Spencer stared at him, trying to put herself in Lady Macbeth's position, as Beau had encouraged. *Become one with Lady Macbeth. Put yourself in her place. Surrender to her problems.*

And for Spencer, that meant: surrender to Tabitha. She had aided in Tabitha's murder, after all. Her motives were different from Lady Macbeth's, but it had accomplished the same end. "*Was the hope drunk wherein you dress'd yourself?*" she sputtered. "*Hath it slept since? And wakes it now, to look so green and pale at what it did so freely?*"

They continued to argue. Lady Macbeth told her husband that he wasn't a man if he didn't go through with the murder. Then she revealed her plan: get the king's chambermaids drunk and kill him while they slept. Spencer tried to make the argument sound as logical as possible, feeling more and more connected to her character. She'd been the voice of reason with her friends that night in Jamaica, too, telling her friends Tabitha needed to be stopped. And when Aria pushed Tabitha off the roof, Spencer had been the one who rallied them together, telling them they'd done the right thing.

Suddenly, she noticed a flutter out of the corner of her eye and looked up. Standing beyond Beau, nearly translucent against the strong stage lights, was a blond girl in a yellow sundress. Her face was ashen and bloodless, her eyes were lifeless, and her head hung at a strange angle on her neck, as if it had been broken.

Spencer gasped. It was Tabitha.

Fear streaked through her. She glanced down at the floor, afraid to look in the corner again. Beau shifted on the stage, waiting for Spencer to deliver her final set of lines. Finally, she peeked across the stage where she'd seen the figure. Tabitha was gone.

Spencer straightened up. *"Who dares receive it other, as we shall make our griefs and clamour roar upon his death?"* she sputtered, clutching Beau's hands. And Beau nodded, saying he was going to go through with the vile deed.

Thankfully, the scene was over after that. Spencer scuttled behind the curtain and collapsed on an old couch once used for a set, taking deep, desperate breaths as though she'd just swum the English Channel. *Disaster.* Pierre probably thought that long pause between lines was because she'd lost her place, not because she'd seen an apparition on the stage. She was probably out of the play for good. Maybe she should write to Princeton and forfeit to Spencer F. now. Her future was ruined.

Footsteps approached. "Well, well, well, Miss Hastings," Pierre's voice said above her.

Spencer drew her hands away from her face. Pierre's

waxy, made-up face looked delighted. "It looks like someone's done her homework between then and now. Excellent job."

She blinked at him. "Really?"

Pierre nodded. "I believe you've finally connected with Lady M. Loved the little shrieks, too. And you kept looking off into the distance, as though possessed. You might nail this part yet."

Then Pierre pivoted on his heel and swished back to the stage. Beau ran toward Spencer, a huge smile on his face. "That was awesome!" he gushed, taking Spencer's hands. "You're really getting there!"

Spencer grinned weakly. "I thought I blew the whole thing. I acted like a spaz."

Beau shook his head. "No, you were *amazing*." He stared deeply into her eyes with such intensity that Spencer felt her cheeks get hot. "You really tapped into something scary inside yourself, didn't you? I could tell."

"Um, not really." Spencer peered out beyond the curtain. There was still no one in the corner where Tabitha had stood. "You didn't notice anyone watching backstage, did you?" she asked.

Beau looked around, then shook his head. "I don't think so." He squeezed her hands. "Anyway, I think with a few more practice sessions, you'll be amazing. Let's meet at your house next time. How about Thursday afternoon?"

"That sounds good," Spencer said shakily. And then Beau leaned close, a shy look on his face. Spencer closed her eyes, certain he was going to kiss her lips, but then a faint whisper sounded in her ears.

Murderer.

She opened her eyes again and pulled away. The hair on her arms stood on end. "Did you just hear that?"

Beau looked around. "No . . ."

Spencer listened hard, but heard nothing else. Maybe it was her imagination. Or maybe, just maybe, it was something—someone—much more sinister than that.

A.

19

THE BOOK THIEF

Later that same Tuesday night, Aria sat in a secluded nook at Wordsmith's, the bookstore a block away from the Rosewood Day campus. Classical music tinkled over the stereo, and the place smelled like the freshly baked cookies from the bakery next door. But nothing smelled as good as Ezra's cologne, which Aria was inhaling deeply as she snuggled next to him on the oversized loveseat in the café at the back of the store. It was daring for them to cuddle in broad daylight—Aria still thought of Ezra as her taboo, sexy teacher—but no Rosewood Day student came into Wordsmith's unless they were forced to, and absolutely no one from school patronized the café. That was a holdover from the days when Real Ali was still alive—she had started a rumor that someone had found a whole finger in one of the brownies, and everyone, even upperclassmen, had banned the place. Four months into her relationship with Noel, Aria caught him sneaking into Wordsmith's between classes, and he finally confessed that he had a major jones for the café's cranberry nut muffins. Aria had loved him for going against the fray.

Wait. Why was she thinking about *Noel* right now? She straightened up and looked into Ezra's ice-blue eyes. *He* was the guy she was with now.

She hefted Ezra's manuscript out of her bag and plunked it onto the ottoman. "So I read the whole novel," she announced with a smile. "And I *loved* it."

"Really?" Relief flooded Ezra's face.

"Of course!" Aria pushed it toward him. "But I was so . . . *surprised* at the subject matter."

Ezra cupped his chin in his hand. "The subject matter is all I've been thinking about for the last year."

"It was so . . . *vivid*," Aria continued. "The writing was amazing—I felt like I was there." Of course, she kind of *had* been there, but whatever. "I couldn't believe the turn it took. And then the ending! Wow!"

At the end of the novel, Jack moved to New York City. Anita moved with him, and they lived happily ever after. Until a bizarre twist at the end: Jack was mailed anthrax spores from an unknown international terrorist and died. But even *that* was romantic: There were heartfelt scenes of Jack dying in the hospital, Anita at his side.

Then her gaze fell back to the novel. "So . . . how much of this did you want to be true, anyway?"

"I wanted all of it to be true," Ezra answered, running

his fingers up and down her arm. "Well, except for the anthrax part."

Aria's heart pounded, and she chose her next words carefully. "So . . . when Jack asks Anita to move to New York . . ." She trailed off, not able to look him in the eye.

Ezra's voice grew intense. "I don't want to be without you again, Aria. I would love it if you moved there with me."

Aria's eyes widened. "Really?"

Ezra leaned toward her. "I've thought about you so much this year. I mean, I wrote a *book* about you. You could come for the summer at first, see how you like it. You could get an internship, maybe, a job at an art gallery. And you applied to FIT and Parsons, right?" He didn't even wait for Aria to nod. "If you get in—and I'm sure you will—that's where you could go next year."

All of a sudden, the overhead lights felt way too bright, and the oaky scent of wine made Aria's head spin. She chanced an excited smile. "A-are you *sure*?"

"Of course I'm sure." Ezra kissed her lips. Then he sat back and tapped the manuscript. "I want you to tell me everything you thought of it. Be honest."

Aria pushed her hair behind her ears and tried to focus. "Well, I loved it. Every sentence. Every detail."

"Surely there was *something* you didn't like."

The milk steamer switched on behind the counter, filling the café space with noise. "Well, I suppose there were a *few* things," Aria said tentatively. "Like I'm not sure Anita should write Jack ten haikus–that seems a bit much. Just one or two would do, don't you think? *I* certainly didn't write you that many."

Ezra frowned. "It's called creative license."

"True," Aria said quickly. "And . . . well, I *loved* Jack, I really did. But why was he so obsessed with building model train vignettes in his bedroom?" She grinned and touched his lips lightly with her finger. "You would never have done something as dorky as that."

Two sharp lines appeared on the sides of Ezra's mouth. "The model train scenes he created were symbolic. They were of the life he *wanted,* the perfect life he couldn't attain."

Aria stared fixedly at the stack of papers in her lap. "Oh. Okay. I guess I didn't understand that."

"It seems like you didn't understand a lot."

His acidic tone made Aria's heart drop. "You told me you wanted me to be honest," she squeaked. "I mean, those things are so *minor,* really."

"No, they're not." Ezra turned away from Aria, staring at an ad on the wall for filterless French cigarettes. "Maybe the book sucks, like all the agents said. Maybe that's why no one wants to represent me. And here I hoped to be the new Great American Novelist."

"Ezra!" Aria laid her palms flat on her thighs. "The book is awesome. I promise." But when she tried to grab his hand, he pulled it away and curled it in his lap.

"Hallo?"

A shadow fell over them, and Aria looked up. Standing over the loveseat was Klaudia. She wore a fitted blouse unbuttoned just enough to show off her cleavage, and her Rosewood Day skirt was rolled up a few times at the waist to accentuate her long legs. A pair of dark-framed eyeglasses perched on her head, making her look like a naughty librarian.

Aria jumped so hard the manuscript fell off her lap and onto the floor. "W-what are you doing here?" She scrambled to pick up the pages and secure them with a rubber band.

Klaudia shaped her long blond hair into a ponytail. "I meet you here for art history project, remember?"

It took Aria a moment to remember their conversation in the library. "I said we should meet here *tomorrow*, not today."

"Oops!" Klaudia covered her hand with her mouth. "My bad!" Her eyes flicked from Aria to Ezra. An intrigued smile spread across her face. "Hi there!"

"Hi." Ezra half rose, extended his hand, and gave Klaudia a much kindlier smile than Aria would have liked. "I'm Ezra Fitz."

"I Klaudia Huusko. Exchange student from Finland." Instead of shaking Ezra's hand, Klaudia leaned down and kissed him on both cheeks, European-style. Then she knitted her brow. "Why I know you? Your name sound familiar."

"I was a teacher at Rosewood Day last year," Ezra offered in a friendly voice.

"No, that not it." Klaudia shook her head, making her ponytail wobble. She squinted. "You not Ezra Fitz who writes the poetry, are you?"

Ezra looked startled. "Well, I've only published one poem—in a foreign journal."

"Was it called 'B-26'?" Klaudia's eyes brightened.

"Well, *yeah*." Ezra's smile grew broader and more skeptical. "You've . . . *read* that?"

"*Se tytto, se laulu!*" Klaudia quoted in melodic Finnish. "Is beautiful! I have it pinned up on bedroom wall in Helsinki!"

Ezra's mouth hung open. He glanced at Aria in an amazed way as if to say, *Can you believe it? I have a fan!* Aria wanted to smack him upside the head. Didn't he see that this was merely part of Klaudia's sex kitten act? She'd never read his poetry—she'd probably seen his name on the manuscript at the library earlier today and Googled him!

"I've read that poem, too," Aria boasted, suddenly feeling competitive. "It was really beautiful."

"Oh, but it even prettier translated into Finnish," Klaudia insisted.

A barista approached and Klaudia moved closer to Ezra to let him pass. "I have always wanted to be a writer, so this is very exciting for me to talk to a real published poet! Have you written other beautiful poetries?"

"I don't know how beautiful they are," Ezra said mock-bashfully, clearly enjoying being admired. "I'm working on a novel right now." He pointed at the manuscript that now sat on the ottoman next to them.

"Oof!" Klaudia pressed her hand to her ample chest. "A whole novel? Is *amazing*! I hope to read it someday!"

"Well, actually, if you're really interested . . ." He placed the novel in Klaudia's hands. "I'd love to hear your thoughts."

"What?" Aria shrieked. "She can't read it!"

Klaudia's eyes widened innocently. Ezra cocked his head, looking stricken. "Why not?" he asked, sounding hurt.

"Because . . ." Aria trailed off, trying to communicate with her eyes that Klaudia was a psychopath. *Because it's my novel, not hers*, she wanted to say, but she realized how petty and immature that sounded. Still, the novel was so personal. Aria didn't want Klaudia reading it, knowing about the most important relationship of her life.

Ezra waved his hand. "It's a rough draft," he said gently. "I need as many people giving me feedback as I can." He turned to Klaudia and smiled. "Maybe you'll like it as much as 'B-26.'"

"I'm sure I love it!" Klaudia cradled the manuscript in her hands. She backed away, giving Ezra a three-finger wave. "Okay, I go now! Sorry I bother you! See you in school tomorrow, Aria!"

"You were no bother," Ezra called, waving back. There was a slight, satisfied smile on his face, and his gaze followed Klaudia as she sashayed out of the café and through the bookstore. Aria reached for his hand again, but he squeezed only lightly and distractedly, like there were far more important things—or perhaps girls—on his mind.

20

ALL LOVING FATHERS STICK THEIR DAUGHTERS IN TALL TOWERS

Mr. Marin flung open the door to his house and greeted Hanna with a huge smile. "Come in, come in!"

"Thanks." Hanna dragged a Jack Spade duffel, stuffed with enough clothes for a three-night stay, over the threshold. Then she picked up the little doggie carrier that held Dot, her miniature Doberman, and hustled him inside, too. "Do you mind letting him out of there?"

"No problem." Mr. Marin bent over and unlocked the metal latch. The little dog, which Hanna had dressed in a Chanel-logo sweater, immediately scuttled out of the carrier and ran crazily around the living room, sniffing everything.

"*Uch*," a voice said. Isabel, whose salmon-colored twin set matched her orangey, fake-tanned skin, glared at Dot as though he were a sewer rat. "That thing doesn't shed, does it?"

"No, *he* doesn't," Hanna said in the most friendly

voice she could muster. "Perhaps you remember Dot from when you stayed in *my* house?"

"I suppose," Isabel said absently. Isabel had been wary of Dot when she'd lived at Hanna's when Ms. Marin went to Singapore on business, wrinkling her nose when he lifted his leg on the trees in the backyard, pretending to gag when Hanna spooned organic doggie food into his ceramic bowl, and always backing away from him like he was about to bite her. Hanna *wished* Dot would bite Isabel, but Dot loved everyone.

"Well, we're glad to have you," Isabel went on in a tone Hanna wasn't sure was sincere.

"Glad to be here," Hanna said, peeking at her father's expression. He looked so happy that she was honoring his request to stay with them a couple nights a week. It seemed like impeccably bad timing, though, what with her new entanglement with Liam. What if Hanna yelled out his name in her sleep? What if her dad scrolled through her phone and found all their texts to one another, including the steamy ones Liam had sent today?

"C'mon, I'll show you your room." Mr. Marin hefted Hanna's bags and started up the curved staircase. The house had a fussy, Christmas-store smell about it—Hanna had forgotten how obsessed Isabel was with putting lavender sachets into the drawers and bowls of potpourri on every available surface.

Her dad passed the second level, then started up the third. "The bedrooms are all the way up here?" Hanna

asked nervously. When she was little, she'd had an irra-
tional fear that their house was going to catch on fire
and lobbied to have their bedrooms on the first floor for
easy escape—not that her parents went for it. Maybe she
had a sixth sense, even back then, that someday she'd be
trapped in a burning building.

"Ours are on the second floor, but the guest room is
on the third." Mr. Marin glanced over his shoulder and
raised his eyebrows. "We call it the loft." He opened a
door at the end of the hall. "Here we are."

They entered a plain, white room with sloping ceil-
ings and small, square windows. It felt like he was a father
in a fairy tale, sticking Hanna in a tall tower, but the
room did have a hotel-quality duvet on the queen bed, a
huge bureau, an ample-sized closet, and a flat-screen TV
mounted on the wall. And was that . . . a Juliet balcony?
Hanna rushed across the room and opened the French
doors. Sure enough, a tiny balcony protruded from the
room, offering a view of the landscaped backyard. She'd
always wanted one of those.

"Is it okay?" Mr. Marin asked.

"It's great." It was definitely private, anyway.

"Glad you think so." Mr. Marin dropped Hanna's bags
by the closet, patted Dot on the head, and turned on his
heel toward the door. "Now, c'mon. We're going to review
the new campaign commercials. I'd love your input."

Hanna followed him back down the stairs. On the
third riser from the bottom, she noticed a flicker out the

window. It was pitch-black outside, not exactly prime time for a stroll around the neighborhood. Her thoughts flashed back to A's latest note: *Both of them die in Act V.* Was that a threat?

Her father led her into the family room, which contained a cognac-colored leather sectional, a matching leather ottoman/coffee table, and a large television against the wall tuned to CNN. Kate sat in the corner of one of the couches, her coltish legs tucked under her. Sitting next to her, his hand entwined in Kate's, was none other than Sean Ackard.

"Oh," Hanna said, stopping short.

Sean's face paled, too. "Hanna. I didn't know you'd be here."

Hanna looked at Kate, and Kate gave her a saccharine smile. It was clear *she* knew Hanna was coming . . . and that she had invited Sean to reemphasize that he was hers now.

"Hey, Sean," Hanna said coolly, throwing back her shoulders and sitting as far away from the happy couple as she could. What did she care if Kate and Sean were dating? She had an amazing boyfriend now, too, after all.

Not that she could tell anyone about him.

She peeked at Kate again. Her stepsister's brow was furrowed as though she'd expected more of a reaction. She tilted her body toward Sean and nuzzled her chin into his neck. Sean flinched, looking uncomfortable. Hanna wished she could drop a hint about seeing them at the V Club meeting, but she didn't dare.

Suddenly, a familiar girl popped on the TV screen, and Hanna almost screamed. It was a photo of Tabitha. "Drinking during spring break: Should we crack down?" the anchor said. Hanna jumped up and pressed a button on the remote, and the TV went blank. Kate gave her a bizarre look.

"I guess *someone's* ready to see my commercials," Mr. Marin joked. He pushed a DVD into the player, and his new campaign commercials popped onto the screen. Hanna sat back on the couch, trying to calm her nerves. Whenever she closed her eyes she saw an imprint of Tabitha's picture in her mind.

The first commercial was done with quick camera cuts, like an action film. The second one was done in mockumentary style, like *The Office.* "I want everyone to give me their honest opinion," Mr. Marin said. "Do you think young people will respond to these?"

"They're really fun and creative," Kate said thoughtfully, leaning forward. "But I'm not sure kids really watch commercials. They usually DVR right through them."

"You could post them on YouTube, though," Hanna said shakily, finding her voice.

Mr. Marin looked stressed. "We should keep tweeting though, right? And should we stage more flash mobs? The one last week worked so well."

"It did, didn't it, Hanna?" Kate simpered, glancing at Hanna pointedly. Hanna flinched. What did *that* look mean? Had Kate noticed that Hanna wasn't there for most of the presentation? Had she seen the guy Hanna had run off with?

"We could try Hollis this time." Mr. Marin stopped the video. "Or maybe Bryn Mawr? Or we could go into the city, try Temple or Drexel."

Kate raked her hand through her long chestnut hair. "What does the competition think about the flash mobs?" Yet again, she stared straight at Hanna.

Hanna's skin prickled. "How should I know?"

Kate shrugged. "I wasn't asking you specifically."

Biting her lip, Hanna reviewed the various times she'd been with Liam. Had Kate seen them at the church after all? Did she *know*?

Hanna stared at her. Kate stared back as if daring Hanna to blink. Sean tugged on his collar, his gaze ping-ponging between the girls. Mr. Marin shifted his weight, one eyebrow raised. "What's going on, girls?"

"Nothing," Hanna said quickly.

"Don't ask me." Kate threw up her hands. "*She's* the one acting weird."

Suddenly, Hanna felt overwhelmed. She was hiding way too much. "Um, I have to . . ." Hanna jumped up from the couch and ran toward the door. Kate let out a half sniff, half sigh behind her.

She rushed down the hall and paused outside the powder room, noticing a half-unpacked box and some-thing propped on the back of the living room sofa. It was a well-worn stuffed Rottweiler, one of its ears almost missing and a patch of fur on its back worn away. Her father had bought Hanna this stuffed dog after they made up the Cornelius Maximilian dog character, a long-running inside joke between them. Hanna had lost track of the stuffed Cornelius through the years and figured he'd been lost forever. Had her dad really hung on to him this long?

She touched Cornelius's plush head, guilt and regret surging through her veins. Her dad was trying to make an effort to restore their relationship, and Hanna was paying him back by fraternizing with the enemy. She needed to break it off with Liam now, before she got in deeper. She was juggling too many secrets right now. It was all catching up with her.

She reached into her pocket for her phone. But when she opened a new text message, she stopped. The thought of never seeing Liam again made her stomach tighten and tears well in her eyes.

A hand touched Hanna's arm, and she squealed and whirled around. Kate stood behind her, hand on one hip. "Everything okay?" she asked in a faux-concerned voice. Her gaze flicked from Hanna's face to her cell phone.

"Everything's fine," Hanna said tightly, covering the screen with her fingers. Thankfully, she hadn't pulled up Liam's information yet.

"Uh huh." Kate narrowed her eyes. "You don't *look* fine."

"Why do you care?"

Kate stepped closer, and Hanna could smell her Jo Malone Fig and Cassis body lotion. "You're hiding something, aren't you?"

Hanna looked away, trying to remain calm. "I don't know what you're talking about."

A nasty smile wriggled onto Kate's face. "You heard what Tom said," she warned, shaking her finger. "If any of us have secrets, the enemy will find them out. You don't want *that* to happen, do you?"

And then, before Hanna could answer, Kate tossed her long chestnut hair, spun around, and strolled back to the family room. She let out a high, lilting giggle as she walked, a sound that made every cell in Hanna's body quiver.

It sounded exactly like Ali's. *A's.*

21

SAME BAG, SCARIER CONTENTS

"Let's take it from the eighth measure." Amelia's voice floated out from the den as Spencer walked in the door and dropped her bag by the umbrella stand the following afternoon. A few seconds later, clarinets tooted and violins screeched. The classical piece lumbered forward, sounding like a funereal mess. Then it stopped abruptly. "Maybe we should take a break," another voice said.

Spencer froze. Kelsey was here. Again.

Part of her wanted to run up to her bedroom and slam the door tight, but she remembered her promise to the others—and herself. If she studied Kelsey carefully enough, maybe she'd be able to figure out what Kelsey knew about last summer—and if she really was A.

Slowly, she crept toward the den. The door was slightly ajar. Inside the room, Amelia fingered her clarinet. Kelsey held her violin in her lap. Then, as if sensing a presence,

Kelsey raised her head, saw Spencer, and flinched. Her mouth made a small *O*.

Spencer shot back and pressed her body against the wall. Some spy *she* was. But after taking several deep breaths, she peeked around the doorway and looked again. Kelsey's head was down now, concentrating on the sheet music. There was a tiny flower tattoo behind her ear—perhaps temporary, or perhaps real. Spencer wondered if she'd gotten it in juvie.

She thought about the night of their arrest. It had begun like any other. Spencer had grabbed her books from her desk and climbed one floor to Kelsey's room. The dorm was trying out a new keypad system of entry into the rooms instead of keys, and Kelsey had given Spencer her room's code. She'd typed it in and let herself into the empty room—Kelsey was still at the gym. Spencer decided that she might as well pop an Easy A now so it would kick in when they were starting to cram. But when she rifled through her purse, the pill bottle was empty. She checked inside Kelsey's Buddha statue, where she always kept her stash. Kelsey was out of pills, too.

Panic overcame her. Their AP exams were in three days, and she was only through chapter seventeen of thirty-one in AP Ancient History. Phineas had warned her that if she went off the pills cold turkey, she'd suffer a major crash. The most logical thing to do was call Phineas for more, but Spencer had no idea where he'd gone. Two days ago, he didn't show up to class. When Spencer and Kelsey went to his dorm room, it was empty, the sheets stripped from the bed, the clothes removed from the hangers in the closet. Spencer had tried his cell phone, but there was no answer. An automated voice said that his voice mail inbox was full.

A beep of the room's electronic keypad entry system sounded, and Kelsey let herself in, looking fresh-faced and relaxed. Spencer sprang to her feet. "We're out of pills," she blurted. "We need to get more."

Kelsey frowned. "How?"

Spencer tapped her lips, thinking. Phineas had mentioned reputable dealers in North Philly and given her one of the guy's cards in case of emergencies. She pulled it out and started dialing the number. Kelsey stared at her. "What are you doing?"

"We need those pills to study," Spencer said.

Kelsey shifted her weight. "Maybe we can do this without them, Spence."

But then someone answered on the other end. Spencer straightened up, uttered the code words Phineas said would gain the guy's trust, and then told him what she wanted. He gave her his address, and they arranged to meet. "We're set," she said after a moment, hanging up. "Come on."

Kelsey remained on the bed, her shoes off. "I think I'll stay here."

"I can't do this alone." Spencer pulled her car keys out of her pocket. "It'll take a half hour, tops."

But Kelsey shook her head. "I'm fine without the pills, Spence."

Groaning, Spencer stomped over to Kelsey and pulled her to her feet. "You won't be saying that a few hours from now. Put on your flip-flops. Let's go."

Finally, Kelsey relented. They drove through the dark streets into a derelict neighborhood, passing boarded-up windows and graffiti-marred walls. Kids sat on stoops, glaring at everything. A fight broke out on the corner, and Kelsey whimpered. Spencer wondered if she'd been right—maybe this was a bad idea.

But soon enough they were back in the car, pill bottle in hand, heading toward campus once more. Spencer handed Kelsey an Easy A, and they both washed them down with warm Diet Sprite. As they rolled into a safer neighborhood, Kelsey let out a long sigh. "We're never doing that again."

"Agreed," Spencer said.

They were pulling through the Penn gates when two bright lights hit the rear-view mirror. Sirens blared. Kelsey and Spencer turned around to see the campus police bearing down on them. "*Shit*," Spencer hissed, tossing the bottle of pills out the window.

The police car pulled over and signaled for Spencer to do the same. Kelsey looked at Spencer, her eyes bulging wide. "What the hell are we going to do?"

Spencer stared into Kelsey's frantic face. Suddenly, a calm feeling washed over her. Everything she'd been through with Ali, all those A notes and near-death experiences she'd had to endure, made this moment seem manageable in comparison. "Listen," she said forcefully to Kelsey. "We didn't do anything wrong."

"What if they followed us from the deal? What if it was a sting? What if they find the pills?"

"We—" A cop tapped on the window. She rolled it down and gazed innocently into his stern face.

The cop glared hard at the girls. "Can you two get out of the car?"

Kelsey and Spencer looked at each other. Neither said anything. The cop sighed loudly. "Get. Out. Of. The. Car."

"Kelsey's right. Let's take a break, guys," Amelia said. Spencer looked up, snapping instantly out of the memory. All of the orchestra girls rose from the couches.

Panicked, she stepped backward and slipped into the hall closet, which held winter coats, an old dog gate, and three different vacuum cleaners for various types of dust and pet hair. She waited until everyone filed into the kitchen, praying no one would open the door and find her here. Through a slit in the door, she could see the guests' bags and coats piled on the wooden bench across the hall. Amid the Burberry trenches, J. Crew puffer coats, and Kate Spade satchels, was a shimmery gold tote that matched hers.

We're twinsies! Kelsey had said a few days ago when she'd seen the bag.

Maybe there *was* a way to see if Kelsey knew more.

Spencer waited until the break was over, then darted to the front door and grabbed her own Dior bag. Then she scurried to the pile of coats, set down her Dior bag in place of Kelsey's, and lifted Kelsey's bag into her arms. It smelled different from hers, like a fruity candle. It would only take her minutes to go through it. Kelsey wouldn't even know it was gone.

She took the stairs two at a time, slammed her bedroom door shut, and upended Kelsey's purse on the bed. There was the same snakeskin leather wallet Kelsey had used at Penn last summer and a pair of Tweezerman tweezers—she never went anywhere without them. Out tumbled an extra set of violin strings, a flyer for a band called The Chambermaids with a phone number for someone named Rob scrawled across the top, a tube of lip gloss, and a bunch of different-colored pens.

Spencer sat back. There was nothing incriminating in here. Maybe she was being paranoid.

Then she noticed Kelsey's iPhone tucked into the front pocket. She yanked it out, scrolling through the sent-texts folder for notes from A. There weren't any, but that didn't mean anything—Kelsey could own a second phone, like Mona had. On the main screen was a folder titled "Photos." Spencer tapped it, and several subfolders appeared. There were shots from prom, a graduation, and Kelsey with a bunch of smiling girls from St. Agnes, none of whom Spencer recognized from orchestra practice. But then she noticed a folder that made her blood run cold.

Jamaica, Spring Break.

Downstairs, the orchestra music ramped up again, clumsy and dissonant. Spencer stared at the folder icon. It was a coincidence, right? Lots of people went to Jamaica during spring break—hadn't she'd read in *Us Weekly* that it was the number one party location for high school and college students?

With a shaking finger, she pressed the button to access the folder's contents. When the first photo appeared on the screen, Spencer saw the familiar cliffs that she, Aria, Emily, and Hanna had jumped from their first day at the resort. The next photo featured the rooftop deck where the four of them had dined almost every night. There was a photo of Kelsey posing with Jacques, the Rastafarian bartender who made a mean rum punch.

Her stomach roiled. It was The Cliffs.

She scrolled through more pictures at breakneck speed, revisiting the huge pool, the blue mosaic hallway to the spa, the speckled pygmy goats that wandered outside the resort's high stucco walls. In a picture of a crowd at the restaurant, a face stuck out among the rest. There, clear as day, looking sunburned and wearing the lacrosse T-shirt he'd had on the day they'd arrived, was Noel Kahn. Mike Montgomery stood next to him, holding a Red Stripe. If a few random guests had moved out of the way, Kelsey would have gotten Spencer, Aria, Emily, and Hanna in the shot, too.

She scrolled to the next photo and almost screamed.

Tabitha stared back at her, happy and alive, wearing the golden sundress she'd worn the night Spencer and the others had killed her.

The iPhone slipped from her hands. It felt like something heavy and hard was sitting on her chest, preventing air from reaching her lungs. Details crystallized in her mind. Kelsey had been at The Cliffs the same time as she and her friends were. Perhaps Kelsey knew Tabitha. Perhaps Kelsey saw what Spencer and the others did to her. And then, when she met Spencer again at Penn, she made the connection. And when Spencer framed Kelsey for something *she* was responsible for, Kelsey had decided to exact revenge . . . as the new A.

She had her proof. Kelsey was A. And she wasn't going to stop until she brought Spencer down once and for all.

22

NOTHING LIKE A THREAT
TO HELP WITH A DECISION

Later that night, Aria sat on the couch at Byron's house, rain pounding on the windowpanes. She should have been looking at her art history project–Klaudia had cancelled their second Wordsmith's meeting and rescheduled for a coffee shop on Friday–but instead she was on a website called BrooklynLofts, which featured gorgeous apartments in the Brooklyn Heights, Cobble Hill, Williamsburg, and Red Hook neighborhoods. The more she read about Brooklyn, the more she was convinced that it was where she and Ezra belonged. Practically every writer who mattered lived in Brooklyn. Ezra could probably get his book published just by walking to the local coffee shop.

Mike strolled into the room wearing a remarkably clean T-shirt and dark jeans. "Going somewhere?" Aria asked, looking up.

"Just out," Mike mumbled, grabbing an organic, sugar-free candy from the bowl Meredith had set on the side table. She was one of those people who believed sugar consumption shortened one's life span.

"On a *date*?" Aria goaded. Mike was wearing his nice Vans after all—the ones that weren't covered in dirt.

Mike made a big deal of unwrapping the plastic on the candy. "Colleen and I are hanging out. It's not a big deal."

"Are you two getting cozy at play practice?"

Mike winced. "It's not like that. And, I mean, she's not . . ." He clamped his mouth shut and stared off at the teardrop-shaped prism that Meredith had hung in the window.

Aria sat up straighter. "She's not . . . *Hanna*?"

"No," Mike said quickly. "I was going to say she isn't, like, the Hooters honey who's totally digging me on Skype." Then he plopped down in the ancient Stickley chair Byron claimed to have found on the street in his college days. "Okay. Maybe I *was* going to say that."

"If you miss Hanna so much, why don't you tell her?"

Mike looked horrified. "Because guys don't do that. That'd make me look girly."

Aria snorted. Where did guys *get* these nonsensical ideas? She shifted closer to him. "Look, I can't really talk about it, but I'm back with someone I was with last year. Someone I really, really missed, who I'd thought had forgotten me. But he came back and said he missed me, too. It was *romantic*, Mike. Not lame or wussy."

Mike crunched loudly on the candy, looking unconvinced. "So it's really over between you and Noel?"

Aria lowered her eyes. It was still weird to hear talk of their breakup. "Yeah."

"So are you with Sean Ackard again?"

Aria wrinkled her nose, surprised at his assumption. Most of the time she forgot she'd dated Sean last year . . . and that she'd *lived* with him for a while.

"Then who is it?" Mike's brow furrowed.

Aria looked at the BrooklynLofts site, then clicked the lid shut before Mike could see. She should tell him about Ezra, but it felt . . . awkward. Last year, Mike had found out about her fling with Ezra and had called her a freakish Shakespeare-lover. Maybe, to him, it would still be weird.

The doorbell rang. Aria glanced at Mike. "Is that Colleen?"

Mike shook his head. "I'm meeting her at the King James. I'm going to try to convince her to go into Agent Provocateur with me—apparently there's a lingerie runway show tonight. I got two words for you: *Double. Dees.*"

Rolling her eyes, Aria pushed her books aside and walked to the front door, dodging Lola's baby toys, swing, and bouncer that littered the hall. When she pulled the door open, Spencer, Hanna, and Emily were huddled under the small porch overhang, dripping wet from the rain. Aria blinked at them in surprise.

"Can we come in?" Spencer asked.

"Of course." The wind gusted as Aria opened the door wider. The girls stepped inside, peeling off their soaked jackets. Mike hovered in the doorway, though when he saw Hanna, he turned on his heel and retreated to the den.

"We need to talk," Spencer said after hanging up her coat. "Can we go to your room?"

"Um, okay." Aria turned, led them up the stairs to her bedroom, and shut the door. Everyone milled around awkwardly. After Real Ali tried to kill them and they'd reunited, they'd spent tons of time up here, but they hadn't been in Aria's room since shortly after Jamaica. Even Emily, whom Aria still called almost every night, looked twitchy and uncomfortable, like she'd rather be anywhere else.

Spencer slumped down on the floor, pushed Aria's stuffed pig, Pigtunia, out of the way, and pulled an iPad out of her bag. "I need to show you guys something."

A series of photos appeared on the screen. When Spencer tapped the first one, Aria immediately recognized the pink stucco building from the resort they'd stayed at in Jamaica. Then she saw a picture of the mosaic-tiled tables where they ate breakfast every morning. When Spencer touched the screen once more, Noel's face appeared in a crowd of drunken kids. And then came a shot of Tabitha in her yellow sundress. The blond girl grinned straight into the camera, wearing a faded blue string bracelet that looked so much like the one Their Ali had made for Aria and the others after The Jenna Thing.

Aria's heart somersaulted. "Who took these?"

"They were on Kelsey's phone." Spencer's face was

pale. "I stole her bag while she was at my house, then loaded these onto a flash drive."

Emily looked appalled. "You stole her photos?"

"I had to," Spencer said defensively. "Don't you see what this means? She was in Jamaica the same time as we were. She's definitely A. She knows what we did in Jamaica, and now she's out to get us."

Emily cleared her throat. "I really don't think Kelsey's A. I mentioned you to her the other day, Spencer, and she didn't get angry. She just shrugged. I really don't think she knows anything."

Spencer's eyes flashed. "You *saw* her again?"

Emily cowered a little. "I . . ."

Aria swiveled around to face Emily. "Wait, you know Kelsey?"

"It's a long story," Emily mumbled. "I met her at a party before I knew about what Spencer did to her. But she's really, really nice. I think Spencer's wrong about her."

"Em, you have to stay away from her!" Spencer shrieked. "She knows everything about Jamaica! She has a picture of *Tabitha*!"

"But why didn't she start threatening you as soon as she met you at Penn?" Emily chewed on a thumbnail. "If she knew you'd done something awful, wouldn't she have mentioned it?"

"She didn't *need* to threaten me at Penn," Spencer explained. "I hadn't done anything to her to warrant it—yet. Maybe she didn't even realize what she saw in Jamaica—but then, later, after I screwed her over, she put the pieces together. Maybe she spent all her time in juvie gathering information about us . . . *and* Tabitha!"

"That seems a little far-fetched." Emily pulled her knees to her chest. "Just because she was in Jamaica doesn't necessarily make her guilty *or* mean she saw anything. Noel and Mike were there, too, and we don't assume *they* saw."

"Noel and Mike don't have a reason to hate us," Spencer pointed out. "Kelsey does."

Everyone exchanged nervous glances. A gust of wind bellowed outside, sending a series of humanlike creaks and moans through the house. Aria stared down at Tabitha's photo. One of her eyes was closed in a *gotcha!* wink. Aria shut her eyes, remembering Tabitha's twisted expression when she'd pushed her off the roof. The guilt descended upon her like an avalanche.

"What do you think we should do, Spencer?" Hanna whispered. "If Kelsey is A, and she figured out what happened with Tabitha, why isn't she going to the police? What's stopping her?"

Spencer shrugged. "Maybe she doesn't want the cops involved. Maybe she wants to do things her own way."

Aria's stomach swooped. Mona Vanderwaal had tried to take matters into her own hands. So had Real Ali. And the four of them had nearly ended up dead both times.

"Aria?" Meredith called from downstairs. "Dinner's ready!"

Aria looked at her three old friends, feeling awkward. "Do you guys want to stay?"

Hanna rose to her feet. "I should go."

"I have homework," Spencer said, and Emily murmured an equally lame excuse. The three of them stomped down the stairs, fumbled into their jackets, and disappeared into the rainy night. Aria shut the door tight and leaned against it, feeling empty and scared. Nothing had been accomplished. They knew who A might be . . . but what were they supposed to do about it? Wait around in Rosewood for Kelsey to tell on them? Pack their bags for jail?

She listened to her friends' cars start at the curb, suddenly feeling a rush of hatred for Rosewood so strong it made her toes curl in her shoes. What good had come out of living here besides Ezra? So many terrible secrets she harbored, so many moments she'd rather forget, had happened in Rosewood. Well, and Jamaica. And Iceland, too, but she quickly put that thought out of her mind.

She headed back to the den. Mike was gone, probably having snuck out when Aria and the others were upstairs. When she opened the laptop, she began an email to Ezra.

What do you say I move back to NYC with you NOW? I could finish up my high-school credits online. I don't want to wait. I want to start our lives together.

She hit SEND and shut the laptop again. It was a win-win situation: Not only was Aria in love with Ezra, but he was also her ticket out of Rosewood. And she needed to get away as soon as possible.

23

EMILY'S SUCH A PUSHOVER

The following afternoon, Emily pulled into the parking lot of the Stockbridge trail and immediately spotted Kelsey's black Toyota hatchback in one of the front spaces. Last night's rain had stopped, and the sun had come out again, making all of the trees look extra green and lush.

Before she got out of the car, she turned and squinted at the vehicles swishing back and forth on the winding road. When a Mercedes coupe whizzed past, she watched it carefully. Was that Spencer's car, or was hers more silvery? Emily bit a fingernail. What would Spencer say if she saw Emily and Kelsey together? When Kelsey had emailed Emily that morning asking if she wanted to go on a hike after school, Emily had hesitated, thinking about her meeting with Spencer and the others last night. But after a moment, she'd said yes. Spencer couldn't tell her who she could or couldn't be friends with. The photo of Tabitha on Kelsey's phone worried Emily, but just because Kelsey had been to Jamaica at the same time as Emily and her friends didn't mean she was A. Either way, hanging out with Kelsey today was Emily's chance to suss out some information and prove Spencer wrong once and for all.

She locked her car and strode across the lot toward Kelsey. Kelsey was taking a big swig of water, dressed in khaki cargo pants, hiking shoes, and a black North Face hoodie that looked almost exactly the same as the one Emily was wearing. There was something jittery about her walk, her legs moving choppily, her body having lots of bounce. It was as though she'd just drunk a bunch of cups of espresso.

"This is one of my favorite places," Kelsey said, her voice a little on the peppy side, too. "I used to camp up here all the time."

"The trail is gorgeous." Emily followed Kelsey past the large sign that listed the path's hours of use and a bunch of warnings about Lyme disease and ticks. "I was never allowed to come here when I was younger. My mom was sure it was full of kidnappers."

"And did you believe it, too?" Kelsey teased.

"Maybe," Emily admitted.

"And here I thought you were a badass." Kelsey pinched Emily's arm. "Don't worry. I'll keep you safe from the big bad kidnappers."

They started to climb the narrow slope. An older couple with a golden retriever passed them in the other direction, and three runners disappeared around the bend. Emily paid close attention to her footsteps, careful not to trip over any of the scraggly branches that had fallen across the path. The coconut scent of sunscreen wafted down from a higher point on the trail, and the photos from Jamaica Spencer had stolen from Kelsey's phone flashed in Emily's mind again. She cleared her throat. "I like camping, but it's not my ideal vacation. I'd rather go to the ocean."

"I *love* the beach," Kelsey gushed.

"Have you ever been to the Caribbean?" Emily asked. Her heart pounded hard, anticipating Kelsey's answer.

Kelsey skirted around a large rock. "A couple times. I was in Jamaica just last year."

"I was in Jamaica last year, too." Emily prayed she sounded sufficiently surprised. "Did you go during spring break?"

"Uh huh." Kelsey turned around, an intrigued smile spreading across her face. "You too?"

Emily nodded. "Next we'll discover we stayed at the same hotel," she joked. Or at least she hoped it sounded like a joke. "I stayed at a place called The Cliffs. It had these amazing rocks you could dive off into the ocean. And a really great restaurant."

Kelsey stopped on the trail and blinked. "You're kidding me, right?"

Emily shook her head, her mouth bone-dry. She searched her friend's face for any signs of awkwardness or deceit, but Kelsey looked so guileless, truly caught off guard. *If I see a squirrel in that tree, Kelsey is innocent,* she told herself, gazing at a big oak in front of her. Sure enough, a squirrel scampered along one of the high branches.

"What week did your school go on spring break?" Kelsey asked.

Emily told her, and Kelsey exclaimed that was when St. Agnes had been off, too. "I can't believe I didn't notice you," Kelsey said after a moment. "Just think. We could have become friends so much sooner." She touched Emily's arm. "Or maybe *more* than friends."

All the nerve endings in Emily's arm tingled. When she breathed in, the air smelled dewy and fertile, like everything on the trail was sprouting. She gazed into Kelsey's bright green eyes. Either she was an incredibly skilled liar, or she really knew nothing. She might have met Tabitha at The Cliffs, but there was no way she knew what had happened to her. She certainly didn't know what Emily and the others had done.

Suddenly, Emily noticed a familiar fork in the path. "Can we make a detour for a sec? I want to see if something is still here."

Kelsey nodded, and Emily trekked a few steps down the fork and came upon a small stone water fountain that stood on the side of a sharp, muddy slope. There were two handprints in the cement. One print was labeled *Emily.* The other said *Ali.*

Kelsey bent down and touched the cement palm. "Is this yours?"

"Uh huh." Emily felt choked up looking at Ali's slender hands, preserved in perpetuity. "Ali and I sneaked out here once. They'd just poured the cement for this fountain, and she suggested we leave our mark."

She remembered that day like it was yesterday. It had been spring, a few months before Emily's fateful kiss with Ali in Ali's tree house. On their walk up the trail, Ali had listed off boys in their grade, asking Emily if she thought any of them were cute. "You need a boyfriend, Em," Ali had chided. "Or are you saving yourself for someone special?"

Now, Kelsey shook her head solemnly. "I don't know what that must be like to lose such a close friend."

A bunch of kids passed on the main trail, laughing loudly. "I miss her, but now I'm not sure what I *can* miss," Emily said in a small voice.

"What do you mean?"

"Well, take the bowling alley we went to the other day. Ali brought me and my three other friends there when we first started hanging out. She was all, 'I want us to spend some alone time to bond.' I used to think that was so cool, like she really wanted to get to know us, but now I wonder if it was just because she was *Courtney*, stepping into Ali's life and pretending to be her. Maybe hanging out there had nothing to do with new friendships but just needing some time to get her bearings and not hang around the popular Rosewood Day kids her sister had once known so well."

"That's a lot to take in," Kelsey said, eyes wide.

"I know." Emily stared up at the canopy of trees. "I miss my *old* memories of Ali. The ones where I just thought she was an amazing new friend. Now I have to revise my entire history with her. Everything I thought was true was a lie."

"It must mess with your mind."

"It does. Especially because . . ." Emily trailed off, thinking about all the dreams she'd had about Real Ali this year. All the flashes of blond hair she swore she'd seen, all the haunting whiffs of vanilla soap she'd smelled. Her firm belief that she was still out there, watching her every move. "I try to think only about the good stuff with Ali and block out what really happened. It's easier that way. So, like, in my head, My Ali is still this bubbly, intoxicating girl who had everyone wrapped around her finger."

"I guess that's one way to cope."

Emily tilted her head and smiled at Kelsey. "You remind me of her a little."

"I do?" Kelsey pressed a hand to her chest, looking a little sickened.

Emily touched Kelsey's shoulder. "In a good way. Nothing fazed her. She was kind of . . . amazing."

Kelsey pulled her bottom lip into her mouth. She eased a little bit closer to Emily until Emily could smell the faint tinge of bug spray on her skin. "Well, I think *you're* pretty amazing, too."

Lightning bolts zinged up and down Emily's arms. She leaned closer. She expected Kelsey to pull away, but she remained where she was, inches from Emily's face. Emily stared at Kelsey's long, pale eyelashes. The freckles on her earlobes. The tiny speck of gold in her green eyes. Their lips touched. Emily's heart banged hard.

After a beat, Kelsey pulled away, a shy smile on her face. "Wow."

They leaned into each other, about to kiss again, when a group of boys pushed through the clearing for the water fountain. Kelsey turned away. The boys ogled Kelsey and Emily and grunted out hellos. Kelsey glanced at them, her fingers twitching. Her expression was nervous, a complete transformation from what it had been moments before.

"Do you mind waiting here for a sec?" Kelsey whispered in Emily's ear after a moment. "I have to pee."

"Sure," Emily said.

As Kelsey trekked off into the bushes, Emily remained where she was, studying her phone so she wouldn't have to make conversation with the boys. After they'd all had a drink of water, they disappeared through the bushes again and started back up the trail.

Footsteps sounded down the slope, followed by the screech of a hawk. Then, all went silent. The trees seemed to close in around her, making her claustrophobic. When the sun went behind a cloud, it was downright dark out. Emily stared into the trees, wondering what was taking Kelsey so long.

All of a sudden, Emily heard a whooshing sound of a body moving through the brush. A split second later, two strong hands shoved her between her shoulder blades. "Hey!" she screamed, staggering forward. Her feet went out from under her, slipping in the soft mud. Before she knew what was happening, she was tumbling down the sharp, muddy hill, her arms flailing to grab on to something to stop her fall. Branches and shrubs and stumps rose up before her, and she barreled into them, sharp brambles cutting her skin. She rolled onto her side, hitting her elbow hard. Sharp pain shot through her, and she screamed out. Finally, after digging her nails into the earth, she felt her body slow. She came to a stop at the bottom of the hill, caught in a tangle of briars and dead tree limbs, mud covering her jeans, her hands and her arms. She tasted blood in her mouth and felt something wet and sticky on her cheek.

Heart pounding, she turned and looked up. A figure stood at the top of the hill next to the water fountain, half in the shadows. Emily gasped, taking in the person's blond hair and lithe frame. A haunting giggle snaked through the trees, filling Emily's body with shivers. *Ali?*

"Emily!"

When Emily blinked, the blonde was gone. A moment later, Kelsey was standing in her place, her hand over her mouth. "Oh my God!" she screamed. She started down the hill, grabbing on to branches for balance, her shoes sliding in the mud. By the time she'd reached Emily,

Emily had stood up and determined that no bones were broken. But she was still practically hyperventilating at what had just happened . . . and who she'd just seen.

Kelsey studied Emily at arm's length. The corners of her mouth turned down anxiously, and beads of sweat stippled her forehead. She still had that same jittery look on her face, and her hands were trembling. "Are you okay? What happened?"

Emily's chest heaved in and out. The scratches on her skin from the brambles burned every time she moved. "Someone . . . *pushed* me."

Kelsey's eyes widened. "One of those boys?"

Emily shook her head, still finding it hard to draw in a full breath. The giggle echoed in her ears. She could sense someone else's presence, someone looming close, watching. On instinct, she reached for her phone in her pocket. Sure enough, there was a new text message. With trembling fingers, she pressed READ.

Sometimes we all need a little push, Emily. You and your friends know all about that, huh? —A

24

LIFE IMITATES ART

On Thursday afternoon, Spencer was flipping through the newspaper when a splashy ad caught her eye. TONIGHT AT 8 P.M., A CNN SPECIAL: ARE YOUR CHILDREN SAFE ON SPRING BREAK? THREE CASES OF FUN SPRING HOLIDAYS GONE TERRIBLY WRONG.

There was a picture of Tabitha in the corner. Spencer immediately turned the paper over, and then, because that wasn't quite good enough, she tore it into tiny pieces and threw it in the trash. Even that didn't seem safe. She stared at the pieces, wondering if she should burn them.

Something flickered out of the corner of her eye, and she shot up and glanced out the window. A shape moved behind the trees. It looked like someone with blond hair.

Murderer.

Spencer spun around, clutching the sides of her head. The kitchen was empty. Beatrice and Rufus dozed on the floor, their paws twitching. If someone were here, they'd be barking their heads off, right? What the hell was *happening* to her?

Her cell phone let out a loud dog-barking sound, and Spencer jumped. She picked it up from the side table and saw that Emily had sent a text. *I'm really freaked. A just shoved me down a hill at the Stockbridge trail.*

Spencer glanced toward the den, thinking again of the flashes and voice she'd just heard. Amelia and the orchestra nerds weren't here right now, but they were scheduled to come over later this evening. *Kelsey wasn't there, was she?* she wrote back.

There was a long pause. Finally, Emily's reply popped up on the screen: *No.*

And you're not hanging out with her anymore, right? Spencer typed.

Emily replied again with a one-word *No.*

Good, Spencer responded.

"So this was where that Alison stuff went down, huh?"

It was forty minutes later, and Spencer and Beau were standing in the Hastingses' backyard, preparing for another *Macbeth* coaching session. Spencer was sure she'd be more than ready after today. She'd already made arrangements with the school's videographer to pay special attention to her in her scenes in the play performance on Saturday night. She'd even composed a draft email to the admissions committee talking about the play; all she needed now was to attach a movie file of her brilliantly executed scenes.

Beau gazed around at the twisted, blackened, ruined tree branches from the fire Real Ali had set here over a year ago. To the left was the property's original barn, which had once housed a lovingly restored guest suite . . . until Real Ali burned that down, too.

"Yeah," Spencer said softly. "I rarely come out here anymore. It's too creepy."

"I hear you. This place feels haunted." Beau toed the dirty slate path that used to lead to the barn. It was on this very path that she and Their Ali fought almost five years ago on the last night of seventh grade. The argument had been over Ian Thomas, whom they'd both had a crush on. Spencer had shoved Ali, who'd fallen, then quickly leapt back up and run down the path. For a long time, Spencer had assumed Ali had gone to meet Ian, her secret boyfriend, and Ian had killed her. But it was her twin sister who had intercepted her and murdered her.

"Anyway." Beau turned around and faced Spencer. "Are you ready to get into character?"

Spencer shrugged. "As ready as I'll ever be."

Beau smiled. "You did awesome yesterday, but there's another exercise I think we should try. You know how I said I connected being bullied to my role as Macbeth? It's your turn to do that, too. Try to really become her. Imagine getting rid of the person standing in the way of your success. Maybe you didn't mean to do it, but you carried it out anyway."

Spencer stared at him. That sounded like what had happened with Tabitha . . . and Kelsey, too. "I guess I could try," she said quietly.

"*Go* there," Beau instructed. "Repeat the lines Lady Macbeth says when she's overcome with guilt."

"*Out, damned spot,*" Spencer chanted.

"Good. Now, close your eyes and say them again."

"*Out, damned spot,*" Spencer repeated, shutting her eyes. "*Out, damned spot.*" She thought of Lady Macbeth wandering in the night, trying to clean her bloody hands of the shame she could never wash away. "*Out, damned spot!*" She thought of the guilt she felt for Tabitha. She opened her eyes and stared at her palms, imagining they were covered with blood—Tabitha's blood, fresh from her fall from the roof.

She forced herself to relive that awful night in Jamaica. How Tabitha had lashed out at Hanna. How she'd fought with Aria. How Aria had shoved her over the edge. Searching for Tabitha's body on the shore and not finding a trace. Feeling terrified to go out to the ocean each and every morning, certain the girl's body would have washed ashore in the night. Seeing that horrible newscast about Tabitha on television a few weeks ago.

But as she said the line a few more times, a different memory overtook her thoughts. She saw herself in that hot, poorly lit police station on Penn's campus. It was about a half hour after she'd spoken to Hanna and outlined her plan. Spencer didn't know if Hanna had gone through with it, but she had heard a lot of scuffling and ringing phones outside. Finally, the cop burst back in and looked at her. "You're free to go," he said gruffly, holding the door open for her.

"I-I am?" Spencer had sputtered.

He handed her back her iPhone. "Take my advice, Miss Hastings. Finish your summer program and go home to the suburbs. Be a good girl. You don't want to get mixed up with pills."

"What about Kelsey?" Spencer had blurted as she walked into the hall.

The corners of the cop's mouth curled into an ugly smile. At that very moment, a second holding room door opened. Two cops walked Kelsey down the hall. She screamed and flailed. "What are you talking about?" she said. "What did I do?"

"You know what you did," the cops growled at her.

Kelsey met Spencer's eyes for a moment and gave her a pleading look. *What are they talking about?* But there was something else in her expression, too, something Spencer hadn't wanted to think about until now.

It was fury. Like she knew exactly what Spencer had done.

"Out, damned spot," Spencer repeated once more now, staring down at her hands, just as Lady Macbeth did in the play. Suddenly, her palms were filled with small, white, round pills. Were those . . . *Easy As?* Shrieking, she flung them into the air. Where had they come from?

She looked for Beau, but Beau was gone. The yard was empty. "Beau?" she cried. No answer. It was dark out now. How much time had passed?

The trees whispered in the wind. An owl hooted in the distance, and the faintest smell of smoke from last year's fire tickled Spencer's nostrils. She looked down at her palms again; somehow, the Easy A pills had returned. "Get off!" She tried to jettison them away, but they remained glued to her skin. "Get off!" she shrieked, scratching at her palms with her fingernails until red, jagged lines appeared on her skin. "I can't be seen with these!" she screamed. "They can't catch me!"

But the pills wouldn't budge from her palms. Whirling around and breathing hard, Spencer staggered toward the small pond behind the barn. "Get off, get off, get *off*!" she shrieked, plunging her hands into the stagnant, half-frozen water. She barely felt the cold. She swished her hands around for a moment and then drew them back. The pills were *still* there. "No!" she screamed, running her wet palms through her hair. Frigid, fetid water streamed down her face and dripped into her ears and mouth.

Another twig snapped. Spencer shot to her feet, hands and hair dripping. "Who's there?" she cried out, her heart pounding hard. Was it the cops? Were they here for her?

Would they see the Easy As on her palm and take her away?

Someone snickered behind a bush. *Shh*, another voice said. Two figures stepped out from the trees. One was Kelsey. The other was Tabitha. They stood hand in hand, staring at Spencer.

"Hey, Spence," Kelsey teased, staring at Spencer's dripping palms. "Feeling guilty about something, murderer?"

"You can't run from us," Tabitha whispered. "We know what you did."

She smiled mysteriously and advanced down the slope. Spencer wheeled back, her ankle catching on a thick, twisted root. Within seconds, her butt hit the creek bank and her head and right shoulder plunged into the icy water. Her face instantly went numb. When she opened her eyes, Kelsey and Tabitha stood over her, their arms outstretched. Ready to drown her. Ready to exact their revenge.

"I'm sorry!" Spencer sputtered, flailing in the freezing water.

"Not sorry enough," Kelsey growled, plunging her chest down.

"You weren't sorry when you did it," Tabitha screamed, holding her neck.

"I'm sorry now!" Spencer struggled to break free of the girls, but they held her tight. "Please! Don't!"

"Spencer?"

Someone lifted her out of the creek. Ice slid down her back. Cold air slapped her cheeks. When she opened her eyes again, Kelsey and Tabitha were gone. Instead she saw Beau standing before her, wrapping his jacket around her shoulders. "It's okay," he cooed. "It's okay."

Spencer felt Beau leading her out of the woods. After a moment, she opened her eyes and looked around, half crying, half hyperventilating. She was in her backyard again. When she looked at her palms, they were empty. But while the visions she'd had of Kelsey and Tabitha had vanished, the *real* Kelsey stood a few feet away on the lawn with Amelia and some of the other orchestra girls, here for their evening practice. Her eyes were wide and there was a satisfied smirk on her face.

"What's *wrong* with her?" Amelia said in a disgusted voice.

"She's fine," Beau answered, walking Spencer toward the house. "We were doing a drama exercise."

"W-what *happened*?" Spencer whispered dazedly as they climbed the patio stairs.

Beau grinned. "You were amazing. You totally went for it. You immersed yourself in the Method—*literally*. Most actors have to study for years to make that much of an emotional connection. You're going to rock the part tomorrow."

As he helped her through the sliding door, Spencer

tried to smile as if she'd known what she'd been doing all along, but her insides felt weak and decimated, like a town ravaged by a tornado. And when she turned around, the real Kelsey was still watching her. That smirk was still there, as if she knew the root of Spencer's bizarre behavior.

As if she knew everything.

25

"BUT SOFT! WHAT LIGHT THROUGH YONDER WINDOW BREAKS?"

Hanna opened her eyes. A digital clock blazed a big red 2:14 A.M. across the room. A huge poster for a band called Beach House hung on the wall, and the windows were covered with blackout shades. This wasn't either of her bedrooms. Where the hell was she?

The bedsprings squeaked as she sat up. Pale light from the hallway glinted on a mirror across the room. A beaded curtain hung from the closet door. A four-leaf clover air freshener swung from the lamp switch. Hanna saw a picture of a girl with red hair in a silver Tiffany frame on the desk. Next to it were four AP textbooks.

Hanna inhaled sharply. This was Kelsey's dorm room at Penn—she recalled some of the details from when she'd snuck in there last summer. But how was she here now . . . and why?

A hand touched her shoulder. Hanna swung around and almost screamed. There, standing before her, was a familiar blond girl with a heart-shaped face and a haunt-ing smile. It was Real Ali. She was dressed in a blue oxford shirt and a white blazer, which she'd worn to the press con-ference last year when the DiLaurentises had announced her return to Rosewood.

"Looking to plant something?" Ali teased, tilting her hips.

"Of course not!" Hanna hid the pill bottle behind her back. "And what are you doing here? You're supposed to be . . ."

"Dead?" Ali covered her mouth and giggled. "You know better than that, don't you, Han?" And then she rushed for Hanna, her arms outstretched.

Hanna shot straight up in bed, gasping for air. She ran her fingers along the cool sheets and waited for her heart-beat to slow down. She was in the little loft room at her dad's house again. The heater hissed softly in the corner. Her door was closed, and the TV was muted to a late-late showing of *The Hangover*.

But Ali's presence still felt so *real*. She could practically smell her vanilla soap.

Bzzz. Hanna looked over. Her iPhone glowed with a new text from Liam.

Hey. Go to your balcony.

She cautiously slipped out of her sheets and tiptoed to the double doors that led to the Juliet balcony. Dot rose from his dog bed and followed her. The latch made a squeak when it turned. The doors groaned as she pulled them open. A whoosh of frigid air swept in, bringing with it the cold, dead smell of winter.

"Boo."

Hanna screamed. Dot let out a sharp yap. "Whoa!" Liam said, grabbing Hanna's shoulders. "It's okay! It's just me!"

"You *scared* me!" Hanna cried. Dot started barking hysterically.

"*Shhh*." Liam leaned down to pet the dog. "This is supposed to be a secret rendezvous, not a party for all the neighbors!"

Hanna stared at Liam. He was wearing a J. Crew anorak, a thick black scarf, dark jeans, and hiking boots. Then she looked at the long drop to the yard. "How did you know where I lived? And how did you get up here?"

"I looked you up on Google," Liam answered. "And I climbed." He gestured to a trellis on the side of the house.

"You can't be here," Hanna whispered. "My dad's one flight down! And I think my stepsister's onto us!"

Liam tucked a lock of hair behind Hanna's ear. "I thought we could have a sleepover."

"Are you insane?" Hanna glanced at her closed bedroom door, half expecting Kate to poke her head in—or worse, for her dad and Isabel to appear. What would she do with Liam then? Push him off the balcony? Stuff him under the bed?

Liam grabbed her hands. "Tell me you haven't missed me."

Hanna stared down at her pale feet sticking out of her pajama pants, then glanced at the Cornelius Maximilian stuffed Rottweiler in the bed. She stood to lose everything if she let Liam stay here. But when she looked at Liam's soft, warm eyes, his devilish grin, and the adorable dimple in his right cheek again, her heart melted.

Without a word, Hanna pulled him into the bedroom. They tumbled into Hanna's bed and immediately started making out. Liam's hands roamed all over Hanna's body, and his lips devoured her skin. She felt him suck hard on her neck, surely creating a hickey, but she didn't care.

Then he flopped back on the bed and looked at her. "I feel so comfortable with you, like I can tell you anything and you won't judge me. No other girl has made me feel like this before."

"I feel the same way about you," Hanna gushed. "It's incredible."

"*Magical*," Liam whispered. "I never used to believe in soul mates before, but now I've changed my mind."

Hanna propped up her head on her hand. "Tell me something you've never told anyone."

"Like my fear of spiders admission wasn't enough?" Liam rolled onto his back. A few moments passed before he spoke. "I had an imaginary friend when I was little. He was a vampire."

Hanna wrinkled her nose. "Seriously?"

"Uh huh. His name was Frank, and he looked like Dracula. He slept in my closet, upside down like a bat. I used to make my mom set an extra plate for him at dinner."

A little giggle escaped out of Hanna's mouth. "Why a vampire?"

Liam shrugged. "I don't know. It seemed like a cool idea. I wanted Frank to be my dad instead of my *real* dad. We didn't exactly get along." He shot Hanna an uneasy look. "We still don't."

Hanna shifted on the pillow, not wanting to talk about Liam's father. "I had a lot of imaginary friends, too. My dad and I invented some of them, actually. Like this big owl named Hortense who watched over me when I slept— I was afraid of the dark, afraid of being alone. When I was in fourth grade and had no *real* friends, my dad used to draw pictures of Hortense on my lunch bag. It was really sweet." She closed her eyes and pictured her father's crude, shaky drawings on the brown paper bags. She'd stashed a lot of them in her school binder, looking at them when she felt particularly lonely. But then, in fifth grade, the drawings abruptly stopped. That was about the time her parents started fighting.

"That's so great that your dad was there for you," Liam said quietly.

Hanna sniffed. "Well, he used to be."

"What happened?"

Dot snored in the corner, fast asleep again. The small strip of light under the door was an unwavering yellow.

Hanna pictured her father in his king-sized bed downstairs, Isabel next to him. She imagined Kate in her queen bed in the room next to them, a sleeping mask over her eyes. Hanna's father said there were no guest rooms on their floor, but when Hanna had passed down that hall, she'd noticed a bedroom on the other side of her dad's, full of Isabel's quilting supplies. Why hadn't he put Hanna in that room instead? Didn't he remember how Hanna used to be afraid of the dark and suffered from bad dreams? Hanna would've been mortally embarrassed if he would've pointed it out, but it would've been nice if he'd offered.

It was sweet that he'd found Cornelius, but was that really enough? It still felt like he was holding her at arm's length, still considering her separate from his *real* family.

Hanna looked at Liam, feeling overcome with sadness. "My dad and I used to be really close," she said, "but then things changed." She told him how she'd become friends with Ali in the midst of her parents' divorce, but even being the most popular girl at Rosewood Day didn't make up for her father leaving. She recounted the mortifying episode in Annapolis when she and Ali first met Kate. "When Kate came along, I never felt good enough," she sighed. "I always thought my dad liked her better."

Liam nodded and asked questions, holding Hanna's hand when she felt like she was about to cry. "Things are a lot better between us now, and I shouldn't complain," she said. "But I just wish I could go back to when my dad and I were tight. The thing is, that time I want to go back to? I wasn't happy. I might have been popular, but I was still fat and ugly and ruthlessly teased by my best friend. So would I *really* want to go back to that? It's like I'm pining for this time that doesn't exist."

Liam sighed. "I pine for the time when my parents got along."

"I'm so sorry about everything that happened between them," Hanna whispered. "That must be so hard."

A faraway look swept over Liam's face. He sighed deeply and took Hanna's hands. "You're the only positive thing in my life right now. Promise me we'll never let anything come between us. And promise me you'll tell me everything. I don't want there to be any secrets between us."

"Of course." A niggling thought poked the back of Hanna's brain. She certainly *hadn't* told Liam everything—not yet. He didn't know about New A. Or Kelsey. Or Tabitha.

The dorm room from her dream swirled in her mind, fresh and vivid. On the night Spencer had summoned her to Penn, the drive from Rosewood to Philly had been a blur. Hanna parked where Spencer instructed her to and found the propped-open entrance without any trouble. No one stopped her when she punched in the key code to Kelsey's room. No one said anything when the latch clicked and she slipped inside. Hanna had removed the

pills from her pocket and shoved them under Kelsey's pillow, then changed her mind and pushed them into an
empty bedside drawer instead. She was out of the room
again a half minute later. Two minutes after that, she was
on the phone to the police, telling them exactly what
Spencer had wanted her to say.

The guilt hadn't hit her until she was driving home
and passed a cop on the side of the highway administer-
ing a drunk-driving test to two kids. One of them looked
a little like Kelsey, with gingery hair and thin, compact
legs. Suddenly, Hanna imagined what the real Kelsey was
probably going through that very moment, all because of
Hanna. Didn't Hanna have enough to feel guilty for from
Jamaica? Should she pull over, call the cops, and tell them
she'd made a mistake?

Hanna breathed in sharply now. If she *had* told the
cops it was a mistake, would A—Kelsey—be haunting them
now? Maybe they deserved New A's wrath. Maybe they'd
brought this on themselves.

"What are you thinking about?"

Hanna blinked, returning to the room. Liam had
stopped rubbing her shoulders and was inspecting her
face carefully. The secret lingered so close, almost like
a third party in the bed. Maybe it would be safe to tell
Liam. Maybe he would help her figure out what to do.

But then a car passed outside, its motor revving.
Something tickled in her nose, and she let out a sneeze.
Just those two simple actions shifted the moment. She

couldn't tell Liam. Not any of it. "Nothing," she said softly. "I'm just so happy to be with you right now."

Liam engulfed Hanna in a huge hug. "I'm happy to be with you, too."

He sounded calm and content. But even after he fell asleep in Hanna's arms, Hanna stared at the ceiling, wide awake. No matter how hard she tried, she had a feeling none of her secrets would remain hidden for long.

Not if A had anything to do with it.

26

DIDN'T ARIA'S MOM TELL HER NO BOYS IN HER ROOM?

On Friday afternoon, Ezra poked his head into Aria's bedroom at Ella's house and smiled. "Wow. It's just how I pictured it."

"Really?" Aria said, thrilled that he'd bothered to picture her bedroom.

A school bus rumbled at the corner, letting kids off. Ella was at the gallery, and Mike was at a lacrosse clinic, which meant Aria and Ezra had the place to themselves for the hour. Then Aria had to meet Klaudia to talk about the art history project. Now, Aria gazed around her bedroom, trying to see it through Ezra's eyes. There were the old bookshelves Byron had found at a flea market, stuffed with books and magazines. A jumble of necklaces, makeup, perfume bottles, and hats sat atop an antique dressing table Ella had started refinishing before getting bored halfway through. On her bureau was her collection of stuffed animals, which she'd hastily gathered up from her bed this morning, when she had an inkling that Ezra might be coming this afternoon. Ezra didn't have to know she still slept with Pigtunia, Mr. Knitted Cat, Mr. Knitted Goat, and Ms. Knitted Square-Thing-With-Noodly Arms, which Noel had won for Aria at a carnival last summer. In fact, Aria didn't know why she still had Ms. Knitted Square Thing sitting out anymore. Noel might have been cute that day, throwing darts at the balloons until he got Aria exactly the toy she wanted, but she was sure Ezra would be even cuter at a carnival if given the opportunity.

Ezra ran his fingers over a pleated lampshade she'd found at a vintage shop, smiled at the pen-and-ink self-portrait Aria had drawn in tenth grade, and gazed at the Canada geese in the pond out the window. "This is such a great little hideaway. Are you sure you want to leave it?"

"You mean to go to New York?" Aria flopped down on the bed. "I have to leave sometime."

"But . . . so soon? Finishing up high school online? Have you talked to your parents about it?"

Aria bristled, irritated that Ezra was bringing up her parents like she was a child. "They'll understand. They lived in New York once, too, when they were young." She tilted her head, sudden panic gripping her heart. "Why? Do you not want me to come back with you?" The run-in with Klaudia flashed through her mind. Though she'd promised herself not to bring up the fact that he had let

Klaudia read his manuscript, she couldn't help but still feel a jealous twinge.

"Of course I want you to come." Ezra squeezed her thigh. "It's just . . . you're not leaving for some other reason, are you? I saw Noel Kahn yesterday at the McDonald's drive-thru. . . ."

Aria laughed awkwardly. "This isn't because of Noel."

What else could she say? *Well, there's a certain someone named A who knows about the most horrible thing I've ever done? And, oh yeah, A also wants to kill me?* Emily had called last night and told her that A had pushed her down a steep hill at the Stockbridge trail. It scared the hell out of her. She needed to get out of town, away from psycho A, and enormous, anonymous New York seemed like a perfect hiding place.

She took Ezra's face in her hands. "I want to go because of you and only you. I've been looking at places in Brooklyn—we could get something amazing there. Maybe we could get a dog. Or a cat, if you're more of a cat person. We could walk the cat around on a little leash."

"That sounds perfect," Ezra murmured, brushing a piece of hair out of Aria's eyes. "If you're serious about this, I'll start making arrangements, and we can leave in a couple of days."

Aria leaned forward to kiss him, and Ezra kissed her back. But when she opened her eyes for a moment, his were open, too. He was staring at something across the room.

"Is that a first edition?" He sat back and pointed at a book on the bookshelf. *The Sun Also Rises*, it said in gold lettering on the spine. "It looks really old."

"Nah, my dad stole that from the Hollis library." Aria rose, pulled the book out, and brought it to him. When he opened to the title page, a musty, old-book smell wafted out. "It's one of my favorites, though."

Ezra poked her knee. "I thought *my* book was your favorite."

His tone was light and joking, but he looked serious. Was he really asking her to compare him to *Hemingway*? "Well, I mean, *The Sun Also Rises* was a literary masterpiece," she blurted. "But yours was good, too. *Really* good."

Ezra pulled his hands away from hers and balled them in his lap. "Maybe it's not."

Aria resisted a groan. Had he always had this insecure streak, or was his novel bringing it out in him? "Your book is awesome," she said, kissing his nose. "Now come lie next to me."

Ezra reluctantly flopped onto Aria's pillow. She began to stroke his hair. Seconds later, the door slammed downstairs. "Aria?" Ella's voice called out.

Aria shot up, her heart in her throat. "*Shit.*"

"What?" Ezra sat up too.

"It's my mom. She wasn't supposed to be back for hours." Aria jumped up from the bed and pressed her feet into her shoes. She handed Ezra his wingtips. "We have to get out of here."

A corner of Ezra's mouth drooped. "You don't want to introduce me to her?"

Downstairs, Ella's heels clacked on the wood floor. Aria's mind scattered in ten different directions. "I . . . I haven't had time to prep her." She stared at Ezra's blank expression. "You were my *teacher* last year. My mom went to a parent-teacher conference with you. Don't you think that's a little awkward?"

Ezra lifted a shoulder. "Not really."

Aria gawked at him, surprised. But there was no time to argue. "Come on," she said, grabbing his hand and pulling him down the stairs just as Ella shut herself inside the powder room. She grabbed Ezra's coat from the hall closet, thrust it at him, and shoved him out the door.

Outside, the world smelled like sunbaked sidewalks and smoking chimneys. Aria walked down the stone path toward Ezra's Volkswagen, which was parked at the curb. "We'll talk about New York soon, okay?" she babbled. "I have a ton of cool apartments to show you."

"Aria, wait."

Aria turned. Ezra had stopped at the edge of the porch, his hands in his pockets. "Are you *embarrassed* to be seen with me?"

"Of course not." Aria took a few steps toward him. "But I'm not ready to explain to my mom what's going on right now. I'd rather do it alone, when I can compose my thoughts."

Ezra stared at her for a few beats more, his eyes dark, then nodded. "Okay. I'll see you tomorrow?"

"Yeah. Or . . . wait." Aria squeezed her eyes shut. "I have a school thing tomorrow." It was the only performance of *Macbeth*, and Aria and Ella were going to watch Mike and then go to the cast party. There was no way Aria was bringing Ezra to something at Rosewood Day. "How about Sunday?"

"Sunday it is." Ezra kissed her cheek, climbed into his car, and drove off.

Aria watched him go, hugging her arms to her chest. A shadow shifted to her left, and she turned. In the thick brush that separated her house from the neighbor's, something moved. Aria caught a flash of blond hair. Footsteps slid across the wet leaves.

"Hello?" she called.

But the woods suddenly went still, the figure gone. Aria closed her eyes tight. The sooner she and Ezra got away from Rosewood, the better.

An hour later, Aria strode into Bixby's, a local coffee shop on the Hollis campus, and found Klaudia sitting at one of the back tables, dressed in a tight black sweater, an even tighter denim skirt, and black booties with heels. Her white-blond hair shone, her skin was porcelain-doll flawless, and every guy in the café was sneaking looks at her.

"It take you long enough," Klaudia said prissily when

she noticed Aria, the corners of her perfectly lined lips arching into a scowl. "I wait almost fifteen minutes!"

"Sorry," Aria slammed her art history text on the table, then walked to a counter for coffee, which made Klaudia squeak indignantly. The line was long, with everyone ordering complex lattes and mochas, and when she returned, there were bright splotches on Klaudia's cheeks.

"I have plans, you know!" Klaudia protested. "I am meeting for date with Noel!"

I get it, Aria wanted to say. *You stole Noel from me. You won.* She leaned forward. "Look, do you mind if you spoke like a normal person around me? I know you can."

A slimy smile appeared on Klaudia's face. "Suit yourself," she said evenly, instantly losing the ditzy accent. She tapped her own art history textbook with a hot pink pen. "Since we're being honest, I was wondering if you could do my half of the project. My ankle still *really* hurts."

Aria stared at Klaudia's ankle, propped up on a spare chair. It didn't even have a cast on it anymore. "You can't milk that forever," she said. "I'm doing my half of the project, and that's it. We can work together, but I'm not doing the work for you."

Klaudia sat up straighter and narrowed her eyes. "Then maybe I'll tell Noel what you did to me."

Aria shut her eyes, suddenly so sick of being pushed around. "You know what? Tell him. It's not like we're together anymore." Just saying it made her feel light and free. Soon enough, she would be out of Rosewood for good. What did it matter?

Klaudia sat back, her mouth making a small *O*. "I'll tell your new boyfriend, too. Mr. Novelist. Wasn't it so nice that he let me read his book? Isn't it so sad how the male character dies in the end?"

Aria flinched at the mention of Ezra's novel—she so wasn't playing Book Club with Klaudia right now. "Well if you tell them what I did, I'll tell them what *you* told me on the chair lift and that your whole blond bimbo thing is an act. Remember how you said you wanted to sleep with Noel? Remember how you *threatened* me?"

Klaudia's brow crinkled. She jammed her book into her purse and stood. "I strongly suggest you think about doing my half of the report. I'd hate to be the one to ruin things between you and your new poet boy."

"I've *already* thought about it," Aria said firmly. "And I'm not doing your half."

Klaudia slung her bag over her shoulder and wove angrily around the tables, nearly knocking into a college-age guy carrying a coffee and a muffin on a plate. "See ya!" Aria called after her triumphantly.

A folk singer in the front window launched into a Ray LaMontagne cover as Klaudia flounced out. Aria opened her textbook, enormously satisfied. Working alone was a much better idea, anyway. Consulting the index, she found the section on Caravaggio and flipped to the page about his life.

She began to read. *In 1606, Caravaggio killed a young man in a brawl. But he got away with it, fleeing Rome with a price on his head.*

Yikes. Aria flipped to the next page. Three more paragraphs described how violent and murderous Caravaggio was. Then, Aria noticed that someone had affixed a yellow Post-it note to the lower right-hand corner of the page. A hand-drawn arrow pointed to the word *killer* in the text. There was also a note.

Looks like you and Caravaggio have something in common, Aria! Don't think you'll be spared from my wrath, murderess. You're the guiltiest of all. —A

27

BREAK A LEG, LADY MACBETH

On Saturday night, Rosewood students, parents, and townspeople crowded into the Rosewood Day auditorium for the one and only performance of *Macbeth*. The air had an electrified, anticipatory quality about it, and within minutes, the lights dimmed, the crowd quieted, the three witches took their places for the first scene, and the curtain opened. Dry ice swirled around the stage. The witches cackled and prophesized. To the audience, everything seemed composed and flawless, but backstage it was chaos.

"Pierre, I still need makeup!" Kirsten Cullen hissed to Pierre, running up to him in a servant's uniform.

"Pierre, where do they keep the armored vests?" Ryan Schiffer asked quietly.

Seconds later, Scott Chin approached, too. "Pierre, this sword looks really lame." He held up the blunt, foil-decorated ninth-grade art project and made a face.

Pierre glared at all of them, his cheeks turning a darker

shade of pink. His hair stood up in peaks on his head, his shirttail was untucked, and he had a single women's high-heeled shoe in his hand for reasons Spencer couldn't even begin to surmise. Maybe it was another *Macbeth* superstition.

"Why didn't you people figure these things out a little earlier than *five minutes before your scene*?" Pierre groaned.

Spencer sat on a props box, smoothing down the hem of the velvet Lady Macbeth dress. Usually, backstage on opening night was one of her favorite times, but today, as she listened to the witches on stage, she felt nervous for her entrance, which was in a matter of minutes. *Thy met me in the day of success*, she kept repeating to herself, her first line. But what came after that?

She rose from the box and peeked around the curtain. Younger brothers and sisters squirmed in seats, already bored. Kids snacked on popcorn from Steam, the school's coffee bar that had been transformed into a refreshment stand for the night. She could just make out the school videographer, staring into the lens of a camera on a tripod. If all went well tonight, Spencer's performance tape would sway Princeton to choose Spencer J. over Spencer F.

But what if it *didn't* go well?

A blond head in the audience caught Spencer's eye. Mrs. Hastings sat four rows from the front, her diamond earrings sparkling in the lights. Melissa and Darren Wilden were in the seats next to her, their eyes trained on the witches on the stage. Astonishingly, Amelia sat beside Wilden, leafing apathetically through the program. And Mr. Pennythistle was on the other side, dressed in a gray suit and tie, which made Spencer's heart warm a little. It was cute that he'd dressed up for this.

Two aisles back, Spencer's gaze halted on another face. A redheaded girl watched the stage, chewing feverishly on a piece of gum. Spencer clapped a hand over her mouth.

It was Kelsey.

Spencer's legs felt wobbly beneath her. Then she saw the girl next to her and almost fell over. Emily's open, kind face stared back. They were here *together*.

Slowly, Kelsey's gaze turned toward Spencer. Her eyes narrowed. She raised one hand and gave Spencer a three-fingered wave, her smile large and off-kilter. Spencer lowered the curtain and staggered backward, tripping over a pile of discarded petticoats.

"Hey."

Spencer shrieked and whirled around. Beau stepped back and covered his face. He was wearing a suit of armor that was molded perfectly to his body. "You all right? Not too nervous?"

"Of course not." But Spencer's heart was thrumming like an out-of-control needle on a sewing machine. She was dying to peek around the curtain again. Why was Kelsey here? Was she hoping Spencer would have a repeat of last night's performance in the woods with Beau and blurt out all of her secrets on stage?

"Spencer!" Pierre strutted forward and looked Spencer up and down. "Get over here and take your place for your first scene!"

For a moment, Spencer's limbs wouldn't move. She wanted to run out the back door and all the way home. She couldn't go out there—not with Kelsey in the audience. But then everything went into warp-speed. Pierre guided her toward the wings and out onto the stage. The lights felt like hard, iron weights on her skin. Faces from the audience tilted up at her; all of their smiles looked jagged and cruel. She spied Kelsey in the audience immediately. Kelsey was staring right at her, the same maniacal grin on her face.

Feeling guilty about something, murderer? Kelsey's voice from her vision cackled in her ear.

We know what you did! Tabitha crowed.

The crowd was quiet, waiting. Someone coughed. Spencer knew she was supposed to say her first line, but she couldn't remember what it was. Pierre made frantic gesticulations off-stage. Then, a small voice whispered from behind the curtain. *"They met me in the day of success."* It was Edith, the assistant drama coach and prompter, delivering Spencer's first line. Spencer had *never* had to use a prompter before.

Her mouth flopped open like a fish's. A small squeak escaped from the back of her throat, amplified by the many microphones set up around the stage. Someone in the audience snickered.

Edith whispered her lines again. Finally, Spencer opened her mouth and managed to start talking. She got through her first speech, but it took great effort to say each word. She felt like she was moving through mud, yelling from the bottom of a very deep well.

Felicity McDowell, who was playing her attendant, entered the scene. Spencer fumbled her next line, then the next. She gazed desperately at the blinking eye of the videographer, recording everything. Her nervousness was infectious; Felicity missed a line, too, then tripped over a set piece. By the time Beau strutted onto the stage, announcing that the king was coming to see them tonight, Spencer felt like she was going to cry. At the end of the scene, Spencer staggered off stage, feeling like she'd completed an Iron Man triathlon.

Pierre blocked her way, hands on hips. "What the hell was *that*?"

Spencer kept her head down. "I'll get it together. I promise."

"You *promise*? It was unacceptable!"

Pierre snapped his fingers, and Phi Templeton scurried over like an eager dog. She was dressed in a similar gown to Spencer's. In her hand was the *Macbeth* script, Lady Macbeth's parts underlined.

"Why is she dressed like me?" Spencer exclaimed.

"Thank *God* I told her to get dressed," Pierre spat. "I

was afraid something like this might happen, so I told her to get ready to take over the role."

Spencer's jaw dropped. "You can't switch out actresses in the middle of a play!"

Pierre put his hands on his hips. "Watch me. You get one more chance. If you choke again, Phi's in."

Spencer sank dizzily against a low table as Pierre stormed away, wondering if she should give the role over to Phi now. There was no way she could send the scene she'd just performed to Princeton. She'd hear them laughing all the way from New Jersey.

"Hey."

Spencer looked up and saw Beau standing next to her, his jaw clenched and his green eyes hard. "Don't listen to that asshole, okay?" he whispered. "So you psyched yourself out. It happens to everyone from time to time. You can still turn it around. Go to that place you were in yesterday. Access that fire."

"I *can't* access that fire." Tears welled in Spencer's eyes. "It made me crazy!"

"No, it didn't." Beau clutched her hands and squeezed them hard. "It made you *good*. Whatever baggage you have, use it. Conquer it. Don't let it stop you."

Spencer stared at him. Beau was leaning so close, almost like he was about to kiss her.

But then Pierre swept through the backstage again, and the two of them shot apart. "Lady M, you're on again shortly. Are you up for it, or do you want to save yourself the embarrassment now?"

Spencer glanced at Beau in desperation, wishing he'd make the decision for her. "If you get nervous, look for me offstage, okay?" he whispered.

Spencer nodded. "I can do it," she told Pierre.

In no time, it was her cue to step on the stage again. The hot lights were punishing. The actors turned to Spencer, and Seth Cardiff, who was playing Duncan, said his first line.

It was Spencer's turn to speak next, but the same icy freeze immobilized her. For a split second, she was afraid she was going to choke again. The actors shifted uncomfortably. The crowd covered their eyes. Pierre shook his fists in fury. And suddenly, Spencer realized. *This* was exactly what A—what Kelsey—wanted. For her to bomb. To make sure Princeton wouldn't happen.

Spencer peeked backstage and found Beau's encouraging face. And then, like a light switch snapping on, fire flooded into her veins. She'd worked too damn hard for Kelsey to bring her down. That bitch wasn't going to win.

"*All our service in every point twice done, and then done double,*" she said loudly, and she was off. The words flowed easily out of her mouth and her gestures were sharp and precise. The other actors and the audience relaxed. By the time Beau entered and the two of them argued about whether or not killing the king was a good idea, Spencer felt almost like her old self again. When she exited the stage, there was even a smattering of relieved applause.

Pierre loomed in the wings, tapping his lips with a pen. "Well, I suppose that was *better*."

Spencer swept past him, not really caring what he thought anymore. Then, Beau caught her arm and whirled her around. "You were amazing." At first, she thought he was just pulling her into a hug, but then he gave her a long, passionate kiss. Spencer was so startled that she just stood there for a few seconds. Then, she kissed him back. Despite the fact that she was wearing a heavy velvet dress, she felt chills.

Someone nearby let out a gasp. Spencer turned and saw Naomi, Riley, and Kate gawking at her. Triumphant, she leaned in and kissed Beau even deeper. Deep down, she wished the curtain would open so the audience could see this, too—so Kelsey would know just how badly her plan had failed.

28

THE TRUTH WILL OUT

After the play was over, Emily walked through the double doors of Otto, the upscale Italian restaurant where the *Macbeth* cast party was being held. The familiar scents of rosemary, olive oil, and warm mozzarella tickled her nostrils, and she recognized the gray-haired, no-nonsense woman behind the hostess stand. Emily had been to Otto with her family after Carolyn, Beth, and Jake had each graduated from Rosewood Day, sitting in one of the large banquettes and sharing the family-style portions of *penne alla vodka* and Caprese salad. For Beth's graduation, when Emily was in sixth grade, she'd brought Her Ali along, too, and the two of them had sent silly texts to one another and then snuck off to the patio area to flirt with a bunch of graduates from the boys' basketball team. Well, more accurately, *Ali* flirted with them. Emily had stood around feeling uncomfortable.

Tonight, Otto looked utterly different from how it had

during those graduation dinners. The drama class had decorated the Italian-tiled rooms with happy-sad drama masks and big posters of *Macbeth* playbills. The room was stuffed with people, and a large buffet table had been set up on one end, bearing a zillion types of pasta, a huge bowl of salad, eight different kinds of breads, and a bevy of desserts.

"Your school is exactly like mine," Kelsey groaned good-naturedly, squeezing into the room behind Emily and taking in the scenery. "It's only a school play, but they treat it like it's opening night on Broadway."

"Seriously," Emily giggled, turning around and giving Kelsey a shaky smile. She felt a little nervous bringing Kelsey here, but when Kelsey had asked what Emily was doing tonight and Emily told her, Kelsey had gotten so excited. "I love *Macbeth*!" she'd said. "Can I come?"

"Um, sure," Emily had said tentatively, quickly adding, "You should know that Spencer is playing the lead. Will that be weird?" Kelsey said it wouldn't, and Emily had no idea how to tell her that it might be weird for *Spencer*. What was she supposed to say? *Spencer thinks you're our new psychopath text-messager?*

They moved past the hostess stand, and lo and behold, Emily spied Spencer across the room, smiling bashfully at Mrs. Eckles, a ninth-grade English teacher. A streak of nerves went through her, but she straightened up and took a deep breath. "I'll be right back," she said over her shoulder to Kelsey. She needed to explain to Spencer why she'd brought Kelsey before Spencer randomly saw them together and freaked. Maybe if she leveled with Spencer, Spencer would understand. And maybe, if they all talked rationally, Spencer would realize that Kelsey wasn't A.

Emily wove through the crowd and tapped on Spencer's shoulder. Spencer's expression soured. "Oh."

A sick feeling washed over Emily. "I can explain," she blurted.

Spencer pulled her into a little nook that held a trolley for forks, spoons, and other utensils. Her face was pinched and angry. "You told me you weren't hanging out with Kelsey anymore."

"I know I did, but . . ."

"And then you bring her to *my* play?"

Emily gritted her teeth. "Kelsey's nice, Spencer. She even said she wanted to see your performance."

"She wanted to *ruin* my performance, you mean."

"She's not A," Emily urged.

"Of course she is!" Spencer slammed a fist on the trolley, making the utensils jump. "How many times do I have to explain this to you? Does what I say not *matter* anymore? Have you become the kind of person who flat-out *lies* when asked a question?"

"I'm sorry I lied when you asked if I'd seen Kelsey," Emily said in a small voice. She'd panicked when she'd texted with Spencer after the incident on the trail. It had been easier to say Kelsey hadn't been there. "But you're not seeing things clearly. Kelsey doesn't want to hurt us.

In fact, she has no idea what you did to her. And the other day, when someone pushed me down the hill, Kelsey *was* there. But she was the one who ran down the slope and helped me up."

Spencer's mouth dropped open. "Are you high? She was probably the one who pushed you in the first place!"

Emily peered around the room, feeling weary. Some of the drama extras blew straw wrappers at one another and chanted the witches' lines from the beginning of the play. "Kelsey isn't A," she said. "*Ali* is. I think I saw her at the top of the hill, and I keep seeing flashes of blond hair everywhere."

Spencer groaned. "Would you stop it with Ali? She's gone."

"No, she's not!"

"Why are you so convinced?"

A sour taste welled in Emily's mouth. *Tell her,* she thought. *Tell her what you did.* But her mouth wouldn't move. And then a waitress skirted around them, grabbing some forks and knives from the console, and she lost her nerve.

"Kelsey is A," Spencer repeated. "She's got the perfect motive. I sent her to juvie, Emily. I ruined her shot at a good college—at *life*. And this is how she's getting her revenge."

"She doesn't *know* you did that," Emily argued. "But while we're on that subject, don't you feel bad about what you did to her? Don't you think you should come clean and apologize?"

Spencer backed up until her butt hit the little silverware caddy. "Jesus, whose side are you on?"

A group of parents cackled nearby, sipping from glasses of red wine. Three sophomore boys plucked unattended beer mugs off the bar and took quick, covert swigs. "This isn't about picking sides," Emily said wearily. "I just think you should say something. She's right over there." Emily pointed to where Kelsey had been standing, but she couldn't see her anymore through the thick crowd.

"She's *here*?" Spencer stood on her tiptoes and looked out at the mob, too. "Are you *trying* to get us killed?"

"Spencer, you're—"

Spencer held up her hand, stopping her. Realization flooded over her face. "Oh my god. Are you in love with her?"

Emily stared down at the terra-cotta-tiled floor. "No."

Spencer clapped her hands. "You *are*! You've fallen for her just like you fell for Ali! *That's* why you're acting like this!" A desperate look flashed over her face. "Kelsey's not into girls, Emily. She hooked up with a million guys last summer."

A stab of pain shot through Emily's gut. "People can change."

Spencer leaned against the wall, looking incredulous. "Like Ali changed? Because she *really* loved you, Emily. You were her dream girl."

Tears pricked Emily's eyes. "Take that back!"

"Ali never cared about you." Spencer's tone was matter-of-fact. "She *used* you. Just like Kelsey's using you now."

Emily blinked hard. Rage bubbled up inside of her, fiercer and sharper than anything she'd felt before. How dare Spencer?

She whipped around and marched across the room. "Emily!" Spencer yelled. But Emily didn't turn. Her nose itched, like it always did when she was about to sob.

She pushed into the girls' bathroom and placed both palms on the sink, nostrils flaring. In the mirror, she noticed Kelsey behind her, quickly shoving a small object back into her purse. "Uh, hey," Kelsey said nervously.

Emily grunted out a reply. Then Kelsey turned and noticed Emily's tear-streaked face, her angry triangle of a mouth. She rushed to the sink. "Are you okay?"

Emily stared at their reflections, her emotions a huge jumble. Spencer's words burned in her brain: *Ali never cared about you. She used you. Just like Kelsey's using you now.*

Then Emily raised her head, suddenly knowing what she should do. "There's something you should know," she said in a strong, clear voice. "About last summer."

Kelsey's face suddenly looked guarded. "What?"

"Spencer Hastings framed you the night of your arrest. She was the one who arranged for the pills to be planted in your room. She had someone call the cops and tell them you were trouble."

Kelsey stiffened. "*What?*" She took a big step back, looking positively flummoxed. Emily had been right all along. Kelsey clearly hadn't known this before.

"I'm sorry," Emily said. "I didn't find out that long ago, but I thought I should tell you. You deserve to know the truth."

She moved toward Kelsey to embrace her, but Kelsey pulled her purse higher on her shoulder. "I have to go." She hurried, head down, out of the room.

29

SHE WARNED YOU, ARIA . . .

At the cast party, Aria was sandwiched between the jazz band, who were playing a very loud rendition of "The Girl From Ipanema," and a huge poster of *Macbeth*, which featured Spencer's and the guy who played Macbeth's faces in huge black-and-white relief. Ella, her boyfriend Thaddeus, Mike, and Colleen were at her side.

"You were a wonderful doctor, Michelangelo," Ella had to yell over the music. Her long beaded earrings swung wildly. "If I had known you had such an interest in acting, I would've enrolled you in the Hollis Happy Hooray Day Camp with Aria when she was little!"

Aria bleated out a laugh. "Mike would have hated it!" The Hollis Happy Hooray Day Camp put on a lot of plays, but campers were also required to put on marionette shows regularly. Mike had been deathly afraid of puppets when he was younger.

"I think he should audition for a bigger role next year,"

Colleen piped up, leaning over and pecking Mike on the cheek. Everyone beamed. Mike stiffened for a moment, then forced a smile.

Aria gazed around the crowded room. She'd called Hanna and Emily earlier, asking if either of them were coming. Both had said yes—Hanna's dad was making her since Kate was in the play, and Emily was coming to support Spencer. But she didn't see them anywhere. The cute guy who'd played Macbeth was schmoozing with the director by the bar. Naomi, Riley, and Klaudia were dancing on a small square of wood floor near the front of the restaurant. Kate was trying to get Sean Ackard to join in, but he kept shaking his head.

Someone tapped her shoulder, and Aria spun around. Ezra stood behind her, wearing a suit jacket, a clean blue button-down, and unrumpled khakis. "Surprise!"

Aria nearly dropped the ginger ale she was holding. "What are you doing here?"

Ezra leaned into her. "I wanted to see you tonight. I called your dad's house, and your stepmom said you were at the cast party." He looked her up and down appreciatively, taking in the purple sweater dress she'd thrown on for the occasion.

Aria backed away. Everyone could *see* them. She whipped around, feeling her family's gaze upon her. Mike looked disgusted. "Mr. . . . Fitz?" Ella said, blinking hard.

Aria grabbed Ezra by the hand and pulled him across

the room. They snaked around Mrs. Jonson, one of the English teachers, who did a double take. Mr. McAdam, the AP Econ teacher, raised a suspicious eyebrow. It felt as though everyone in the restaurant was suddenly whispering about them.

"This isn't a good time," she hissed when they finally got to the narrow hallway that led to the bathroom.

"Why not?" Ezra stepped aside for a group of kids to pass. It was Devon Arliss, James Freed, and Mason Byers. Their eyes bulged at the sight of Aria and Ezra together—they'd all been in Aria's English class last year and had surely heard the rumors.

"This would be the perfect time to tell your mom about us," Ezra said. "And to talk to her about New York." He took her hand and began to pull her back in Ella's direction. "C'mon. What are you so afraid of?"

The jazz band shifted into a slow number. Aria planted her feet. Something in the front archway caught her eye. Noel Kahn and his brother, Erik, had just come in. Noel was looking from Aria to Ezra, his mouth open.

Aria turned back to Ezra. "Look, I can't talk to my mom about this right now. And I don't do well with ambushes, okay?"

Ezra shoved his hands in his pockets. "Are you saying you don't want me here?"

"It's not that I don't *want* you here. But you seriously don't think this is weird?" She gestured into the dining room. "All of your old colleagues are here. I still go to school with all of these people. Now everyone's going to talk."

Ezra's eyes narrowed. "You *are* embarrassed of me."

"I'm not!" Aria cried. "But did you see the way they all looked at us? Didn't that make you uncomfortable?"

"Since when do you care what people think?" Ezra poked his head into the dining room. As soon as he looked, everyone's head turned away instantly, to hide that they'd been staring.

"I don't care what people think," Aria insisted. Although, in this case, maybe she did.

"And you're eighteen," Ezra continued. "Everything we're doing is legal. There's nothing to worry about. Is it because I haven't made anything of myself? Because my novel sucks?"

Aria almost screamed. "This has nothing to do with your novel."

"Then what is it?"

At a nearby table, a waiter set a dome-shaped dessert on fire, and blue flames shot up into the air. The table applauded. Unconsciously, Aria's gaze drifted toward the entranceway once more. Noel hadn't moved. His blue eyes were fixed, unblinking, on Aria.

Ezra followed her gaze. "I knew it. Things aren't over between you, are they?"

"They are. I swear." Aria shut her eyes. "I just . . . I can't do this with you right now. I can't be in public with you. Not with all these people here. In New York, it'll be different."

But Ezra pulled away from her angrily. "Find me when you grow up and sort out all your baggage, Aria." Then he stormed into the crowd.

Aria felt too weary to follow him. Despair rippled through her. Was love always this complicated? It certainly hadn't been with Noel. If she truly loved Ezra, would she have been oblivious to everyone's confused and gossipy stares?

She drifted toward the buffet and ate a tofu skewer without tasting it. A hand touched her arm again. It was Mrs. Kittinger, her art history teacher, dressed in a bowler hat, a checked men's vest, and billowing black pants.

"Aria! Just the person I'd like to see." Mrs. Kittinger pulled a typewritten paper halfway out of her leather bag. "I wanted to thank you for handing in your Caravaggio project early and tell you what a lovely job you did. I was reading it before the performance tonight."

"Oh." Aria smiled faintly. She'd finished her portion of the report and emailed it to Mrs. Kittinger this morning, adding a note that she'd tried to get Klaudia to help her with the project, but Klaudia hadn't been interested. Okay, so it was kind of a tattletale thing to do, but she wasn't letting Klaudia off the hook.

"I haven't received anything from your partner yet, though," Mrs. Kittinger added, as if reading Aria's mind. "Let's hope she turns something in by Monday, or else I'll have to fail her." She looked like she wanted to say something more, but then she shot Aria a sad smile, slipped the paper back into her bag, and moved down the line.

The band started playing "'Round Midnight," one of Aria's favorite songs. A heady, soothing smell of olive oil drifted through the air. When Aria looked up at the collection of knickknacks lined up on the high shelves over the tables, she noticed a familiar Shakespeare bobble head figure. It was the very same one Ezra had given her before he left last year. She'd treasured that gift, jiggling its head often, longing for Ezra to write to her and reconnect. After a while, she'd figured he'd long forgotten about their relationship, but all that time, he'd been writing a novel—about just that.

The world seemed to brighten a little. Maybe Aria *was* being juvenile and paranoid about Ezra. Since when did she care what other people thought? She was Kooky Aria, the girl who wore pink streaks in her hair and made up dance routines in gym class. Rosewood hadn't changed her *that* much.

Squaring her shoulders, she marched through the crowd. Hopefully, Ezra was still here. She would find him, bring him to Ella, and tell her their plans. She would dance with Ezra on the tiny dance floor, students' and teachers' stares be damned. She'd pined for him for so long. She couldn't let him slip away now.

"Ezra?" Aria called, sticking her head into the men's bathroom. No answer. "Ezra?" she called again, peeking out the back door, but there were only a series of green

Dumpsters and a couple of line cooks smoking cigarettes. She looked in the back dining room, the hostess area, and even the front parking lot. Luckily Ezra's blue Bug was still parked next to a Jeep Cherokee. He had to be inside somewhere.

As Aria walked back into the restaurant, a faint, familiar laugh greeted her. She paused, icy fear shooting through her.

The laughter was coming from the coatroom. She tiptoed around the unmanned coat-check desk. A figure moved in the blue-black darkness at the very back of the space, hidden behind overcoats and leather jackets and furs. "Hello?" Aria whispered, her heart pounding hard.

Aria heard a sigh, then the smacking sounds of two people kissing. *Oops.* Aria backed away, but her ankle turned, and she lurched to the side, banging into some empty hangers on the rack. They clanged together loudly.

"What was that?" a voice said from the back of the coat closet. Aria stopped, recognizing it instantly. In seconds, a figure stepped into the light. "Oh my God."

Aria's eyes widened. Ezra stared back at her. His lips parted, but no words came out.

"Mr. Poet Man?" a second voice lilted. A blond girl stepped out of the shadows and wound her arms around Ezra's waist. Her hair was mussed, her bright lipstick was smudged, and the straps of her low-cut dress hung off her shoulders. When she saw Aria, she burst into

a triumphant smile. "Oh, hallo!" she teased, squeezing
Ezra harder.

Klaudia.

Aria backed away, banging into more coat hangers.
Then she turned and ran.

30

KILL HER BEFORE SHE KILLS YOU

"I must say I'm impressed." Mr. Pennythistle swirled his dirty martini and beamed at Spencer. "That Lady Macbeth performance rivaled the Royal Shakespeare Company."

Melissa stepped forward and gave Spencer a hug. "It was *amazing*." She nudged Wilden, who nodded too. "You seemed utterly transformed! Especially for the scene where she can't wash the blood off her hands!"

Spencer smiled shakily, pushing her heavily hair-sprayed blond hair off her neck. Dozens of people had come up to her since the play ended and told her what an amazing job she'd done, her rocky start forgotten. By the time she'd reached the *Out, damned spot* scene, she was fully immersed in the role, channeling all of her guilty energy into the character. She'd received the loudest applause at the end, even beating out Beau, and she'd already spoken with the videographer, asking him to edit out her first disastrous scene. The rest of her performance would make the perfect package for Princeton.

But now she felt off-kilter again, all because of the conversation she'd just had with Emily. She hadn't meant to lash out at her, but Emily needed to understand. She was dying to apologize, but Emily was nowhere to be seen. She couldn't find Kelsey, either.

A woman with dark hair and a long, thin face appeared next to Spencer. "Lady Macbeth?" She extended her hand. "I'm Jennifer Williams, from the *Philadelphia Sentinel*. Mind if we do an interview and some pictures?"

Mrs. Hastings's eyes lit up. "How exciting, Spence!" Even Amelia looked impressed.

Spencer said good-bye to her family, even giving Mr. Pennythistle an awkward little hug. As she wove through the crowd, drama kids, girls she knew from field hockey, and even Naomi, Riley, and Kate clapped her on the back and told her she'd done an amazing job. She scanned the room for Emily, but she still didn't see her.

The reporter led Spencer to a booth at the back. Beau was already waiting with a small cup of espresso. He'd changed out of his armor and into a black cashmere sweater and the sexiest fitted corduroys Spencer had ever seen on a guy. She sat next to him, and Beau squeezed her hand. "How about we sneak out of this party after the interview is done?"

Just feeling Beau's hand in hers steadied Spencer's nerves. She raised an eyebrow in mock disapproval. "Does

Mr. Yale Drama dare ditch out on his own cast party? I would've thought you'd want to hang around and listen to people kiss your ass."

"I'm full of surprises." Beau winked.

Jennifer Williams slid into the booth across from them and flipped her notepad to a fresh page. As she looked at Beau and asked him the first question, Spencer's cell phone beeped. Spencer reached into her pocket. There were at least twenty texts on her phone from people congratulating her. The latest text, however, was from a jumble of letters and numbers.

Spencer swallowed a lump in her throat, slouched down in the booth, covered the screen, and pressed READ.

You hurt both of us. Now I'm going to hurt you. –A

Attached was a photograph of a blond girl in a goldenrod-colored sundress lying on her stomach on a beach at night. Her head was turned to the side, and there was a huge gash at her temple. Blood trickled down her chin and onto the sand. The waves crashed ominously near her head, ready to wash her away.

The phone dropped to Spencer's lap. It was a picture of Tabitha just after Aria had pushed her off the roof. Neither Spencer nor the others had seen her on the ground—it had been too dark, and her body had disappeared by the time they got down to the beach.

But someone had seen. And photographed it. *Kelsey.*

A tortured noise escaped from Spencer's throat. Jennifer Williams looked up from her notes. "Are you okay?"

"I . . ." Spencer pushed out of the booth, feeling dizzy. She needed to get out of here. She needed to hide. The reporter called for her, but she couldn't turn back. She fumbled toward the exit. Every face she passed looked warped and crazed, even dangerous. She burst through the back door, emerging into an empty alley. A line of metal garbage cans stood by the wall. The overpowering scent of rotting vegetables and meat roiled Spencer's stomach. It was eerily quiet out here, a sharp contrast to the raucous atmosphere inside the restaurant.

"Hey."

Spencer turned and saw Kelsey standing at the back door. Her eyes were narrowed. Her mouth was a pale line. Spencer gasped. She wanted to run, but her limbs wouldn't move.

Kelsey placed her hands on her hips. "Did you get my text?"

Spencer let out a tiny whimper. The image of Tabitha, dead on the sand, swam before her eyes. "Yes," she whispered.

"You're so sick," Kelsey hissed, her eyes round. "Did you really think you were going to get away with it?"

Spencer's heart leapt to her throat. "I'm—"

"You're what?" Kelsey cocked her head. "You're sorry? Sorry doesn't cut it, Spencer."

She grabbed Spencer's elbow hard. Spencer wrenched away, desperate to get free, but Kelsey let out a frustrated noise and tackled Spencer against the brick wall. Spencer yelled out, her voice echoing through the alley. Suddenly, a hideous, jumbled mix of all the visions that had appeared to Spencer over the past few days swirled through her mind. She saw Tabitha leering at her from the Rosewood Day stage. She saw Kelsey advancing toward her in the creek, ready to drown her.

"You can't get away from me," the Kelsey in her dreams had said. Or maybe it was the real Kelsey, here now. "You deserve to pay for what you did."

"No!" Spencer screamed, smacking Kelsey hard.

Kelsey wheeled back, but then lunged for Spencer again. Panicked, Spencer thrust her hands out and wrapped them around Kelsey's neck and squeezed harder and harder, feeling the tendons give way, feeling the air stop in her throat, feeling the delicate bones break. It was the only option. She had to stop Kelsey before Kelsey hurt her.

"Jesus!" a voice called. Spencer felt a fist in her spine. Her feet slipped out from under her, and her hands flailed at her sides. All at once, she was on her back on the ground. Various cast members stood above her, their mouths triangles of shock. Behind them, a second group of people clustered around a sobbing girl. Kelsey was bent over, gasping for air.

Spencer sat up. "Don't let her get away!" she screeched. "She's trying to kill me!"

Everyone stared at her. "What is she talking about?" a voice cried.

"I saw her lash out at that girl for no reason!" someone else said.

"It's the play," Pierre's voice called from the back. "It's taken over her mind."

"She's insane!" a familiar voice screeched. It was Kelsey.

The crowd parted, giving Spencer a clear view of Kelsey's face. Tears streamed down her cheeks. Her chest heaved in and out, frantic for air. One of the waiters was helping her to her feet. A few more people guided her down the alley toward the parking lot.

"Wait!" Spencer cried feebly. "Don't let her go! She's A!"

Beau crouched down. "You've had a long night," he said a bit gruffly. "Maybe you should go before you make more of a scene."

Spencer shook her head feverishly. How could he not get it? But when she looked at Beau's freaked-out face, she understood: Somehow, it looked like this had been all *her* fault. To them, she'd attacked an innocent girl.

"*Freak*," someone whispered.

"She needs to be checked into a mental institution," someone else said.

A woman chased after Kelsey and touched her shoulder. "You should press charges. She *assaulted* you."

Slowly, people began to move away from Spencer. After a moment, only Beau remained standing above her, staring at Spencer like he suddenly had no idea who she was.

"That girl is dangerous," Spencer whispered to him. "You believe me, don't you?"

Beau blinked at her. She wished he'd help her up, give her a big hug, and say he'd protect her. But instead, he backed away with the others. "I'm all for getting into character, Spencer, but you've taken it too far."

He turned around and disappeared back into the restaurant. Spencer wanted to call out, but she felt too disoriented to do so. Then she looked at Kelsey, slowly hobbling out of the alley. After a moment, Kelsey spun around and glanced at Spencer once more. She lifted a pointer finger and slid it evenly across her throat, then pointed straight at Spencer. She mouthed something very distinctly, her lips moving slowly over each word to make sure Spencer understood.

You're dead.

31

EMILY FOLLOWS HER HEART

"Kelsey?" Emily pushed through the crowd, which had gotten even more packed since the party had begun an hour ago. When she turned a corner into one of the smaller dining rooms, everyone was gathered in a thick cluster, murmuring and staring as if something had just happened. Naomi, Riley, Kate, and Klaudia whispered heatedly. A cute, dark-haired guy was standing with them, and Emily did a double take. Was that Mr. Fitz, the old English teacher?

Emily had lost Kelsey as soon as she'd left the bathroom and hadn't been able to find her since. Was Kelsey angry with Emily for knowing what Spencer had done but not saying anything?

Emily rushed past a large poster of Beau and Spencer's portraits as Macbeth and Lady Macbeth, and a guilty twinge twisted her gut. *Spencer.* Once upon a time, Emily had been fiercely loyal to her friends—it was why Her Ali used to call her "Killer." Spencer had said some terrible things, but did that really warrant Emily outing her secret to Spencer's enemy? Suddenly, a memory popped into her head: One night last summer, after her job at Poseidon's, she'd gotten off the subway and spotted Spencer on the street corner, talking with a guy in a black beanie hat.

"Phineas, you've got to get me more," Spencer begged.

The guy, Phineas, just shrugged. Emily had tried to get a good look at him—Spencer had mentioned him countless times—but he was standing in the shadows, his shoulders hunched. He said something Emily couldn't hear.

"I wish you hadn't turned me on to this in the first place," Spencer said. "It's ruined me."

Phineas held up his hands helplessly. When Spencer's shoulders started to shake, he didn't comfort her.

Emily ducked around the corner, astonished. Spencer seemed so . . . weak. Overwhelmed. In trouble. Emily knew she should do something, make her presence known, throw her arms around Spencer and help her, but all she could think of was her scandalous pregnant belly. She didn't want Spencer to see. It was just too horrifying.

Now, that reaction felt ridiculous. Spencer had found out Emily's condition in the end—she, along with their other friends, had helped her when she had needed them most. If Emily had gone to Spencer in that moment, would she have gotten arrested? Would Kelsey have gone to juvie? Could Emily have prevented that horrible trajectory?

Suddenly, Aria's face swam into view, breaking Emily from her thoughts. "I've been looking for you. Where have you been?"

Emily made a vague gesture. "Around. Listen, have you seen . . ." She was about to say *Kelsey* but stopped. ". . . Spencer?"

A strange look came over Aria's face. "Didn't you *see* what happened?"

Emily glanced into the shaken crowd again. "No . . ."

"I saw the tail end of it." Aria's eyes were wide. "But Spencer *freaked*. She attacked someone. I think it was that girl she's convinced is A–Kelsey. She's *here*."

"Oh my God." It was because of what Emily said about Spencer–Emily knew it. "Is anyone hurt?"

Aria shook her head. "But we need to find Spencer. Maybe she had a good reason to lash out like that."

Emily stared around the room again. Suddenly, she saw a redheaded girl near the door, receiving her jacket from the coat-check girl. *Kelsey.*

She touched Aria's arm. "I'll be right back."

Aria frowned. "Where are you *going*?"

"I'll just be a sec." Emily maneuvered awkwardly through the crowd of kids. By the time she got to Kelsey, Kelsey's hand was on the front door. "Are you leaving?" Emily said breathlessly.

Kelsey turned and gave Emily a frazzled, almost puzzled look, as if she couldn't exactly place who Emily was. Her lips were cracked, and her eyes bulged unnaturally. "Uh, yeah. I guess cast parties aren't really my thing."

"Did something happen?" Emily's voice rose in pitch. "Did you talk to Spencer? You're not mad at me, are you? For knowing? For not saying anything? I didn't know how to tell you, but I should have."

Kelsey's lips parted. A muscle in her cheek twitched violently. Even though it was chilly in the coat-check area, beads of sweat had formed on her forehead. Wordlessly, she turned and started out the door to the parking lot.

"Where are you going?" Emily followed after her.

"Anywhere but here." Kelsey stopped at her car and unlocked it with two sharp bleats. She pointed to the passenger side. "If you want to come, get in."

Emily let out a long, relieved breath. She glanced back toward the restaurant, wondering if she should tell Aria where she was going. But Aria was looking for Spencer, and Emily doubted Spencer would want to see her right now. Emily wasn't sure she was ready to see Spencer, either.

"I'm coming," Emily said. She wrenched the door open and slid into the bucket seat.

Kelsey gave Emily a quick, twitchy grin. "Good," she whispered, and then pulled out into the dark night.

32

NOT YOUR USUAL FLYER
ON THE DASHBOARD

The clock on the dashboard of Hanna's Prius said 9:08 when Hanna and Liam pulled into Otto for the *Macbeth* cast party. Hanna shifted into park, and Liam brushed a strand of hair out of her eyes. "Are you *sure* you have to go in there?"

"I'm sure." Hanna rubbed his neck. "It's bad enough I didn't go to the play. I'm going to have to lie and tell my dad I sat in the back or something. What do the witches do, anyway? Just in case my dad quizzes me."

"They bring Macbeth a prophesy." Liam traced his finger up Hanna's bare arm. For their secret date tonight, she was wearing a brand-new silky minidress from Otter that showed off lots of skin. They'd gone to the college theater in Hollis and made out in the back seats. "They tell him he's going to be king and give him all kinds of other creepy warnings," Liam went on. "And they do a lot of cackling."

Hanna touched the tip of his nose. "I love how sexy you sound when you talk about Shakespeare."

"Well I love *everything* about you," Liam answered, kissing her lips.

Hanna's insides swirled. Had he just said he *loved* her?

After six more kisses good-bye, Hanna kicked Liam out of the car—he'd parked his own in the church lot across the street a few hours earlier. She watched him lope across Lancaster Avenue, shivering with pleasure. Then she climbed out of the Prius and crossed the parking lot toward the restaurant. A Toyota hatchback pulled out in front of her, seemingly not noticing she was there.

"Hey!" Hanna yelled at the vehicle, jumping out of the way. A familiar face stared at her from the passenger seat. "Emily?" Next to Emily was a red-haired girl Hanna knew she'd seen before, too. But where?

The car peeled out of the parking lot before Hanna could figure it out. Turning, she walked into the restaurant, which was filled with kids and smelled like roasted garlic and fresh bread. There were so many people jamming the door that Hanna nearly fell into someone on her way to the coatroom. "*Watch* it," the person snapped when Hanna accidentally elbowed his back.

"Watch it yourself," Hanna snapped. Then the figure turned. It was Mike.

Hanna stepped back. "Oh. Hey."

"Hey." Mike blinked hard, looking startled. This was the closest Hanna had been to him in weeks. He still smelled like the Kiehl's cucumber hand lotion she'd bought him for Christmas. "How . . . are you?"

Hanna raised an eyebrow. "So you're speaking to me again?"

Mike shifted awkwardly. "I've been kind of . . . stupid." He glanced at her imploringly, then touched his hand to her wrist. "I miss you."

Hanna stared at his long, thin fingers, suddenly annoyed. Why couldn't Mike have come to this conclusion a week ago when Hanna was leaving him those messages? Was Mike only interested in Hanna again because her messages had stopped? That was *so* like guys.

She pulled her hand away. "Actually, Mike, I'm with someone."

The light drained from Mike's eyes. "Oh. Well. Good for you. I have a girlfriend, too."

Hanna flinched. He *did*? "Good for you, too," she said stiffly.

They eyed each other cagily. Then someone tugged Hanna's arm. Hanna turned and saw Aria and Spencer standing next to her. Both of them looked frazzled and pale.

"We need to talk to you," Aria said. They whisked her back into the parking lot once more. Hanna glanced over her shoulder at Mike, but he'd already turned toward Mason Byers and James Freed.

"You need to see this," Spencer said when they got to a secluded spot at the corner of the lot. She pulled out her iPhone and waved it in Hanna's face.

Hanna's vision took a while to adjust. On the screen was a picture of a girl's body lying in the sand. Blood pooled around her head. "Is this . . . ?" Hanna gasped, too afraid to even say Tabitha's name.

"Yes. It's from A. From *Kelsey*."

Spencer told Hanna how Kelsey had marched up to her and asked if she'd received her text—*this* text. "She knows what we did," she said. "She knows everything. She came after me, and I tried to protect myself, but people pulled me off her saying *I* attacked *her*. And then, when it was all over, Kelsey looked at me one more time and mouthed *You're dead*."

Hanna gasped. "Are you sure?"

Spencer nodded. "We have to find her and stop her before she does something terrible. But I have no idea where she's gone. I can't find her anywhere."

An engine sputtered on the road, reminding Hanna of the car that had almost sideswiped her moments before. Suddenly, synapses connected in her brain. She gasped. "I think I just saw Kelsey. But I didn't realize it was her."

"Where?" Aria shrieked.

Hanna swallowed hard and gestured to the restaurant's exit. "In her car. Leaving. And, guys, she wasn't alone."

Spencer widened her eyes. "She was with Emily, wasn't she?"

Aria reached into her bag for her car keys. "We have to find them. *Now*."

She started across the parking lot, and Hanna followed.

But after a few paces, Hanna turned and noticed that Spencer had remained on the sidewalk, shifting from one foot to the other. "What is it?" Hanna asked.

Spencer chewed on her bottom lip. "I . . . I had a fight with Emily in the restaurant. I said some pretty horrible stuff to her. She might not want to see me."

"Yes, she will." Hanna grabbed Spencer's arm. "It's *Emily*—and she's in danger. We're all in this together, right?"

Spencer nodded, zipped up her coat, and stepped off the curb toward Aria's car. Aria hit the UNLOCK button on her keychain, and they all climbed in. Just as Aria was revving the engine, Hanna pointed to a piece of paper skewered through the antenna on the hood. "What's *that*?"

Spencer jumped out of the car and ripped the paper free. She climbed back inside and spread it out on her lap. Everyone gathered around to look. Collectively, they let out a long, nervous gasp.

Hurry, girls! Before it's too late! —A

33

A FALLEN IDOL

Emily and Kelsey sped past the quaint shops on the main drive, the Hollis clock tower, the covered bridge, the upscale hair salon where Their Ali had taken Emily and her friends to get eyebrow waxes for seventh-grade graduation. Ali had tried to talk Emily into getting a bikini wax, too, but Emily had refused.

Kelsey didn't say a word, just drove, staring straight ahead. Every so often, her whole body shivered and spasmed, like Emily's body did when she was waking from a bad dream.

"Is everything okay?" Emily asked tentatively.

"Everything's fine," Kelsey answered. "Never better! On top of the world! Why do you ask?"

Whoa. She'd said all that in the span of about two seconds. Emily eased back in her seat, feeling the seat belt cut against her chest. "You confronted Spencer about what happened, right? How did that go? Are you upset?"

Kelsey took her hands off the wheel, leaned over, and started to stroke Emily's shoulder. "You're so cute. Do you always get this worried about people, or am I special?"

"Uh, can you watch the road?" Emily warned as the car drifted over the dotted yellow line. A car speeding toward them honked and swerved.

"I *hope* I'm special to you." Kelsey faced front again. "Because you're special to me."

"Good," Emily answered, but she still felt a little unnerved. She stared out the window at the dark telephone poles rushing past. Where were they, anyway? This was a part of Rosewood she rarely visited.

Just after an old, ramshackle Quaker church came into view, Kelsey wrenched the wheel, sending the car onto a hidden turnoff. A sign swept past, written in crooked capital letters. FLOATING MAN QUARRY.

"W-why are we going here?" Emily stammered.

"Have you ever been to this place?" Kelsey gunned up the steep hill. "It's awesome. I haven't been here in ages. Not since before I went to juvie."

Emily peeked out the window. She hadn't been here in a while, either: The last time was when she and the others had discovered Mona Vanderwaal was the original A. Mona had been about to push Spencer over the cliff into the jagged rocks below, but Mona had slipped to her death instead.

"There are cooler places than this, you know," Emily

said shakily. "There's a spot near the train tracks where you can see the whole Main Line."

"Nah, I like it here." Kelsey pulled into the empty parking lot next to a big trash barrel. "Come on!" She ran over to Emily's side and pulled her out. "You've got to see this view!"

"That's okay." Emily wriggled her arm from Kelsey's grasp. Her heels sank in the wet grass. "I'm not really good with heights."

"But it's so beautiful, Emily!" Kelsey gestured toward the edge of the ravine. Her eyes were bulging and a little crossed, and she was still twitching and shaking. "This should be on your bucket list! You haven't lived until you've stood on the precipice of a cliff!"

Kelsey punctuated the last line with a faint giggle. The hair on the back of Emily's neck stood on end. She thought of Spencer's warnings. The coincidental overlap in Jamaica. The two hands pushing Emily over the hill, Kelsey appearing at the top seconds later. Kelsey's sudden bizarre behavior.

"Kelsey, what's going on?" Emily whispered.

Kelsey broke into a broad, off-kilter smile. "Nothing! Why would you say that?"

"You seem so . . . *different*. Like you're . . . I don't know . . . you're drunk or something."

"Just drunk on life!" Kelsey spread out her arms. "Ready to do something huge! I thought you were brave, Emily. Don't you want to stand on the cliff with me?"

Kelsey skipped toward the edge of the gulch, leaving her bag gaping open on the driver's seat. The lights over the dashboard were still on, and Emily could see the bag's contents. Sitting right on top was a huge vial of pills. There was no name on the prescription label.

All kinds of alarms were going off inside her. Slowly, without making any sound, she felt around in her pocket for her cell phone. When she found it, she tapped in a quick message to Aria. *SOS. At Floating Man. Please come.*

She pressed SEND and waited for the confirmation that Aria had received the message. But then Kelsey turned around. "Who are you calling?"

"No one." Emily dropped her phone back into her pocket.

Kelsey went limp. "You don't want to be here, do you? You don't want to hang out with me."

"Of course I do. But I'm worried about you tonight. You seem . . . upset. Kind of weird. Is it because of what I told you? I should've come clean from the start. I'm sorry."

Kelsey sniffed sharply. "Well, I should've come clean, too."

Emily cocked her head. "What do you mean?"

"I'm a liar, just like you." Kelsey giggled, retreating toward Emily. "You know when I told you I didn't realize you were Spencer's best friend? Or that you went through all that stuff with Alison? I knew all along, Emily. I was just pretending I didn't."

Emily pressed her hand against her temple, trying to take this in. "Why?"

"Because I was trying to be nice." The wind picked up strands of Kelsey's hair. "Not gawk at you like you were some freak. What's *your* excuse, Emily? Did you want to laugh at me behind my back? Did you and Spencer giggle about what she did to me?"

"Of course not!" Emily cried. "I only found out after we met!"

Kelsey's eyes flashed. "You have all kinds of secrets up your sleeve, don't you?" She shook her head in disgust. "I can't believe you did what you did. You're a horrible person, Emily. *Horrible.*"

Emily pressed her hand to her heart and felt it thudding through her dress. Kelsey's features had transformed. Now she stared at Emily with pure, clean hate, the same self-loathing Emily felt ever since Tabitha's remains had turned up on the shore. All at once, every theory Spencer had proposed about this girl seemed possible. More than possible—right. She thought about the picture of Tabitha on Kelsey's phone. And about Tabitha's face as Aria shoved her off the roof. The soft *thud* as she hit the ground. The resort had seemed so desolate, as though every guest had vacated the island for the night. But someone had been watching. Kelsey.

How had Emily not seen it before? Was Spencer right? Had Emily been blinded by her crush?

In any case Kelsey was right: Emily was a horrible person. The most horrible person in the world.

"I didn't mean for it to happen," Emily whispered. "You don't understand."

Kelsey shook her head in disgust. "You *let* it happen. And you said nothing."

Emily covered her face in her hands, thinking of the Tabitha memorial pages online, her grieving friends and family. "I know. I should have. It's awful."

A faint sound of tires on gravel rang out, and Emily turned. Headlights appeared above the crest, and Aria's Subaru gunned up the hill. Aria gripped the wheel. Hanna sat next to her, frantically pointing when she saw Emily.

Emily lifted her hands above her head to wave them over, but Kelsey caught her wrist. "You're coming with me." She yanked Emily toward the cliff.

"No!" Emily tried to pull away, but Kelsey gripped her hard, dragging her so forcefully Emily's feet left the ground.

"I want you to see this," Kelsey said, marching her toward the ravine. Emily's ankles turned several times in her uncomfortable shoes, and when one of them fell off she left it there and went the rest of the way in one stockinged foot. Tears streamed down her face, and she could barely breathe she was so afraid.

"I'm so sorry," she whimpered. Her voice was trembling so badly she could hardly get the words out. "I thought we were friends. *More* than friends."

"We *were*." Kelsey pushed Emily over a series of rocks.

"But this is going to hurt me more than it's going to hurt you."

They arrived at the edge of the quarry. Gravel spilled down the long rock face. When Emily looked over the side, all she could see was deep, infinite darkness. She glanced over her shoulder then and saw Aria getting out of the car. "Emily!" she cried. "Oh my God!"

Kelsey nudged Emily closer to the edge, and Emily let out a scream. Kelsey was going to do to Emily exactly what Mona had tried to do to Spencer, what Tabitha had tried to do to Hanna, what Ali had tried to do to all of them. Except this time, A would live . . . and A's victim would die.

"Please," Emily glanced imploringly at Kelsey. "You don't want to do this. Maybe we can talk this over. Figure it out."

"There's nothing to figure out," Kelsey said in a deflated voice. "This is the way it has to be."

"Emily!" Aria screamed, running closer.

But she wasn't close enough. Kelsey's fingers curled around Emily's shoulder. Her breath was hot in her ear. Her whole body seemed to stiffen, as though preparing to push Emily over. Emily shut her eyes, realizing these were her last few seconds of being alive.

"Please," she whispered one more time.

And then, suddenly, Kelsey released her grip from Emily's arm. Emily turned in time to see Kelsey walking to the edge of the precipice. She caught Emily's eye, but the crazy, dangerous look was gone. She seemed exhausted and incredibly sad.

"Good-bye," Kelsey said in the most pathetic voice Emily had ever heard. There were tears in her eyes. Her hands were shaking so violently they smacked against her waist. A thin trickle of blood dripped from her nose. She looked over the edge and took a deep breath.

"Kelsey!" It took Emily only a second to realize what was happening. "Don't jump!"

Kelsey ignored her, inching forward until her toes dangled over the edge. More rocks cascaded into the quarry. "It's too late. I'm so sick of how shitty life is." She was slurring her words so badly Emily could barely understand her. "I'm so sick of *everything*." She shut her eyes and took a step into the darkness.

"No!" Emily wrapped her arms around Kelsey's waist. Kelsey tried to elbow her away, but Emily mustered up all her strength and ripped Kelsey backward. They both staggered onto the grass. Kelsey grunted, trying to break free. Emily pulled her even tighter. Her ankle turned once more, and all of a sudden, she was on the wet, slick ground with Kelsey on top of her. Pain cracked through her head and her tailbone. Coldness from the rocks seeped straight through her coat and into her skin.

She blacked out for a few moments, hearing only faint sobs and the vague sounds of footsteps. When she came to, Hanna was leaning over her. "Emily? *Emily!* Oh my God!"

Emily blinked hard. Kelsey was no longer on top of her. She looked around frantically, afraid Kelsey had thrown herself into the quarry, but the girl was only a few feet away, curled into a ball.

"Are you okay?" Aria appeared above Emily, too.

"I-I don't know," Emily said dazedly. And then everything swarmed back to her. The fear. The certainty that she had been about to die. How Kelsey knew *everything*. Tears streamed down her face. Her body heaved and bucked. Her sobs sounded messy and ugly.

Hanna and Aria knelt down and hugged her tight. "It's okay," they whispered. "You're safe now. We promise."

"Hey," another voice said a few feet away. Emily opened her eyes and saw a third figure squatting next to Kelsey. "Wake up."

Emily's jaw dropped. It was Spencer. She'd doubted Spencer and double-crossed her, and she'd come anyway.

"You guys?" Spencer looked up and pushed her blond hair away from her face. "*Look.*"

She moved out of the way for the girls to see. Kelsey's back was arched, her head was flung to the side, and her arms and legs danced as though they were being pumped with a million volts of electric power. Bile bubbled out of her mouth. Cords stood out prominently on her neck.

"What's wrong with her?" Hanna screamed.

"I'm calling 911." Aria pulled out her phone.

"I think she's OD'ing." Spencer kneeled down to Kelsey's face. "She must have taken something."

Emily stood up weakly and staggered to Kelsey's bag, which was still sitting on the driver's seat of her car. Inside was the vial of pills, half empty. "This." She showed the others.

Spencer looked at them and nodded. "Easy A."

An ambulance screamed up the gulch road minutes after Aria's call. EMTs surrounded Kelsey and immediately started treatment, telling the girls to step back. Emily hugged her chest, feeling cold and numb. Aria watched the EMTs with a hand over her mouth. Hanna kept shaking her head and saying, "Oh my God." Spencer looked like she was going to be sick.

After a while, the ambulance driver, an athletic woman with shoulder-length brown hair, walked over to the girls. "What happened?"

"I think she was trying to kill herself," Emily answered, her voice still weak. "I guess she took too many pills . . . and she was going to jump into the gulch."

The EMTs checked Emily for any injuries, but besides feeling bruised and banged up, she was fine. Then they loaded Kelsey in the ambulance and drove off. Emily silently watched the red lights swirl down the hill. She listened to the sirens until the sound disappeared.

A deafening silence followed. Emily walked over to Spencer, who was staring across the huge ravine. This was the same view she'd looked out upon over a year ago, just when Mona was about to kill her. It didn't seem like a coincidence that they were back here, fighting A again.

"I'm sorry," Emily said quietly. "I shouldn't have doubted you."

"It's okay," Spencer answered.

"But I told her everything." Emily shut her eyes. "I told Kelsey what you did at Penn. How you sent her to juvie."

Spencer whipped her head up. All kinds of emotions played across her face. "You *did?*"

Emily frowned. "She didn't mention that when she talked to you tonight?"

Spencer shook her head. "Everything moved so fast. We just screamed at each other."

Emily placed her head in her hands. "I'm so sorry. I never should have . . ." She trailed off, choking with sobs. Everything felt so wrong. "I'm a terrible friend. I wasn't there for you." She meant it in more ways than one.

"Hey, it's okay." Spencer touched Emily's shoulder. "I get it. And it *was* a horrible thing I did. Maybe I deserved it, too, after what I said to you."

The wind howled. Far off, Emily thought she could still hear the sirens. Hanna and Aria crunched over, quiet and solemn. "Kelsey's going to tell everyone what we did to Tabitha," Hanna said.

"No one will believe her," Spencer said. "She's on drugs. They'll think she hallucinated the whole thing."

"But she has proof," Hanna argued. "She has that picture of Tabitha dead on the beach."

"What picture?" Emily shrieked.

Spencer reached for her phone, then shrugged and seemed to change her mind. "It's a long story. Honestly, I should delete it. Pretend I never got it. But even a picture of Tabitha doesn't prove *we* did anything. It might even make *her* look guilty. Who takes a picture of a dead body and doesn't report it? Everyone will think she's just . . . crazy."

An airplane flew silently overhead, its red light blinking on and off. A bird let out a long, hollow call somewhere in the ravine. Everyone turned back toward Aria's car, feeling shaken but slightly relieved. But then, Kelsey's words whipped through Emily's mind once more. *You let it happen. You're a horrible person.*

Just because no one believed Kelsey didn't mean it hadn't happened. Emily *was* a horrible person. That guilt would never go away.

34

FAMILY STICKS TOGETHER

Hanna awoke the next morning to the sound of Dot's nails scratching against her bedroom door. "I'll be there in a second, sweetie," she moaned, sitting up.

The sun streamed through the windows of the Juliet balcony. Birds chirped in the trees. It seemed like a perfectly pleasant morning . . . until Hanna remembered what had happened the night before. Kelsey. Floating Man. The ambulance taking her away. She'd looked so fragile. So helpless. Once again, they'd narrowly escaped A ruining their lives.

But it was over now. She grabbed her iPhone and scrolled through her texts. Strangely, Liam hadn't written her a note this morning—that was a first. Had he gotten home okay? It was 9:23 A.M., a little early, but she could call him, right? She dialed his number, but it went to voice mail.

"Wake up, sleepyhead," Hanna cooed after the beep.

"I hope I can see you today. I miss you already. Call me back when you get this."

After changing into a pair of skinny jeans and a Petit Bateau T-shirt, she walked down three flights of stairs to the kitchen carrying Dot in her arms. Her father sat at the breakfast bar, looking over a pile of spreadsheets. Kate hunched over half a grapefruit at the table, staring at the paper. When she saw Hanna enter, she gave her a strange look. Hanna pretended to fix a tag on Dot's collar. Kate had probably found out that Hanna ditched the play and was pissed, but the last thing Hanna wanted was a petty fight.

Kate wouldn't stop staring, though, even as Hanna let out Dot, poured herself a cup of coffee, and added a splash of soy milk. "*What?*" Hanna snapped finally. God, it wasn't like it had been Kate's Broadway debut.

"Um . . ." Kate looked down at the Style section of the newspaper and pushed it toward Hanna with one finger. Hanna stared at it. When she saw the image on the open page, she spit up a mouthful of coffee all over the floor.

"Are you all right?" Mr. Marin turned and slid off the stool.

"Fine." Hanna dabbed the coffee with a napkin. "Just fine."

But she was far from fine. She looked at the image on the newspaper page again, praying she was imagining things. Three pictures of Liam's handsome, smiling face stared back at her. In the first one, he had his arm around a thin blond girl with a pointy nose. In the second, he was kissing a dark-haired girl in a swingy jersey dress. And in the third, he was walking down a busy Philly street, hand-in-hand with a short-haired girl wearing oversized sunglasses and a Burberry trench. *A Real-Life Romeo, In Love With Love*, said the caption next to the montage. *Liam Wilkinson is one of Philly's most eligible bachelors . . . and he loves playing the field.*

A hard, thick ball lodged in Hanna's throat. The photo caption named each of the girls Liam was with and when he'd been seen with them. One of the photos was from earlier this week, on a day Hanna and Liam hadn't seen each other. And the short-haired girl, whose name was Hazel, was described as "Liam's long-term girlfriend he hopes to marry someday."

Hanna's gaze flitted to a quote in the main body of the article. *"He's definitely a charmer,"* said Lucy Richards, one of *Liam's ex-girlfriends from last year. "He made me feel like I was the only girl in the universe. Said that he'd never felt this way before except with me. He kept talking about running away with me, taking me to one of his family's châteaus in France or Italy. It definitely made me feel special . . . until I realized he did that with every girl he dated."*

Hanna reached to the middle of the table, grabbed a piece of toast from the stack, and shoved it in her mouth. Then she grabbed another piece, and then a slice of bacon, even though she hadn't eaten bacon in years. Liam had said all those things to her, too. He'd made those same promises. So it was just a . . . line? A ruse? And she'd fallen for him. She'd let him stay overnight at her father's house. She'd jeopardized her father's career.

Her legs wobbled beneath her as she stood. The room tilted and swayed as though the whole house was on a rocky ocean. Liam's adoring face flashed through her mind. All those romantic things he'd said. The passion that had snapped and crackled between them. *Jesus.*

She staggered out of the kitchen and into the living room. When she dialed Liam's number on her phone, the line rang and rang, once again going to voice mail. "Nice article about you in the *Sentinel*," Hanna sputtered as soon as she heard the *beep*. "Don't call me back. *Ever.*"

When she hung up, the phone slipped from her fingers to the cushion of the couch. Hanna sank down and hugged a pillow to her chest, biting down hard on her tongue so she wouldn't cry. Thank God she hadn't told Liam anything important about her father. Thank God she hadn't told him about Tabitha.

"*Ahem.*"

Hanna turned. Kate stood in the doorway. There was an uncomfortable look on her face. She walked into the living room, perched on the edge of the patterned slipper chair across from Hanna, and waited. Kate *knew.* She'd pushed the Style section to Hanna's place so Hanna would see it, after all.

"How did you find out?" Hanna said in a low, hateful voice.

Kate fiddled with a pearl choker at her throat. "I saw you guys together at the flash mob. And then I heard you, the other night, in your room. I knew he was here."

Hanna winced. "You're going to tell Dad, aren't you?" She glanced into the kitchen. Her father was now pacing around the island, his phone to his ear.

Kate turned away. "He doesn't need to know."

Hanna blinked at her incredulously. This was a perfect opportunity for Kate to be Daddy's favorite again. Her father would never forgive Hanna for this.

"I've been cheated on, too," Kate said quietly.

Hanna looked up in surprise. "By Sean?"

Kate shook her head. "Not by *him*. By someone I dated in Annapolis, before I moved here. His name was Jeffrey. I was so into him. But then I found out through Facebook that he had another girlfriend."

Hanna shifted in her seat. "I'm sorry." She found it hard to believe perfect Kate could've ever been dumped, but she looked so humble. Almost human.

Kate shrugged. She raised her green eyes to Hanna. "I think we should take them down. Not only has that family messed with Tom, but they've messed with you, too."

Then Kate rose and strutted out of the room, her arms swinging, her shoulders back. Hanna slowly counted to ten, waiting for Kate to turn around and say, *Just kidding! I'm totally telling on you, bitch!* But after a moment, Hanna heard the gentle *clunk* of her bedroom door closing. Huh.

"I'll call you back in a bit," Mr. Marin said loudly in

the kitchen, and Hanna heard the *beep* of the call ending. She stood, the tips of her fingers prickling. Kate was right. Maybe Hanna *should* take Liam's family down. Hanna might not have told Liam anything vital about her father—besides typical divorce stuff every family suffers from and a lot of embarrassing stories about her weight—but Liam had told Hanna a whopper of a secret about his family. Something that would cut Tucker Wilkinson out of the campaign for good.

"Dad." Hanna padded into the kitchen. Her father was now standing at the sink, washing his dishes. "There's something I need to tell you. About Tucker Wilkinson."

Her father turned, one eyebrow raised. And then everything Liam had told Hanna spilled out of her: his father's affair, the woman's unwanted pregnancy, the abortion. Her dad's eyes bulged with every word. His jaw dropped lower and lower. The words felt like poison spilling from Hanna's mouth, worse than any piece of gossip she'd ever spread, but then the photos from the paper flashed through her mind once more. They made her think of that line from some random Shakespeare-era play Mr. Fitz had made them read in English class last year: *Hell hath no fury like a woman scorned*.

Liam totally deserved it.

35

WHO CARES ABOUT PERFECT, ANYWAY?

"Mike, cereal is meant to be eaten with a spoon," Ella said that same morning as she, Aria, and Mike sat down to breakfast in the sun-filled nook. The room smelled like organic coffee, freshly squeezed orange juice, and the slightly wilted wildflowers Thaddeus had sent Ella the other day.

Mike begrudgingly grabbed an antique silver spoon from the drawer and slumped back to his seat. Then Ella turned to Aria. "So what happened to you at the cast party last night? I turned around and you were gone."

Aria pushed the big Ray-Ban sunglasses higher on her nose. She was wearing them to hide her red, puffy eyes from a whole night of crying over Ezra, Kelsey, A, and everything else. "I had some stuff to take care of," she mumbled.

"You should've stuck around." Mike chewed his Kashi flakes loudly. "The director got really smashed. People say that's why he had to come and work at a random private school in the suburbs—he's a boozer. And Spencer Hastings freaked out on this random girl. *Psycho!*" He sang the last word and bugged out his eyes.

"She's not psycho." Aria picked at a Fresh Fields waffle, the events of last night whirling in her head. Spencer freaked out, but it was for good reason.

So Kelsey was New A. On one hand, it was a good thing: At least they knew who the notes were coming from. On the other, what if people *did* believe what Kelsey knew about Tabitha? This morning, three more stories had appeared online about Tabitha's death: one about a new forensic procedure the scientists had done to prove once and for all it had been Tabitha's remains, another about a bake sale held in Tabitha's honor, and a third about underage drinking in general, mentioning Tabitha's death as a recent example.

Tabitha was becoming as popular in her community as Ali had been in Rosewood. If her little town in New Jersey caught wind that Tabitha had been murdered, would they really care if the girl crying foul was a drug addict? And what if Kelsey had more photos of Tabitha's body? She thought of A's recent note: *Don't think you'll be spared from my wrath, murderess. You're the guiltiest of all.* Kelsey seemed to even know that *Aria* had done the pushing.

Mike's phone rang, and he jumped up and left the room. Ella balled up her napkin and leaned forward on her elbows. "Honey, is there anything you want to talk about?"

Aria slurped her coffee. "Not really."

Ella cleared her throat. "Are you sure? I couldn't help but notice you talking to a certain ex-teacher of yours last night."

Aria winced. "There's nothing to tell."

And there wasn't. Ezra hadn't called Aria after she'd caught him with Klaudia. There had been no *I'm sorry* texts on her phone or *please take me back* boxes of candy on her doorstep. New York certainly wasn't happening. The love affair wasn't happening. It was like she'd dreamed the whole thing.

Aria sighed and raised her head. "Remember how, before I went to Iceland last summer, everyone kept telling me it was going to be so amazing to be back?"

"Sure." Ella stirred more Sugar in the Raw into her coffee.

"But then, when I came back, I told you it just . . . wasn't the same?" Aria fiddled with the gnome salt and pepper shakers on the table. "It's like, you can dream about something for so long, but sometimes reality doesn't exactly quite live up."

Ella clucked her tongue. "You know, you're going to make someone very happy someday," she said after a moment. "And someone is going to make *you* happy someday, too. You'll know when it's right."

"How?" Aria asked quietly.

"You'll just know it. I promise."

Ella patted Aria's hands, maybe waiting for Aria to say

something else. When Aria didn't, Ella rose to clear the table. Aria remained in her chair, deep in thought. She'd known something was different about Ezra as soon as he'd returned, but she hadn't wanted to admit it. It was the same feeling she'd had about Reykjavik when the airport bus had driven them into town. She'd wanted to love it just as much, but it wasn't the same place she remembered. The bar that sold soup in giant bread bowls was no longer on the corner. Aria's old house had been painted a garish pink and had an ugly satellite dish that took up half the roof.

And then there was what had happened on that trip, something that had more or less ruined Aria's memories of the country forever. It was a secret that only her old best friends knew, a secret she'd take with her to the grave.

When the doorbell rang, Aria straightened her spine. Could it be Ezra? Did she even *want* it to be Ezra? For both Ezra and Iceland some of the old magic was gone.

She rose from the table, cinched the belt of her robe around her waist, and pulled the door open. Noel stood on the porch, wringing his hands. "Hey."

"Oh. Hi," Aria said cautiously. "Are you looking for Mike?"

"No."

Awkward seconds ticked by. The tap in the kitchen turned on, then off. Aria shifted from one foot to the other.

"I've missed you," Noel blurted. "I can't stop thinking

about you. And I'm a complete ass. What I said in the hall the other day, it was bullshit. I didn't mean it."

Aria stared down at the gash in the floor she'd made when she was little by digging a clay knife into the soft wood, thinking she was a sculptor. "You were right, though. We *are* really different. You deserve someone more . . . Rosewood-y. Someone like Klaudia."

Noel winced. "Oh, God. *Not* Klaudia. That girl's crazy."

A small light flickered on in Aria's heart.

"She's had me working like a dog after that ankle injury," Noel said. "And I found out she's a total klepto. She's been stealing stuff from my room! Underwear, CDs, pages from my notebooks . . . and then I realized she took my leather jacket, that one that used to be my grandfather's."

Aria frowned. "I saw her wearing that in school. I figured you gave it to her."

Noel looked horrified. "No way! And when I confronted her about it, she went ballistic. Then she went off about *you*, saying you were spreading lies about her— that you told everyone she threatened you, saying she was determined to sleep with me and that I shouldn't believe it. But I kind of think she *does* want to sleep with me. A couple of nights ago, I woke up to her standing in my doorway, wearing . . ." He trailed off, an awkward look on his face. "I told my mom I wanted her out of the house."

"Wow," Aria said. Part of her wanted to gloat, but part of her just felt tired. "So . . . you didn't sleep with her?"

She couldn't help but ask. It was kind of inconceivable to think Noel had resisted gorgeous Klaudia.

Noel shook his head. "I'm not into her like that, Aria. I like someone else."

A frisson went through her. She didn't dare look at him for fear she'd give too much away.

Noel leaned against the doorjamb. "I should have listened to you. About *everything*. I can understand if you don't want to get back together, but . . . I miss you. Maybe we could at least be friends? I mean, who else will go with me to the rest of those cooking classes?"

Aria raised her head. "You *liked* those cooking classes?"

"They're kind of girly, but they're fun." Noel smiled shyly. "And anyway, we need to have our *Iron Chef* battle at the end of the semester."

The heady scent of the orangey soap Noel always used tickled Aria's nose. What was he asking for: a companion to cooking class . . . or for Aria to be his girlfriend again? Maybe it was too late to get back together. Maybe they really *didn't* have enough in common. Aria would never be a Typical Rosewood, after all. It wasn't even worth trying for.

She must have been taking too long to answer, because Noel breathed in sharply. "You're not back with that teacher dude again, are you? When I saw you guys together last night . . ."

"No," Aria said quickly. "He's . . ." She squeezed her eyes shut. "Actually, he's into Klaudia."

This suddenly struck her as ridiculous. She leaned over and laughed long and hard, tears streaming from her eyes.

Noel laughed awkwardly, not really getting the joke. After a moment, Aria gazed up at him. He looked so sweet, standing on the porch in baggy jeans and an oversized T-shirt and rubber shower shoes over white gym socks, a look Aria had always hated. So Noel would never write a novel. So he'd never roll his eyes at the irony of the suburbs or whine about how everything here was so contrived and pretentious. But then she thought about how, on Christmas Day, Noel had appeared at Aria's doorstep in a Santa Claus outfit with a bag of presents for her, all because she'd told him that her family never "did" Santa when she was little. And how, when Aria dragged Noel to the modern art wing at the Philadelphia Art Museum, he had patiently walked through the rooms with her, even buying a book about Picasso's Blue Period at the gift shop afterward because he thought it was trippy. And he made Aria laugh: When the two of them had gone to the cooking class at Hollis, knives poised over green bell peppers, Noel had pointed out that they looked just like lumpy butts. The other students, mostly old ladies or sad bachelors probably taking the class to meet women, pursed their lips at them, which just made them laugh harder.

She stepped toward Noel. Her heart pounded as he leaned down, his breath sweet and warm on her face. They'd only been broken up for two weeks, but the moment their lips touched it felt like their very first kiss.

Fireworks went off in Aria's chest. Her lips tingled. Noel pulled her in and squeezed her so hard she thought she might burst. And, okay, it was drizzling outside, and Aria was pretty sure her mouth tasted like coffee, and Noel's shower shoes were probably caked in mold. The moment wasn't perfect, but it didn't matter.

It just felt . . . right. Maybe even the *right* that Ella had talked about in the kitchen just moments ago. And for Aria, that was as perfect as perfect could be.

36

THE REAL SPENCER F.

"Sorry it smells like chlorine," Spencer said, lifting the lid of her family's backyard hot tub, which had been closed up since last fall. She fiddled with the tie on her Burberry string bikini.

"I'm used to it," Emily said. She was wearing one of her practice swimsuits, the shoulder straps stretched and the Speedo emblem almost worn off.

"As long as it's warm, I don't care," Hanna seconded, stripping off her T-shirt to reveal a new Missoni bikini. And Aria shrugged, unzipping her hoodie, showing off a polka-dotted maillot that looked like it could have come from a 1950s time capsule.

Steam rose from under the hot tub cover. The water burbled invitingly. Percival, Spencer's old yellow rubber duck, bobbed in the water, left there from the last time she'd taken a soak. Bringing Percival in here was a ritual of hers, back from when she was little and her parents only let her climb in the tub for a few minutes at a time. Their Ali always used to tease her about it, saying it was just as bad as a security blanket, but Spencer loved seeing the duck's happy smiling face bobbing in the bubbles.

One by one, the girls stepped into the warm bath. Spencer had invited them over to rehash what had happened with Kelsey, but as soon as she saw Mr. Pennythistle—she should really start calling him Nicholas—fiddling with the lid to the tub earlier today she thought they might as well get some relaxation out of the visit, too.

"This feels awesome," Aria murmured.

"Such a good idea," Emily agreed. Her pale cheeks and forehead were already red from the heat.

"Remember the last time we were going to get in a hot tub together?" Hanna asked. "At the Poconos?"

Everyone nodded, staring into the steam. Ali had run under the deck to turn on the tub, leaving the girls alone on the porch. They'd all hugged and said how happy they were to be friends again.

"I remember feeling so happy," Emily said.

"And then everything changed so fast," Hanna said, her voice tight.

Spencer arched her neck up and looked for patterns in the gray clouds. That night at the Poconos felt like it was both yesterday and a million years ago. Would they ever get over it, or would it be something that haunted them for the rest of their lives?

"I found out what rehab hospital Kelsey's in," she said after a moment. "The Preserve."

Everyone looked up, startled. The Preserve was where A had sent Hanna last year . . . and where Real Ali had spent all those years.

"The nurse on the phone said she can have visitors starting tomorrow," Spencer went on. "I think we should go."

"Are you serious?" Hanna's eyes were round. "Don't you think we should stay away from her?"

"We need to figure out what she really knows," Spencer said. "Figure out how she became A. What she wanted with us."

"She wanted what every A wanted." Hanna picked at her cuticles. "Revenge."

"But why did she try to kill herself?" Spencer had been running the problem over in her mind all night. "That's unlike Mona or Ali. I would've thought she'd wanted *us* dead instead."

"Maybe she wanted us to know we drove her to suicide," Aria suggested. "It's the ultimate guilt-trip. We'd have it on our conscience for the rest of our lives."

The strong scent of chlorine tickled Spencer's nose. She'd never suspected that Kelsey was suicidal—she'd always seemed so bubbly and carefree at Penn, even in the thick of taking Easy A. Had it been juvie that had changed her? Had it been the addiction to drugs? That was the biggest surprise of all: In Spencer's memories, Kelsey had been resistant to taking the pills, seemingly disgusted by her druggie past. She'd never have thought Kelsey would turn to them again after juvie. After Spencer's near-arrest experience, she'd quit Easy A cold turkey. It had been hard, especially with all the cramming she still needed to do, but she'd powered through her studies, scoring fives on the exams anyway. Nowadays, Spencer didn't even yearn for the pills anymore.

But then, Kelsey's life had taken such a different turn from hers. Even if Kelsey hadn't succeeded in jumping into Floating Man Quarry, just the fact that she'd wanted to do it was more than Spencer could bear. It could have been all her fault, both for getting her back into drugs and for getting her sent to juvie. The visions Spencer had been having of Kelsey and Tabitha weren't because of stress over school, as Spencer had wanted to believe. The guilt over what she'd done was eating her from the inside out. It was a good thing no one important had seen her attack on Kelsey at the cast party, like Wilden or her mother or any of the Rosewood Day teachers—Pierre had been there, but word had it he'd also been drunk. If Spencer didn't find a healthy outlet for this guilt soon, she was a little afraid of what she might see—or do—next.

"Maybe Spencer's right." Emily broke the silence. "Maybe we should go see Kelsey at the Preserve. Try to figure things out."

Hanna chewed on her pinkie. "Guys, I'm not super comfortable about going back there. It's an awful place."

"We'll be with you," Aria said. "And if it gets too hard, I'll take you home." Then she looked at Spencer. "I think we should go, too. Together."

"I'll set up an appointment for us tomorrow when we go back inside," Spencer said.

Fat raindrops began to fall on the hot tub, first slowly, and then fast and steady. Thunder rumbled in the distance. Spencer eyed the steel-colored sky. "So much for our big hot tub idea."

She climbed out of the tub, wrapped herself in an orange towel, and handed three towels to her old friends. Everyone was silent as they padded back toward the kitchen. Hanna and Aria slipped inside, but as Emily passed by, Spencer caught her arm. "Are you okay?"

Emily nodded faintly, her eyes trained on the wood slats on the deck. "I'm so sorry again," she sighed. "It was wrong of me to tell Kelsey what you did. I never should have trusted her over you."

"I should have never said what I said to you, either. I don't know what happened to me."

"Maybe I deserved it," Emily said sadly.

"You didn't." Poor Emily, always thinking she deserved the worst. Spencer leaned into her. "We've been terrible to each other ever since Jamaica. We should know by now that we should stick together, not fight."

"I know." A tiny smile wobbled across Emily's lips. Then, awkwardly, she stepped forward and circled her arms around Spencer's shoulders. Spencer hugged back, feeling tears come to her eyes. In moments, Aria and Hanna returned from inside and looked at them. Spencer wasn't sure if they'd heard the conversation or not, but both girls stepped forward and wrapped their arms around Spencer and Emily, too, becoming a four-girl sandwich, just like they'd hugged in sixth and seventh grade. They were one girl short, but Spencer didn't miss her at all.

An hour later, after Spencer's friends had gone home, she made the call setting up the appointment to visit Kelsey the following day. Then she sat on the living room couch, absently stroking Beatrice's matted fur. For once, the house was dead quiet. Amelia's orchestra group wasn't rehearsing today. Spencer wondered what the songs would sound like with one violinist missing.

When the home phone rang, Spencer started so hugely her whole body twitched. *Princeton Admissions Board*, the Caller ID said. She stared at it for a moment, afraid to pick it up. This was it. The big decision of the Spencers had been made.

"Miss Hastings?" said a brisk voice when Spencer answered. "We haven't met, but my name is Georgia Price. I'm on the admissions board at Princeton University."

"Uh huh." Spencer's hands were shaking so badly she could barely hold the phone. She could just imagine the next sentence. *We regret to inform you, but Spencer F. was a much stronger candidate. . . .*

"I was wondering if you were still planning on joining

us for the early admission mixer next week," Georgia's chipper voice broke through.

Spencer frowned. "Pardon?"

Georgia repeated herself. Spencer laughed confusedly. "I-I thought you were still reviewing my application."

There was the sound of papers flipping. "Uh . . . no. I don't think so. It says here we accepted you six weeks ago. Congratulations again. This was a tough admissions year."

"What about the other Spencer Hastings?" Spencer said. "The boy with my same name who also applied? I got a letter that some of the admissions committee reviewed our applications thinking we were the same person, and . . ."

"You got a letter from *us*?" Georgia sounded appalled. "Miss Hastings, we would never do something like that. Your application is reviewed by five different rounds of readers. Discussed in committees. Approved by the dean himself. I assure you that we don't make mistakes with whom we admit. We are very, *very* careful."

Spencer stared at her reflection in the large mirror in the hall. Her hair was wild around her face. There was a wrinkle in the middle of her forehead she always got when she was utterly confused.

Georgia told Spencer the details about the mixer, then hung up. Afterward, Spencer sat back on the couch, blinking hard. What the hell had just happened?

And then, it came to her. She rose and padded across the hall to her dad's old office, which still contained a bunch of computer and office equipment. It took her five seconds to log onto the Internet, and another five to call up Facebook. With shaking hands, she typed in Spencer F.'s name into the search window. Several Spencer Hastings profiles appeared, but none were for the golden boy from Darien, Connecticut, Spencer had stalked days before.

She pictured the letter from Princeton in her hands. Come to think of it, the seal *had* looked crooked. And it *was* suspicious that Kelsey had known Spencer had gotten into Princeton . . .

Of course. Kelsey had written the letter. She'd created Spencer F.'s profile, too, to mess with her head. Spencer F. didn't exist. It was all a mind game.

Spencer shut her eyes, embarrassed that she'd been so naïve. "Good one, Kelsey," she said into the silent room. She had to hand it to her old friend: It was classic A, through and through.

37

FACE-TO-FACE WITH THE ENEMY

Dread filled Hanna as she walked into the sleek lobby of the Preserve at Addison-Stevens Mental Wellness and Rehab facility on Monday after school. All of a sudden, she was reliving the events of last year: how her dad had shoved her through the revolving doors, certain she needed help for her panic attacks. How Mike had walked with her through the lobby, saying, "Well, *this* doesn't look so bad!" Yeah, the lobby wasn't bad at all. It was the rest of the place that was a nightmare.

Next to her, Aria squinted at a tall potted cactus in the corner. Someone had affixed two eyes, a nose, and a mouth to its long green body. "Where have I seen that before?"

Spencer glanced at it and shook her head. Hanna shrugged. So did Emily, who had dressed up for the occasion in a rumpled gray skirt and a slightly too-small white sweater. She turned and nervously watched a worried-looking couple with a thin, hollow-eyed boy lean their elbows on the check-in desk. "It's so weird to think Ali was *here*," she whispered.

"Seriously," Hanna said. Ali's family had left her in here for years, too, barely even checking on her. They'd assumed she was the crazy twin, ignoring her pleas that she really *was* the Real Ali. That was probably enough to make anyone lose her mind.

Spencer approached the check-in desk and told an attendant that they were here to visit Kelsey Pierce. "Right this way," the attendant said briskly, giving the girls a circumspect look. "Why do I know you?"

Everyone exchanged a glance. *Because a patient here tried to kill us,* Hanna wanted to say. Really, it was a wonder the Preserve hadn't been shut down by a medical review board—they'd let the Real Ali out, thinking she was well, and she'd gone on to murder a bunch of innocent people.

They entered an airy room with round tables. There was a water dispenser in the corner, a coffee machine on the shelf. There were upbeat, self-esteem-affirming sayings written on yellow oaktag on the walls: YOU ARE UNIQUE! REACH FOR THE STARS! Gag.

Hanna recognized the black-and-white photo of the spiral staircase; apparently, some Preserve alum had taken it once he'd recovered. The room had a view to the facility hallway, and she couldn't help but glance at some of the patients walking past, half expecting to recognize some of them. Like Alexis, who never ate anything. Or Tara, who had those huge boobs. Or Iris, who Hanna had thought was A—and who'd also roomed with Real Ali. But even the nurses looked unfamiliar. Betsy, the nurse who administered the meds, was gone. And there was no sign of Dr. Felicia, who'd led the torturous group therapy sessions.

After a moment, the door from the hallway creaked open, and a stout nurse with a hairy mole on her chin led a frail-looking girl in pink hospital pajamas into the room. The girl had bright red hair and small, even features, but it still took Hanna a beat to realize that this was the same person she had briefly met at Noel's party last year . . . *or* the crazed figure she'd seen on the cliff two nights ago. There were circles under Kelsey's eyes. Her hair was matted. Her shoulders slumped, and her arms hung heavy.

Everyone stiffened as Kelsey pulled out a chair and quietly sat down. She looked at them blankly, her face betraying nothing. "Fancy meeting you here."

"Hello," Spencer answered. She gestured at Hanna and the others. "You remember everyone, right? This is Hanna and Aria . . . and you know Emily."

"Uh huh," Kelsey said morosely.

There was a long, punishing silence. Hanna stared at her hands in her lap, suddenly desperate to busy them with a nail file or a cigarette. She and her friends hadn't exactly discussed what they were going to say to Kelsey once they got here. They'd never been in this situation before: face-to-face with A, able to ask her why she was torturing them.

Finally, Kelsey sighed. "So my therapist says I'm supposed to apologize."

Hanna snuck a peek at Aria. *Apologize?*

"I shouldn't have dragged you out to that quarry." Kelsey looked at Emily. "My therapist said I put you in danger."

Emily's throat bobbed as she swallowed. *Wasn't that the point?* Hanna wanted to say.

"And I should thank you, too." Kelsey stared at her fingernails, sounding upset. "For saving my life on Saturday. So . . . *gracias.*"

Emily blinked. "Uh, you're welcome?"

Kelsey pushed a letter into Emily's palm. "This is for you. I wrote it this morning, and it explains . . . everything. We don't have access to phones or computers here, so our shrinks are all about us writing letters to get our feelings out." She rolled her eyes.

"Thanks," Emily said, staring at the folded piece of paper.

Kelsey shrugged. "I'm glad you pulled me back from the cliff, but you shouldn't have called an ambulance."

Emily's mouth dropped open. "You were convulsing! What were we supposed to do?"

"Leave me. I would've come out of it okay. It's happened before." Kelsey started to tear a random napkin that was sitting on the table into pieces. Redness crept into her neck. "The cops had zero tolerance because of my record. This was strike three, so I'm automatically back in rehab.

And after rehab, more juvie."

Emily shook her head slightly. "I had no idea."

"None of us did," Spencer added.

Kelsey didn't say anything, but she looked like she didn't believe them.

Everyone shifted uncomfortably. Then, Spencer leaned forward. "Listen. I'm sorry, you know. About . . . what happened this summer. What I did at the police station."

Kelsey stared down at the table, still not saying a word.

"And I'm sorry, too," Hanna added. There was no way she could bottle it up any longer. "For putting those pills in your room. And for calling the cops and telling on you."

Kelsey let out a choppy laugh. "I already had a bunch of pills in my room, but that was pretty shitty of you to call the cops. I don't even *know* you."

Hanna blinked hard. So . . . Kelsey deserved to go to jail after all?

Spencer looked equally blindsided. "Why didn't you tell me you had pills that night? We wouldn't have gone on that crazy drug deal. We wouldn't have gotten in trouble!"

A sneaky smile appeared on Kelsey's lips. "That was my secret stash, Spencer. *My* ticket to an Ivy League school—not yours. I never thought you'd have the balls to go to North Philly and buy drugs from someone. I mean, *look* at you." She narrowed her eyes at Spencer's blousy Elizabeth and James tunic and J Brand denim leggings, which Hanna had seen on a table at Otter for almost three hundred dollars.

Aria leaned forward. "Why did you do this to us?"

"Do what?" Kelsey asked dumbly, raising her heavy-lidded eyes to the group.

Torture us as A! Hanna wanted to scream.

"This is because of Tabitha, right?" Aria pressed.

"Who's Tabitha?" Kelsey sounded bored.

"You *know*," Spencer urged. "You know everything!"

Kelsey stared at them for a beat, then squeezed her eyes shut. "My head really hurts. They have me on so many meds here." She pushed back her chair and stood. "Frankly, this is kind of weird. I mean, thanks for apologizing and whatever. And . . . here." She reached into the pocket of her pajama pants and pulled out a folded piece of lined paper. "I wrote this for you, too, Spencer."

Kelsey pushed the letter into Spencer's hands. "Have a nice life, guys." And then she shuffled out of the room, her pajama bottoms dragging on the ground. A nurse stopped her outside the guest area and led her into a small office with transparent windows. The girls watched as she slumped onto a blue plastic chair. The nurse said something to her, and Kelsey nodded limply, her face expressionless.

Hanna leaned across the table. "What the hell was that?"

"She seemed so . . . *different*." Emily stared at Kelsey across the hall. "So hopeless."

Spencer twisted her silver ring around her finger. "Why did she say she didn't know Tabitha? She *has* to know her. She had those pictures on her phone. She sent me that text!"

"She was lying," Aria said matter-of-factly. "She had to be."

Then Spencer unfolded the letter Kelsey had given her and laid it flat on the table. Everyone hitched forward in their seats to read it. A single paragraph was written in leaky black pen.

Dear Spencer,

Apparently one of the steps to getting better in rehab is letting go of bad blood between people, so I guess I'll start with you. I'm not mad at you anymore. I mean, I was pissed at you for months after I went to juvie, wondering if you had something to do with getting me in trouble, but I never knew for sure until Emily told me on Friday. So you saved yourself; good for you. I don't really blame you, I guess. When I texted you on Friday about how we needed to talk, I thought I could keep my cool, but then I saw you and I got so angry. Then again, you were angry, too. But I even forgive you for hurting me. I don't know what your problem is, but you seriously need help.

Good luck with everything. Think of me when you're at Princeton—yeah, right.

Kelsey

"Whoa," Hanna said when she finished.

"I don't understand." Spencer looked at Emily. "She *didn't* know what I did until you told her? If she's A, how is that possible?"

"She did seem surprised when I told her at the cast party," Emily murmured. "But then, at the quarry, I fig-ured she was lying–that she knew all along."

Hanna pointed to Emily's letter. "What does yours say?"

Emily looked nervously at each of them, almost as if she'd rather read the missive in private, but then she shrugged and unfolded the letter.

Dear Emily,

I suppose I have some explaining to do. I totally screwed up, and I dragged you into it, and I'm so sorry. But I'm mad at you, too. You kept a huge secret from me.

When I met you, I was clean and sober. Happy. Excited to make a new friend. But then I made the connection of who you were and who you knew. That made me think of Spencer, and all the bad memories flooded back. So I started on pills again. I popped them before we hung out at the bowling alley and before we walked on the trail. I popped them at the play. You asked me what was wrong, but I didn't tell you. I knew you'd try everything in your power to stop me, and I didn't want to stop.

As soon as you told me what Spencer did, I drowned

my sorrows, taking more pills than I could handle. I was out of my mind when we were at the quarry, and I'm sorry if I put you in danger. I can't thank you enough for pulling me back from the edge, and although I'm pissed to be in rehab, my therapist says that if I give it time, maybe I'll really get better. You never know.

The thing is, I'm a liar, too. I've done things I'm not proud of, things no one would ever put on her bad-girl bucket list. I cheated on my SATs. I bribed a teacher sophomore year to give me an A by making out with him in the supply closet. And when I was on spring break in Jamaica, I met this guy the first afternoon and left with him hours after getting there, going to the other side of the island and leaving my friends without a car or money.

So see, you're not alone in being a shitty person. I forgive you, and I hope you can forgive me, too. Maybe someday we can be friends again.

Or maybe life sucks, and then you die.

Kelsey

When everyone finished reading, Emily folded the letter back up, tears in her eyes. "Poor Kelsey."

"Poor *Kelsey*?" Spencer exploded. "Poor *you*!"

"And, you guys, *Jamaica*." Aria pointed to the bottom of the page. "This part where she says she took off with a guy her first day there. Could that be *true*?"

Hanna glanced out into the hall again. Kelsey was still

sitting in the nurse's office, fiddling with the string on her pajama pants. "If it is, she wouldn't have seen us inter-acting with Tabitha. She certainly wouldn't have seen . . . what happened."

"Maybe she was telling the truth when she said she didn't know who Tabitha was," Emily whispered.

Spencer shook her head, her dangling earrings trembling. "It's not possible. What about that photo she sent me of Tabitha on the beach . . . *dead*?"

A light went on in Hanna's mind. "Let me see your phone."

Spencer gave her a strange look, but then turned it over. Hanna opened up Spencer's saved texts and scrolled through her history. A's message was still there: *You hurt both of us. Now I'm going to hurt you.* But Spencer also had at least twenty unopened messages from Friday after the play. Many of them were from her family or friends or that guy who played Macbeth, but one was from an unknown number with a 484 area code.

Hanna opened it up. *Emily told me what you did, bitch*, it said. *We need to talk. Kelsey.*

"Jesus," Hanna whispered, showing it to Spencer. "What if *this* was the text she was talking about in the let-ter? The text she was referring to on Friday night?"

The blood drained from Spencer's face. "B-but I didn't see this on Friday. All I saw was that one from A, and then Kelsey came up, and I put two and two together, and . . ."

She let the phone fall to the table. Her gaze searched

the room, seemingly trying to hold on to something stable and solid. "Kelsey must have sent both texts."

"But what if she didn't?" Hanna whispered. "What if this second one was from someone else?"

Everyone stared at one another, wide-eyed. Then Hanna turned around and peeked into the nurse's office across the hall. They needed to solve this. They needed to ask Kelsey what the hell was going on.

But the office was empty. The nurse was gone . . . and Kelsey was, too.

38

SOMETHING WICKED THIS WAY COMES

"Visiting hours are over," a nurse in crisp medical scrubs said, poking her head into the visitation room. "If you want to schedule another appointment for tomorrow, you're welcome to come between noon and two P.M."

Emily bit the inside of her cheek. They had school tomorrow. "Is there any way we could call Kelsey?" she asked. "We have a quick question for her. It's important."

The woman fingered the badge that hung from her jacket. "I'm sorry, but phone calls are verboten for the patients. We want them concentrating on the work they do inside here, not dealing with anything from the outside world. But like I said, if you'd like to visit again . . ." She opened the door that led to the hall that eventually emptied into the lobby.

There was nothing to do but comply. Emily followed Spencer, Hanna, and Aria through the hall, her mind swarming. Kelsey's letter to Spencer was puzzling, and her letter to Emily was downright heartbreaking. Had Kelsey really not seen what they'd done to Tabitha . . . or was that just another one of her A mind games? If she didn't know, what did Kelsey mean at the quarry when she'd said Emily was a terrible person? Maybe it simply *was* because Emily had kept the secret of what Spencer had done to her. Kelsey had trusted Emily, after all.

"So what do we do?" Emily whispered. "Visit her on another day?"

"I guess so," Spencer said. "If she'll see us."

The girls walked slowly through the corridor, which was lit with harsh overhead fluorescent lights and lined with tightly shut doors. "*Look*," Aria hissed, stopping at a small alcove that held a water fountain. On the inside wall were dozens of scrawled names in different-colored pens. PETRA. ULYSSES. JENNIFER. JUSTIN.

"That was my roommate," Hanna whispered, pointing to the large IRIS in pink marker. "The one I thought was A."

Then Emily spied something in the corner, a signature so hauntingly familiar she felt her knees go wobbly. COURTNEY, it said, in silvery bubble letters. It was the same handwriting that was on the sixth-grade mural where everyone had to stamp their handprints and write a few adjectives about themselves. It was very similar handwriting, too, to the *real* Courtney, the girl Emily had always known as Ali. Emily pictured Her Ali writing her name at the top of a vocab quiz, the *e* in *DiLaurentis* just as loopy as this *e* in *Courtney*, the letters slanted slightly forward in the same way. Courtney had wanted to be just like Ali down to the last detail—and she had been.

The other girls followed Emily's gaze. "So she really was here," Spencer said quietly.

Hanna nodded. "Seeing it makes it so real."

Emily glanced at the signature once more, then looked down the Preserve's joyless, spic-and-span hallway. What must it have been like for Real Ali here with no one believing she was who she said she was for close to four long, miserable years? Ali must have burned with hatred for her sister for making the switch. She must have seethed with rage at Emily, Aria, Spencer, and Hanna for being at the wrong place at the right time, too. While inside these walls, she'd plotted her return, orchestrated her sister's murder, laid out her plans as A, and even masterminded the Poconos fire.

And, if Emily's gut feeling was right, she was still out there. Alive.

Emily turned to her three old best friends, wondering if she should tell them the secret she'd kept for over a year now. If they were going to start off on the right foot and really be close again, it had to come out sometime, right?

But then Hanna sighed and pushed out the exit door at the end of the corridor. Spencer followed, then Aria. Emily took one last look at the inside of the facility. A faint, high-pitched giggle echoed in her ears. She jumped, whirling around. But, of course, no one was there.

The girls walked across the lawn toward the parking

lot. A gardener was on his hands and knees, cleaning out dried grass from one of the flower beds. A Pennsylvania state flag flapped on a pole, making a snapping noise in the wind. For the first time in a while, as they all walked quietly in a line, Emily didn't feel awkward around her old friends. Instead, she felt comfortable. She cleared her throat. "Maybe we could hang out a little later this week," she said softly. "Get coffee or something."

Aria looked up. "I'd like that."

"Me too," Hanna said. Spencer smiled and bumped Emily's hip. A warm sense of satisfaction fell over Emily like a thick blanket. At least one good thing had come out of this. She hadn't realized how desperately she'd missed her old friends.

They passed a wrought-iron bench by the flagpole. It must have been newly installed; the cement base looked freshly poured. A shiny copper plaque lay in front of the bench, a bouquet of lilies next to it. Emily glanced at the plaque idly, her eyes sweeping over the letters but not really taking them in. Then, she stopped short and read them again. "You guys."

The other girls, now a few paces ahead, doubled back. Emily pointed at the sign on the ground.

Everyone stared at the newly chiseled letters. THIS BENCH IS DEDICATED TO TABITHA CLARK, FORMER PRESERVE AT ADDISON-STEVENS PATIENT. REST IN PEACE. Her birth and death years were inscribed below the message. They were the same years as Real Ali's.

"Oh my God," Spencer whispered. Aria clapped her hand over her mouth. Hanna took a wheeling step backward.

"Tabitha was *here*?" Spencer said.

"Why didn't this ever come up in the news articles?" Aria shook her head.

Emily looked around at the others, making a chilling connection. "Do you think she knew . . . *Ali*?"

Everyone exchanged a horrified glance. The wind kicked up, brushing a smattering of dead, dry leaves across Tabitha's name. Then Aria's cell phone let out a beep. Seconds later, Spencer's phone, tucked deep in her bag, chimed. Hanna's phone made a snake-hiss sound, and Emily's phone buzzed in her pocket, making her jump.

Emily knew who the note was from without having to look. She gazed at her friends, confused. "You guys, Kelsey can't make calls from inside the Preserve. She has no cell phone."

"So . . ." Hanna stared at the phone. "Who wrote *this*?"

With shaking hands, Emily pressed READ. And then she shut her eyes, realizing this wasn't over. Not even close.

Dig all you want, bitches. But you'll NEVER find me. —A

WHAT HAPPENS NEXT . . .

These pretty little liars just can't help but be bad, and I can't help but torture them. They call that a symbiotic relationship, right? Spencer would know—unless she was high during that class? Whoopsies!

Just when poor widdle Emily thought she'd made a new bestie, Kelsey went and nearly killed her. Still have a thing for bad girls, Em? Hanna thought she was Juliet in a star-crossed love. How romantic. Maybe she should have listened when I warned her how that one ended up. And Aria—oh, Aria. She fell into some old, bad habits. Those who don't learn from history are doomed to repeat it. Fingers crossed she never learns her lesson.

I'd say these ladies need a vacation, but given what they did on their last getaway, that's probably not the best idea. And besides, watching the drama unfold is like a holiday for *moi*!

Until next time, bitches.

Mwah!

—A

ACKNOWLEDGMENTS

I can't believe I'm writing the acknowledgments for *Pretty Little Liars #10*. I'm beyond lucky that the series has continued on for this long—and that I work with so many amazing editors, brainstormers, and all-around brilliant people who help make the series as compelling and interesting as it is. It's the same cast of characters as always, but I owe a huge debt of gratitude to Lanie Davis, Sara Shandler, Josh Bank, Les Morgenstein, and Kristin Marang at Alloy Entertainment for being supportive, reliable, smart, and savvy during this whole process. You guys make all of this so much easier, and I'm thrilled we're still partners after all these years.

Thanks also to the people to whom I've dedicated this book—Farrin Jacobs, Kari Sutherland, Christina Colangelo, and Marisa Russell at HarperTeen. Farrin and Kari are amazing editors with incredible insight that turn these books from good to great. Christina has been my digital guru—she's the mastermind behind the many Twitter contests! And Marisa put together a great tour for me this summer, where I got to meet so many of my wonderful readers. I feel so safe and nurtured with you guys, and I'm very excited for the future!

Thanks also to Andy McNicol and Jennifer Walsh at William Morris, to the awesome TV people who continue to produce nail-biting episodes of *Pretty Little Liars*, including Marlene King, Oliver Goldstick, Lisa Cochran-Neilan, all of the fantastic writers, directors, producers, and crew, and of course Lucy, Shay, Ashley, Troian . . . and Sasha! Let's not forget the ingénue who plays Ali! Thanks to Andrew Zaeh, who endured recording all those gifts at the baby shower, and to Colleen McGarry for being all-around wonderful—and finding my husband the best cupcakes ever. While we're on the subject, much love to my husband, Joel, and to my parents, Shep and Mindy, and to Ali, who, may I remind everyone, is nothing like the Ali in the books . . . either of them.

I forgot to thank Mia Rusila in *Twisted* for all her help with Finnish translation, so since Klaudia's still in the mix, I'd like to give her a shout-out here. Thanks to all the fans I met this summer on tour, all the fans I speak to on Twitter, and everyone else who is inspired by the books or ʰ˒w. All of you make writing worthwhile. Keep ʲse me to keep your secrets safe from A!

Photo by Austin Hodges

SARA SHEPARD is the author of two *New York Times* bestselling series, Pretty Little Liars and The Lying Game. She graduated from New York University and has an MFA from Brooklyn College. Sara's Pretty Little Liars novels were inspired by her upbringing in Philadelphia's Main Line, where she lives today.

For exclusive information
on your favorite authors and artists,
visit www.authortracker.com.

Stunning

That summer in Rosewood, Pennsylvania, a picturesque, wealthy suburb about twenty minutes from Philadelphia, had been one of the hottest ones on record. To escape the heat, people flocked to the country club pool, gathered around the local Rita's for extra-large strawberry ices, and skinny-dipped in the duck pond at Peck's organic cheese farm, despite the decades-old rumor that a dead body had been found there. But by the third week in August, the weather suddenly turned. "A Midsummer Night's Freeze," the local news called it, because the temperature got down to freezing a few nights in a row. Boys broke out their hoodies, and girls donned their brand-new, back-to-school Joe's jeans and puffer vests. A few leaves on the trees changed to reds and golds overnight. It was as though the Grim Reaper had come and ripped the season clean away.

On a chilly Thursday night, a beat-up Subaru cruised down a dark street in Wessex, a town not far from Rosewood. The glowing green clock on the dashboard read 1:26 AM, but the four girls inside the car were wide awake. Actually, there were five girls: best friends Emily Fields, Aria Montgomery, Spencer Hastings, Hanna Marin . . . and a tiny, nameless baby Emily had given birth to that day.

They drove past house after house, peering at the numbers on the mailboxes. When they approached number 204, Emily sat up straighter. "Stop," she said over the baby's cries. "That's it."

Aria, who was wearing a Fair Isle pullover she'd bought while on vacation in Iceland last month—a vacation she couldn't bear to think about—steered the car toward the curb. "Are you sure?" She eyed the modest white house. It had a basketball hoop in the driveway, a big weeping willow in the side yard, and cheerful flower beds under the front windows.

"I've seen this address on the adoption form a million times." Emily touched the window. "Two-oh-four Ship Lane. This is definitely where they live."

The car grew quiet. Even the baby stopped crying. Hanna glanced at the infant next to her in the backseat. Her tiny, perfect pink lips were pursed. Spencer looked at the baby, too, then shifted uncomfortably. It was obvious what everyone was thinking: How could this have happened to sweet, obedient little Emily Fields? They'd been Emily's best friends since sixth grade, when Alison DiLaurentis, the most popular girl at Rosewood Day, the private school they all attended, recruited them into her new clique. Emily had always been the girl who hated badmouthing people, who never instigated a quarrel, who preferred baggy T-shirts to tight-fitting skirts—*and* girls over guys. Girls like Emily didn't get pregnant.

They'd thought Emily was doing a program at Temple that summer, much like the one Spencer was attending at Penn. But then, one by one, Emily had told each of them the truth: She was hiding in her sister's dorm room in Philly because she was pregnant. Aria, Spencer, and Hanna had all reacted the same way when Emily broke the news: with jaw-dropping, speechless shock. *How long have you known?* they had asked. *I took a pregnancy test when I got back from Jamaica,* Emily had answered. The father was Isaac, a boy she'd dated last winter.

"Are you sure you want to do this?" Spencer asked quietly. A reflection in the window caught her eye, and she cringed. But when she turned to stare at the house opposite them, a similarly modest brick ranch, no one was there.

"What other option do I have?" Emily twisted the pink rubber Jefferson Hospital bracelet around her wrist. The staff didn't even know she was gone—the doctors had wanted her to stay an extra day so they could monitor the incision from her C-section. But if she'd stayed in the hospital a minute longer, her plan wouldn't work.

She couldn't possibly give the baby to Gayle, the wealthy woman who'd paid a huge sum of money for her, so she'd told Gayle she'd pushed back the date for her scheduled C-section to two days later. Then she'd solicited her friends' help to sneak out of the hospital shortly after the baby was born. Everyone had played a part in the escape. Hanna returned Gayle's money. Spencer distracted the nurses while Emily hobbled toward the exit. Aria provided her Subaru and even found an infant car seat at a garage sale. And they'd succeeded: They'd escaped without Gayle finding out and taking away the baby.

Suddenly, as if on cue, Emily's phone bleated, breaking the tense silence inside the car. She pulled it out of the plastic shopping bag the hospital had stashed her clothes in and looked at the screen. *Gayle.*

Emily winced and hit IGNORE. The phone quieted for a moment, then bleated once more. Gayle again.

Hanna eyed the phone warily. "Should you answer that?"

"And say what?" Emily hit IGNORE one more time. "'Sorry, Gayle, I don't want to give you my baby because I think you're psycho'?"

"But isn't this illegal?" Hanna looked up and down the street. There wasn't a car in sight, but she still felt on edge. "What if she turns you in?"

"For what?" Emily asked. "What Gayle did was illegal, too. She can't say anything without incriminating herself."

Hanna bit a thumbnail. "But if the cops do find out

about this, what happens if they investigate other things? Like . . . Jamaica?"

A palpable tension rippled through the car. Although it was always on their minds, the girls had promised each other never to talk about Jamaica again. It was supposed to have been a getaway to forget about Real Ali, the diabolical girl who'd killed her twin sister, Courtney, the Ali they all knew and loved. Last year, Real Ali had returned to Rosewood and tried to pass herself off as the girls' old friend, but it was later revealed that she was the new A, the girls' text-messaging tormenter. She'd killed Ian Thomas, Rosewood Day heartthrob and suspect in the first murder, and Jenna Cavanaugh, who the girls and Their Ali had blinded in sixth grade. Real Ali's master plan was to murder the four girls. She'd brought them to her family's house in the Poconos, locked them in a bedroom, and lit a match. But things hadn't turned out as she'd hoped. The girls escaped, leaving Real Ali trapped in the house when it exploded. Even though her remains had never been found, everyone was positive she was dead.

But *was* she?

The trip to Jamaica had been a chance for the girls to move on with their lives and deepen their friendships. Once they got there, though, they met a girl named Tabitha who reminded them of Real Ali. She knew things only Ali would know. Her mannerisms were chillingly like Ali's. Slowly, they became convinced that she *was* Real Ali. Maybe she'd survived the fire. Maybe she'd come to Jamaica to finish off the girls as planned.

There was only one thing to do: stop her before she got revenge. Just as Real Ali was about to push Hanna off the rooftop deck, Aria had intervened, and Ali fell instead. Her broken body had vanished before the girls got down to the beach to see what they'd done, probably swept away by the tide. The girls vacillated between relief that Ali was gone for good . . . and horror that they'd killed someone.

"No one will ever know about Jamaica," Spencer growled now. "Ali's body is gone."

Emily's phone bleated again. *Gayle*. A beep followed. *Six new voicemail messages*, the screen announced.

"Maybe you should listen to those," Hanna whispered.

Emily shook her head, her hands trembling.

"Put the call on speaker," Aria suggested. "We'll listen with you."

Drawing her bottom lip into her mouth, Emily did as she was told and played the first message. "Heather, it's Gayle." A harsh voice blared through the car. "You haven't returned my calls in days, and I'm worried. You didn't have the baby a few days early, did you? Were there some complications? I'm calling Jefferson to make sure."

"Who's Heather?" Spencer whispered nervously.

"It's the fake name I gave everyone this summer," Emily said. "I even applied for my job using a fake ID I bought on South Street. I didn't want anyone making the connection that I was Alison DiLaurentis's best friend. Someone might have told the press I was pregnant, and then my parents would've found out." She stared at her phone. "God, she sounds really pissed."

Gayle's second message followed. "Heather, it's Gayle again. Okay, I called Jefferson—that *is* where you've scheduled your C-section, right? No one on the staff will tell me what's going on. Can you please pick up and tell me where the hell you are?"

The tones of the third and fourth messages increased in intensity and frustration. "Okay, I'm at Jefferson now," Gayle said in the fifth message. "I just talked to an orderly, and they don't have any record of anyone named Heather in the maternity ward, but then I described what you look like and she said you *are* here. Why didn't you call me? Where the hell is the baby?"

"What do you want to bet she *bribed* the orderly?" Emily murmured. "So much for checking in under my real name to throw Gayle off the scent." Checking in under Emily Fields had been a risk—even though Emily gave a PO box in Philly as her address and planned to use her babysitting savings to pay the hospital bill, what if, for some reason, her parents called Jefferson and found out she'd been there? But since Gayle knew her only as Heather, using her real name seemed like an easy way to lose her.

By the sixth message, Gayle had figured it out. "This was a setup, wasn't it?" she growled. "You had the baby and you left, didn't you? Was this your intention all along, bitch? Did you plan to scam me from the start? Do you think I give out fifty thousand dollars to just anyone? Do you think I'm an idiot? I'm going to *find you*. I'm going to hunt you and that baby down, and then you'll be sorry."

"Whoa," Aria whispered.

"Oh my God." Emily flipped her phone closed. "I should have never promised her anything. I know we gave it back, but I should have never taken her money in the first place. She's crazy. *Now* do you guys see why I'm doing this?"

"Of course we do," Aria said quietly.

The infant started to whimper. Emily stroked her tiny head, and then, steeling herself, pushed open the car door and stepped into the chilly air. "Let's do this."

"Em, don't." Aria opened her own door and grabbed Emily's arm just as Emily fell against the side of the car, clearly in pain. "The doctor said you shouldn't strain, remember?"

"I need to get the baby to the Bakers." Emily pointed woozily to the house.

Aria paused. A truck horn honked far in the distance. Over the sound of the car's chugging engine, she thought she heard a brief, high-pitched laugh.

"Fine," Aria conceded. "But *I'll* carry her." She grabbed the baby seat from the back. A smell of baby powder wafted up to greet her, bringing a lump to her throat. Her father, Byron, and his girlfriend, Meredith, had just had a baby, and she loved Lola with all her heart. If she looked too long at this baby, she might love her just as much.

Emily's phone rang again, and Gayle's name flashed on the screen. She dropped it in her bag. "Come *on*, Aria."

Aria hefted the baby seat higher in her arms, and both girls staggered across the front lawn. Dew wet their feet. They narrowly missed a sprinkler head jutting out of the grass. When they climbed onto the porch, they noticed a cheerful wooden rocking chair and a ceramic dog dish that said GOLDEN RETRIEVERS WELCOME.

"Aw." Aria pointed to it. "Golden retrievers are awesome."

"They told me they have two golden retriever puppies." Emily's voice shook. "I've always wanted one of those."

Aria watched as a million emotions passed across her friend's face in a split second. She reached over and squeezed Emily's hand. "Are you okay?" There was so much to say, but no words with which to say it.

Then Emily's expression hardened again. "Of course," she said through her teeth. Taking a deep breath, she grabbed the baby carrier from Aria and set it on the porch. The baby squeaked. Emily glanced over her shoulder at the street. Aria's Subaru idled at the curb. Something slipped into the shadows near the hedge. For a split second, she thought it was a person, but then her eyes blurred. It was probably the drugs that were still racing through her system.

Even though it made her incision hurt like hell, Emily bent down, pulled out a copy of the baby's birth certificate and the letter she had scribbled down shortly before going into the hospital, and tucked them into the top of the baby carrier. Hopefully, the letter explained everything. Hopefully, the Bakers would understand and love this baby with all their hearts. She kissed the baby's forehead, then let her fingers trail across her impossibly soft cheeks. *It's for the best,* a voice inside her said. *You know that.*

Emily pressed the doorbell. Within seconds, a light flipped on inside, and two sets of footsteps sounded behind the door. Aria grabbed Emily's hand, and they staggered for the car. The front door opened just as they were putting on their seat belts. A figure was silhouetted in the doorway, first looking out, and then looking down at the abandoned baby seat . . . and at the baby inside.

"Drive," Emily growled.

Aria zoomed into the night. As she rounded the first corner, she glanced at Emily in the rearview mirror. "It's okay."

Hanna placed her hand on Emily's arm. Spencer twisted around and squeezed her knee. Emily crumpled and started to sob, first quietly, then in huge, heaving gasps. Everyone's hearts broke for her, but no one knew what to say. This was yet another devastating secret in a long list of secrets they had to keep, along with Jamaica, Spencer's near-arrest for drug possession, what had happened to Aria in Iceland, and Hanna's car accident that summer. At least A was gone—they'd made sure of that. What they'd done might have been terrible, but at least no one would ever know.

They shouldn't be so sure about that, though. After all that had happened, they should know to trust their premonitions, to take those phantom laughs and shadows seriously. Someone *had* been there that night, after all. Watching. Studying. Plotting.

And that someone was just waiting for the opportunity to use all this against them.

PRETTY GIRLS DON'T PLAY
BY THE RULES...

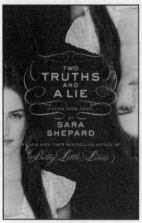

THEY MAKE THEM.

WELCOME TO THE NEW AMERICA

Don't miss a single page of the forbidden love and extraordinary adventure in the Eve Trilogy.

Visit TheEveTrilogy.com to follow Eve's journey.

HARPER
An Imprint of HarperCollinsPublishers